Girls Like Us

ALSO BY JENNIFER DUGAN

Hot Dog Girl

Some Girls Do

Melt With You

The Last Girls Standing

Playing for Keeps

Summer Girls

WITH KIT SEATON

Coven

Full Shift

Bite Me

JENNIFER DUGAN

G. P. PUTNAM'S SONS

G. P. PUTNAM'S SONS
An imprint of Penguin Random House LLC
1745 Broadway, New York, NY 10019
penguinrandomhouse.com

Design by Suki Boynton | Text set in Chronicle Deck

Library of Congress Cataloging-in-Publication Data
Names: Dugan, Jennifer author | Dugan, Jennifer. Some girls do.
Title: Girls like us / Jennifer Dugan.
Description: New York, NY: G. P. Putnam's Sons, 2026. | Summary: "Two teen girls struggle to make things work when long distance complicates their relationship"— Provided by publisher.
Identifiers: LCCN 2025034188 (print) | LCCN 2025034189 (ebook) | ISBN 9798217112555 trade paperback | ISBN 9798217112562 epub
Subjects: CYAC: Long-distance relationships—Fiction | Universities and colleges—Fiction | LGBTQ+ people—Fiction | Romance stories | LCGFT: Romance fiction | Queer fiction | Novels
Classification: LCC PZ7.1.D8343 Gi 2026 (print) | LCC PZ7.1.D8343 (ebook)
LC record available at https://lccn.loc.gov/2025034188
LC ebook record available at https://lccn.loc.gov/2025034189

First published in the United States of America by G. P. Putnam's Sons, 2026

Manufactured in the United States of America
LSCC

ISBN 9798217112555
1st Printing

The authorized representative in the EU for product safety and compliance is Penguin Random House Ireland, Morrison Chambers, 32 Nassau Street, Dublin D02 YH68, Ireland, https://eu-contact.penguin.ie.

To all the readers, bloggers, Bookstagrammers, BookTokkers, teachers, librarians, and booksellers who have supported *Some Girls Do* over the years and to this day. You have changed my life. This one's for you. I hope you love it.

Girls Like Us

1

RUBY

The air ratchet sends vibrations running through my hand as I mess with this stubborn bolt.

The sensation travels up my arm and through my body until I swear I can feel it buzzing inside every single one of my bones. I'm going to scream if I can't get this part unstuck. I drop my arm and wipe some sweat off my brow—I've probably just smeared grease across my forehead, but I don't even care. I need a second to recalibrate before I hoist the air ratchet again. Still, I have to get this done fast . . . or else risk dying of heatstroke.

It's *usually* cold in the garage these days, despite it being fairly mild for early January, but my stepdad—and boss—Billy got a new heat pump for his office and moved his old space heater out here into the main bay. He's *helpfully* pointed it at me as I shift around on my creeper, the small platform with wheels I use to slide back and forth beneath vehicles. That means it's a steamy two thousand degrees in here today, or at least it feels like it, all while I'm stuck wrestling with a shitty stripped bolt beneath this old Jeep Wrangler instead of kissing Morgan on her last full day home for winter break.

In a perfect world, I'd be glued to her side, like I have been almost every second since she got home last month. Her parents even came up here for the week of Christmas, since the old house still holds a lot of bad memories for her. It was nice to have everyone together, even if it does kind of suck to think that Morgan still feels like she doesn't belong in the town she grew up in.

I'm pretty sure my brain short-circuited when my girlfriend informed me that, actually, she didn't think it sucked at all because *I felt like home to her.*

Jesus. You can't just walk around saying stuff like that and expect me not to be a ball of electrical current and dirty thoughts. Unfortunately, she said this on Christmas Eve, in front of her parents, so I had to sit there acting like everything was fine and Morgan hadn't just flipped my universe on its head *again.*

Her parents went home a few days later, and I've pretty much had her to myself since then. I mean, we aren't rude or anything. We hang out with her brother, Dylan, and his girlfriend, Keisha, who has become just as big of a staple around his apartment as I am. But mostly, it's just me and her, soaking up every single second we can.

I'm trying not to begrudge her parents for coming back up

for dinner last night, which I was invited to, and then staying over to take her out shopping today "one- on-one"—which I'm pretty sure was a polite way of saying *no Rubys allowed.*

I get it, fully, and I'm not mad or anything . . . but Morgan had already made afternoon plans with Danny, a friend of hers from the LGBTQ+ resource center that she used to work at. He's been basically spearheading the Rainbow Athlete Coalition they started last year ever since she left for school in August. I guess they need to start figuring out how to adjust things to keep it running, now that he's going to be graduating and going away to school this year too.

Like I said, all good things, but I wish it wasn't so hard to balance friends and family time. I know it's not fair, but if I could keep her all to myself? I selfishly would. I only get to see her for a few short weeks, and then she's gone again, four hours down the highway. A whole hour closer for her parents, I might add, who go and watch her races at school all the time.

With my class and work schedule, and her class and practice schedule, Morgan and I rely on FaceTime and texting to keep the spark alive. It definitely doesn't help that my old Ford Torino is awful on gas and hates long drives. Billy's mostly using whatever cars we're working up on the side as his daily driver—a 1978 Dodge Adventurer in his case, and a 1972 Chevy Camaro in mine—so he's no help either. I took the bus down once last semester, and she took it home once too, but it's a far cry from how much time we used to have together.

I'm just glad Billy had this job for me to do today to help pass the time. I had originally planned for today off until I heard about Morgan's parents' impromptu shopping trip. I'm counting down the time until I can see her tonight—just seven more hours and I'll have her all to myself. But . . . yeah, I'd be lying if I said I didn't want her all to myself now *and* later.

I lift the air ratchet and get back to work.

Before I can get too lost in my head about it all, someone gently kicks at my sneaker, the only visible part of me while I work on the car. I slide out from under it, fully expecting it to be Billy telling me it's time for my lunch break, but I'm delighted to see Morgan there instead. And not just Morgan, but Morgan holding up two greasy bags of takeout from Mama's.

I've never ripped my earbuds out so fast in my life.

"What are you doing here?" I ask, grinning as I sit up and grab a rag to clean my hands.

Her returning smile nearly knocks me off my feet. *God, she's beautiful,* I think as she holds up the bags of food, and suddenly I'm hungry in a whole different way. I take a step closer, getting in one, two, three kisses before she takes a step back with a very amused look on her face.

"Later." She laughs. "I only have a few minutes. I was hoping we could sneak in a quick lunch date before I have to meet Danny. If this is a bad time, though—"

"It's not!" I say. "It's a very, very *good* time, actually. Although it's taking all my willpower not to tackle you into a hug right now."

"Well, remind your *willpower* that this is your favorite sweater of mine, which will be ruined if we get grease on it. Maybe that will help," she teases.

I blush, because yeah, that white fuzzy sweater, the one

that hugs her in all the right ways and has a very, magically deep neckline, truly is my favorite thing that's come out of this holiday season. Sure, Morgan's friend Lydia gave it to her as a Christmas present, but honestly, *Merry Christmas to me too.*

It's possible that I made her wear that the last time we—

"Get your head out of the gutter, Ruby Gold," she says, shoving me toward the sink while she heads over to the picnic table that Billy has dragged into the garage for the winter. It's become a sort of break room area, especially during the holidays, when so many of our regular clients brought us cookies and other treats.

Taking the hint, I head to slather my hands in Gojo and scrub them under the faucet, trying not to think too hard about the fact that this is going to be the last time she shares lunch with me for weeks, if not months. Who knows how many weekends together we'll be able to pull off this semester. It's been a nice routine the last few weeks, eating with her, I mean. The domesticity of it all—I used to think stuff like that would be mind-numbingly claustrophobic for me, but instead it's just kind of . . . nice.

We plan to at least be together for spring break, but there's no way I want to go *that* long without seeing her. We've already got big plans for it, even—a trip to DC where I'll be soaking in all of the automotive exhibits at the Smithsonian's National Museum of American History, and she'll be setting up meetings to talk with representatives on Capitol Hill. Apparently, that's a thing that you can just . . . do? Even though she said most of the meetings will end up being with staffers, I still think it's pretty cool.

I drop down onto the bench across from her and then think better of it, opting to slide in beside her instead. She smirks at me, pressing her leg against mine, and I press back, enjoying the closeness that I hadn't thought we would have until tonight.

"I missed you," she says, hooking our pinkies together the way she does whenever one of us needs reassurance. "I don't want to go back tomorrow."

"Quit school and stay here," I tease, opening up my sandwich with my free hand. "What's one more person living at Billy's?"

She rolls her eyes. "My parents would kill me."

"I happen to know a guy who loves to take in parentless strays. You'd fit right in."

I'm joking, of course. Well, about trying to get her to stay at Billy's, not about him taking in parentless strays. I still haven't talked to my mom since our big blowup. Not for her lack of trying, though. She's been texting me a couple times a week, every week . . . but I'm just not ready. And I'm not sure her intentions are pure either, if I'm being honest, especially considering how she keeps sending me registration links to pageants with captions like "just in case" and "FYI."

Morgan leans into me, swallowing her bite. "I can't wait until we can be together all the time again."

I turn to study her eyes, lost in the sincerity I see in them. She tilts her head, parting her lips slightly in invitation as she apparently gives up her "no time for kissing" stance. *Don't have to ask me twice.* And sure, we both smell like onions from our subs now, but I don't even care. There is less than twenty-four hours before she's gone, and I'm not about to let a little sandwich breath stop me.

She deepens the kiss, clearly thinking the same thing, and I slide closer, holding the side of her neck as I trail my thumb against her cheek, chasing the sensation of her skin against mine. She gently nips my bottom lip and then lets me inside.

I'm a millisecond from laying her down on this picnic table, decorum be damned, when Billy clears his throat behind us. We jump apart, both turning guiltily to look at him.

"I was gonna see if you wanted me to grab you anything for lunch while I was out," he says, crossing his arms as he looks between the both of us. "But I can see you all have plenty to eat."

"Oh my god, I should have gotten you something," Morgan says, thankfully missing the innuendo. "I'm so sorry, Billy. I wasn't thinking—"

He holds up his hand. "It's fine. I've got some parts to ship out right now anyway," he says. "I was already planning on swinging by Mike's Hot Dogs for lunch after."

"I bet you are," I say under my breath, which earns a kick to my side of the bench from him. I fight my smirk as Morgan covers her laughter with her hand. We both know his sudden and constant need for Mike's Hot Dogs is only because he's got a crush on the new manager there.

I may or may not have gone and scoped her out with Morgan when she first got back from school, feeling a little overprotective. It's not that I don't trust Billy; it's just that, well, he *did* decide to marry my mom once upon a time. Like not just date her, but *actually marry her*! Sure, they eventually divorced, but can you blame me for being worried that his partner picker is broken?

The new manager, Shelby according to her name tag, seemed nice enough. He must have shown her pictures of me or something, because she gave me extra fries from day one and introduced herself saying that I must be "Billy's Ruby."

Billy's Ruby. I liked the sound of that, as if I belonged here and wasn't just some rando he felt bad for. Between that and the extra fries, I was fully on board the Shelby train. Billy was mad I went on my own, because I guess he wanted to formally introduce me to Shelby himself. He insisted on taking me right back there the next day after work to do so, but I think he regretted that pretty quick. At least, he sure looked like he was dying when I asked him *right in front of her* if this meant she was going to be my new mom. He's too easy to troll sometimes.

"Tell Shelby we say hello," Morgan says, looking at him innocently. We've been working her name into convos as much as possible lately just to see him trying to hide how pink in the face he gets from it.

"Oh, fuck off, both of you," he groans. "If you're done yanking my chain, I'm gonna head out. Don't do anything I would do," he says, his favorite parting refrain, as he heads to his truck.

Morgan checks the time on her phone, and I try and fail to ignore the way she frowns and then quickly types out a text.

"Do you have to go already?" I whine, crumpling up the

wrappers of our now-finished sandwiches and tossing them in the trash.

She looks up at me with mischief in her eyes as she says, “Hey, do you think Billy would ever make out with someone at your station?”

“Ew, gross, absolutely not. Why would you even ask that?”

She flicks her eyes toward the makeshift office that Billy set up for me, just a couple temporary walls around my old workspace. It’s not much, but it gives me a place to do my homework in peace even if people are moving around in the shop.

“Because . . .” She smiles. “I may have just told Danny I was running about twenty minutes late.”

I look at her, baffled. She widens her eyes like I’m ridiculous for not getting it, and maybe I am, because it takes me another few seconds before it hits me.

“Right,” I say, tugging her up from the table. “We’re not supposed to do anything Billy *would* do.”

She taps me on the side of my head. “Glad you caught up, Ruby Gold. Only nineteen minutes now.”

“Then we better make them count,” I say, grabbing her hand and running to my “office.” And if we’re both laughing too hard to let things get too heated, well, I don’t even mind. Being alone with her, hell, being *near* her, is all I need. Swallowing each other’s laughter with our lips is just the icing on the top of a very, very fantastic cake.

2

MORGAN

I slide my messenger bag over my head and drop it onto the chair by the side table in my brother's apartment, before sitting down to take off my shoes. One of the perks of Dylan being in a serious relationship with Keisha is the addition of a little bench in the entryway so we don't have to try to kick off our shoes without losing our balance. She even added a cute little boot tray under it that's perfect for these dreary, wet winter days.

Other fabulous additions include supersoft throw pillows, plus, like, some of the posters in the living room are down . . . or at least framed. Dylan is still the same old Dylan—she's not trying to change him or take over—he's just slightly more domestic. Less of a bachelor and more of a former feral who's finally embracing things like soft pillows and clean towels. She hasn't officially moved in yet, but she's here so much I suspect the change in address won't be too far off. I can only imagine how much more awesome the place will get with all her stuff here. The girl has taste.

"Honey, I'm home," I call out, setting my shoes on the tray and then padding across the living room.

Dylan pokes his head out of the bathroom down the hall, where he's clearly in the middle of brushing his teeth. He holds up his finger and then disappears, blessing the apartment with the sound of him spitting, followed by water running.

"You could shut the door, you know!" I shout after him. His hand sticks out into the hall, middle finger raised. It's nice that we're back to the annoying big brother / bratty little sister dynamic now that I've graduated and don't live here full-time.

I'll always appreciate the way he stepped up to help me last year, but the panicked-parent vibe he took on when I first moved in with him got old pretty soon after graduation. Like, he's still my best friend and go-to person for life advice, but also, we bicker again like old times and he's stopped treating me like I'm made of glass.

"Keisha coming over?" I ask when he comes out wiping his mouth on his sleeve. *So much for domestication.*

"Why do you think Keisha's coming over?" he asks. "But you're not wrong."

"I knew it as soon as I saw you brushing your teeth." I laugh, heading into the kitchen to grab a can of Bubly—Dylan stopped buying LaCroix when I left for school and is firmly a Bubly man now. I suspect this is another change we can credit to Keisha the Great. It smells amazing in here, and I spy what looks like pasta sauce simmering on the burner. The oven timer is on too. *I hope I'm not interrupting a date or something.*

Dylan walks over to the stove, aggressively stirring the sauce. "I always brush my teeth, Morgan! Don't act like I'm some gross frat boy you met on campus."

"Yes, in the morning and at night," I say, kicking the door to the fridge closed and opening the can. "But not at 7:17, out of the blue, when I can tell you've *definitely* been cooking Mom's pasta sauce recipe all day. Also, do frat boys really not brush their teeth? I don't think that's true."

He playfully shoves me out of the way, reaching into the cabinet to grab some seasonings. "You tell me. I went to barber school, remember? Not too many frats there."

"Liberal arts lesbian, remember?" I laugh, pointing to myself with both thumbs. "Not hanging out with a lot of, or any, frat boys, but . . . you *do* remember your girlfriend was the president of her sorority, right? That makes you almost, like, a frat boy–in-law."

He rolls his eyes as he stirs the sauce, before quickly pulling a fresh spoon out of the drawer beside him. He scoops a little out and passes it to me. "Here, stop talking and try this."

It tastes just like Mom's, and I grin. "You're getting good at this," I say, and Dylan preens a little.

"I'm glad you like, because it's for you."

"What? Seriously? I was legit going to ask you if Ruby and I should try to stay at Billy's tonight. I figured it was like an anniversary or something with Keisha."

My brother raises his eyebrows. "It's your last night home and you thought I was making your favorite food for someone else? Be for real. Keisha *is* coming, but this is all for you. I thought we'd chow down and maybe watch a movie or something, if you can. I'm sure Ruby's coming over, but I thought maybe we'd all . . . Whatever, either way." He goes back to stirring, angling his face away.

"Dylan," I say, "are you . . . are you sad I'm leaving?"

"No," he says, before huffing out an aggrieved sigh and turning back to face me. "Maybe a very little bit. Like microscopically."

"You're *microscopically* sad I'm leaving? Sure, sure," I say. "For what it's worth, I'm going to microscopically miss you too."

"Good. Now that that's settled," he says, "what time is your girlfriend coming? Mine's almost here."

"Pretty soon, I think. I texted her when I was on my way back from the meeting," I say, with a little frown.

Dylan furrows his brows. "Hey, what's that face for? Do you want it to be just us tonight? Or . . . Oh shit, did I completely misread that? If you want Keisha and me out of the house so you two can—"

"No, shut up," I say, blushing furiously. It's one thing to abstractly know that your brother is aware of your physical relationship with your girlfriend, but it's another for him to *mention it in front of your dinner.*

He holds up his hands. "Okay, okay, I'm just saying!"

"Well, stop saying it!" I say, raising my arm like I'm going to fling my seltzer at him. "I wasn't upset because of that. I'm upset because I . . . I'm going to really miss you, more than microscopically, and it's going to be really hard to leave Ruby too. As great as all this is, it just feels a little bittersweet."

"I get that," he says, holding his arms out for a hug.

I step into them, knowing that if I don't, I'll regret it when I get to school. Dylan and I got so much closer since I moved in with him last year. Like, I had no idea he could give Dad-level hugs until then, or that he's a total wife guy . . . er . . . girlfriend guy? He's going to make a great partner and parent someday, probably (hopefully) to Keisha.

He pats me on the back a few times and then turns to check on the sauce before I make it awkward by doing something like bursting into tears from his kindness. "You guys have been glued at the hip this whole break," he says. "I get how that might be making things harder for tomorrow."

"Yeah," I say, dropping into a chair at the table. "You're so lucky your girlfriend lives across town and not across the state."

"Hey, I did the long-distance thing at barber school. Remember Alexa? We were together for a while. I know what it feels like. It sucked when we broke up. Most long-distance relationships do, though," he says absentmindedly, and then, seeming to realize what he just said, he scrambles to overcorrect. "I mean, not *most*! *Some!* Not you and Ruby, obviously. Me, mostly; I couldn't hang. But Alexa and I broke up, like, weeks in. *Weeks!* You guys have a whole semester under your belt already. I'm sure you'll be fine. But even if you guys aren't fine, *you'll* still be fine, you know?" He hangs his head back and lets out a groan when he sees that I'm wincing. "I'm gonna shut up now, if that's cool. That was supposed to be a pep talk."

I snort. "Wow, your pep talks still kinda suck, Dylan."

"I am very well aware, Morgan," he says, looking at me out of the corner of his eye. "That's why I give the hugs, and I let Keisha or Owen do the talking."

"Where is Owen anyway? Is he coming tonight too?" I ask.

Owen is my brother's best friend and business partner. They own a barbershop together, but he also swings by for dinner sometimes—especially on spaghetti nights. Owen loves to say, "I'm not your stepbrother; I'm the brother who stepped up." I haven't bothered pointing out that being Dylan's best friend doesn't make him my stepbrother, but I also can't tell if he's being serious when he says it. Either way, Dylan's right; he does give good pep talks—way better than Dylan's. But if I'm being honest, Keisha's always take the cake.

"He wanted to, but he can't. His cat's super sick, and he doesn't want to leave her alone."

"Not Mogwai!"

"She *is* eighteen," my brother says sadly. "But hey, we're not worrying about that today, okay? Today we're celebrating a great visit home and getting excited for next semester, right?"

"That would be easier if you didn't keep saying sad stuff!"

"Yeah, that's on me," he says. "I'm serious about you and Ruby, though, so forget what I said. You two can and *will* make it work, as long as you both want to. Look at Mom and Dad. They were high school sweethearts and went to different colleges too. It happens."

I shrug. "Yeah, I know we'll be fine," I say, because I desperately hope it's true.

It's nice to think that Ruby and I could be forever, that we could have our own happily ever after, but comparing us to my parents is . . . well, weird, first of all. I know *technically* my parents were my age once and dating, but it's hard to see them as anything besides my middle-aged mom and dad. But also, my parents were pretty much made for each other from day one. According to my grandparents, it would have been weirder if they *didn't* work out.

I'm not saying Ruby and I are *not* made for each other. I can't imagine my life without her and definitely wouldn't ever want to. We're solid. We're great. She's my favorite person on this entire earth, and I love her more than I thought was even possible . . .

But we definitely didn't have that peanut-butter-to-my-jelly start to our relationship the way my parents did. Like, she hit me with her car. *Twice.* (Okay, fine, the first time is a bit of a gray zone on who technically hit who.) The point is, we didn't have the entire world saying we were made for each other and cheering us on from the start. The opposite, actually. Luckily, that only made us stronger . . . but still.

Then there's also the practical stuff, like that we're four hours away from each other during the school year, but it might as well be four hundred. Ruby's car is *really* not made for constant road trips, *and I don't even have one!* We're too close for a plane, too young for rental cars, and the bus is shockingly expensive, although we've tried to make that work. I'm kind of at the mercy of Dylan or my parents helping me afford tickets to get home. With my class load and track practices, I don't have time for a job to help, so I try not to push it.

And that's on top of things like homesickness, and stress from our classes, and trying to paste on a happy face when I'm feeling impossibly lonely.

I wish I didn't have to go back at all. I wish I could just stay home forever instead.

And by "home," I mean this apartment. I mean *Ruby*.

I tried to go to my old house with my parents to stay for a few days at Christmas. Dylan drove me down one afternoon, and we all went out to the café near our house before he had to head back—the holidays are a really busy time for barbers, apparently. Of course, we ran into one of my old private school "friends" there. It sucked.

We were all being fake nice, but I couldn't help but remember how quickly she dropped me after I was outed at my old school, and how she'd never once checked up on me after. I could tell my family was thinking the same thing. I was quiet and uncomfortable until we left.

The second we got back to the house, my parents and Dylan all insisted on packing up everything—even the tree—and coming back here. My mom declared nobody should feel uncomfortable at Christmas. I told them they didn't have to leave their house, but they weren't hearing it. We were back at the apartment by that night. My brother gave my parents his bedroom and slept on the couch, even though I told him he should have my bed because I was the one putting everyone out.

Dylan put me into a headlock and told me it was time for me to realize that my happiness was not putting anyone out, which made me cry.

By the time I woke up the next morning, they had turned Dylan's little apartment into a winter wonderland. Mom and Dad ended up booking an Airbnb with a hot tub the day after Christmas and made a mini vacation for themselves. It was nice having everyone in one place, but even nicer to know I never had to go back to my old town if I didn't want to.

"Smells good in here," Keisha says, stepping inside and kicking off her shoes. She does a double take, noticing me and Dylan in the kitchen both looking like sad sacks. "What's wrong?"

"Dyl tried to give me a pep talk," I groan.

"It looks like it went quite well." She laughs, coming over to ruffle my hair and press a kiss onto my brother's cheek. "Want me to take a stab at it?"

"That's up to her," Dylan says. "I should get back to the pasta."

"Come on." Keisha smiles. "Let's ditch your brother and go in the living room."

It's like she can sense I need to hug one of her throw pillows for this. She probably can, actually; I've been confiding in her more and more as they get more serious. She's bi, like Ruby, who finally settled on a label. Well, mostly. Sometimes she still says pan or queer, but usually it's bi.

Keisha actually helped Ruby this summer when she was still navigating her feelings around being attracted to every gender. Plus, Keisha was president of the Alpha Chapter of Delta Sigma Theta when she was at Howard, so she definitely gets my passion for service work, and doesn't laugh when I say I want to change the world. She's still really involved with her sisters and the work her sorority does. It's pretty awesome.

"Okay, lay it on me," she says, passing me a pillow and then settling in beside me.

"Break went by too fast," I say miserably.

"I know, but spring break will be here before you know it. Are you still planning to head down to DC together?"

"Yeah." I smile. "That part will be awesome, just me and her and—" A loud yelp cuts us off.

Dylan calls out from the kitchen. "Uh, what was that?"

Keisha and I look at each other in confusion, before I realize . . .

"Ruby?" I call out.

"When did you move your frigging hope chest?" she says, limping out of my bedroom. "I fully just fell on the floor because I expected my usual little step down to be there."

Keisha and I both burst out laughing. "Why didn't you use the door?" I say, jumping up to fuss over her.

Ruby wraps me in a hug, kissing me quickly and then burying her head in my shoulder. "I thought it would be fun for old times' sake," she mumbles as I rub her back. "And now my ass hurts."

"Poor baby," I say, trying not to laugh again.

"You know," she says, leaning back to meet my eyes, "you *could* always kiss it better."

My brother snorts from the kitchen, and I notice that Keisha has joined him when I hear her smack his arm. She's too late, though—I can already feel my face going hot all over again. I probably look like a cherry tomato.

As much as Ruby and I have teamed up to tease Billy about

his crush, Dylan and Ruby have *also* teamed up to spend this entire break making me cringe. Dylan made one bad joke about Ruby not getting me pregnant, and—seeing my reaction as I literally died in front of them—apparently, they thought it would be a fun game for the holidays.

Dyl always says if I'm old enough to have sex, I'm old enough to be normal about it when it comes up, but I don't know. It feels like there's a lot of space between "being normal about it" and my girlfriend's and brother's terrible puns and even worse jokes. They never go too, too far, though, and I know I'll miss the teasing when I'm back at school.

"I'm sorry. I had to," she says, kissing me twice in quick succession. "You kinda walked right into that one."

"Technically, you fell into it first," Dylan says, leaning out of the kitchen to point his spoon at Ruby. "Because, you know, the window and the—"

"They get it." Keisha laughs, rolling her eyes. "Now stop eavesdropping or I'll tell them all about the time you farted when I—"

"Okay!" he says. "I am stirring my pasta and minding my business."

I shake my head and look back at Ruby, leaning forward to kiss her once more, just because I can. We opt for the oversized armchair in the corner—it's practically the size of a love seat anyway—instead of the couch. I pull Ruby into my lap so we have no choice but to tangle our limbs together and snuggle in.

I want to be as close as humanly possible to her until the very last second I have here. I wish that I could store the sensations in my skin somehow—that there was a way to hold on to the feeling of her body against mine until we can be together again.

"I'm dreading going back," I say as Ruby snuggles against me, playing with my hair. She's kind of become obsessed with how long it's gotten—shoulder length now after nearly a year of growth. While I decided super short hair was no longer for me, I didn't give up on the pink. It's handy having someone who does hair for a brother, especially when you pick a color that requires so much maintenance. He definitely touched it up in more than one hotel bathroom last semester.

"I told you majoring in public policy was a bad idea."

"Haha," I say, tickling her just enough to make her squirm. She tickles me right back, and then it's a tickle war until we start to fall. She catches us both, propping us up with one hand on the ground while I shimmy my way back into the chair and then pull her in beside me again. I can't help but admire the curves of the muscles in her arms as I do. Mechanic work looks good on her. So does my skintight Under Armour warm-up shirt from college that she's currently wearing.

It's technically meant to go *under* our team shirts, not to be worn alone, but it fits her like a second skin and has my college name printed across it. Seeing her in it always makes the butterflies in my belly spin.

Unfortunately, I'm going to have to take it with me when I leave—it *is* part of our official uniform and all—but I've already decided which hoodie I'm going to leave with her instead, and which of hers I'm stealing.

"I don't want to be sad right now," Ruby says, looking in

my eyes. "Please? We'll have too much time for that after you leave."

"I don't want to be sad either," I say, even though I very much am.

How could I not be? In less than fourteen hours, I'm going to be piled in Dylan's car with all of my stuff, heading four hours away from the girl I love.

"Then we won't be," she says, leaning in for another kiss. "Even if we have to distract each other all night."

Dinner is a relatively quick affair, both Dylan and Keisha sensing that we want to take our leave sooner rather than later and calling off movie night, and after we help load the dishwasher, we find ourselves quickly curled up in my bed, facing each other.

It's an unseasonably mild winter, but we both pretend we're freezing cold and use it as an excuse to cuddle even closer. I would give anything for a good old nor'easter like we used to get. The snow piling up a couple feet would keep me trapped here for another day or two. Sure, I would miss the start of classes. I'm leaving at the absolute last second as it is—I have a lecture at six p.m. tomorrow—but it would all be worth it for one more day in Happy Girlfriend Land.

The first semester was hard, but I had the benefit of not knowing how hard it would be to be away from Ruby. I had an idea, sure, but this time, I know *exactly* how much it's going to suck. It's making things one hundred times worse.

"Hey, no overthinking," Ruby says, tapping my temple gently. "Be here, with me, right now."

I huff out a breath and force a smile. Seemingly unsatisfied with that reaction, she rolls me onto my back and cages me in her arms. "Don't make me punish you," she says. "Your brother might hear and wonder what we're doing."

"No, I'm sure he'll know, given that you've tickle attacked me once already tonight." I giggle.

She raises her eyebrows, before falling to the side of me like she's been struck. "You were supposed to think that was innuendo so I could sneak attack you as the tickle monster. You ruined the surprise."

"I'm sorry, I'm sorry. I knew you were up to something with that horrible impression of a cheesy guy in a romance novel. 'Don't make you punish you,'" I say, lowering my voice to imitate hers. "Where did that even come from?"

"TikTok." She shrugs, looking very serious about it.

I try and fail to pull it together in case I've actually offended her, only for Ruby to burst out laughing instead. Some of it is nerves, I know, and some of it is probably us each trying to put on a good show for the other, but I suspect at least a little of it is because it feels so good to be back together after most of a day apart. The truth is, being around Ruby just makes the smiles and laughter come easier, especially knowing everything we fought through just to be together in the first place. Who cares if we were meant to be at the start or not; we clearly are *now*.

I lean in to kiss her, no TikTok impressions necessary

this time, but Ruby's phone vibrates across my nightstand, interrupting us. I catch the way her eyes narrow, all humor in them dying as she stares at her phone. She must think it's her mother again.

She still hasn't talked to her yet, even though Billy and I both encouraged her to. We just have to trust that Ruby has a handle on it. She knows she can always come to me if she needs to talk about it, so I've been trying to give her space . . . but space is the last thing we need on our final night together.

"Come here," I say, not wanting to have this ruin her night. She curls up beside me, resting her hand over my heart and tapping out the rhythm on my sternum. I catch her fingers with my own and pull them to my lips for a kiss.

"I love you," I say.

"I know," she says back, a habit she picked up when Dylan made us watch *Star Wars* with him on one of our FaceTimes a few weeks after I left for school. Ruby didn't know that I'd seen it before, and I made Dylan swear not to tell. She doesn't know that I spent the entire movie watching her blink and breathe and laugh on the tiny screen, clutching onto the moment like a lifeline in my little extra-long twin bed. She doesn't know how lonely it gets surrounded by cinder block walls, hours away from everyone you know.

The captain of my track team, Mika, is on me all the time to get out of my room more—to join more clubs, or go to parties, or make friends outside of my teammates—but I can't help if I'd rather be FaceTiming Ruby or texting with Dylan or Zooming with my best friend, Aaron. Mostly FaceTiming with Ruby, though, if I'm being honest. Besides, it's not like I have much free time anyway—running for a D-I school is practically a full-time job.

Ruby, on the other hand, did so well without me last semester. At first, I thought she was just putting on a brave face like I was, but no, she is *thriving*. I love my school, I do, and I nailed my classes and my race times, but sometimes it felt like I was falling apart while Ruby was hitting her stride. I tried to hide it as much as I could. I don't ever want to be the reason she has a bad day or be the person that slows her down when she's finally letting herself hit full speed. So I stare when she's not looking, and I send her cheerful texts all the time, using entirely too many smiley-face emojis, and I pretend I've already joined all the clubs that Mika tells me about, even though I only went to one meeting, once, because Mika dragged me there herself, and I . . .

No. Ruby's right. Tonight's not for sadness. That will come in its own time. No use inviting it in early. I kiss the top of her head, trailing my fingers down her side, searching for the little expanse of skin where her shirt has rucked up so I can trace invisible hearts against it.

God, I love her in such a real and true way. I knew she'd be the death of me the second I met her—not just because she literally could not stop hitting me with her car, but because I felt it in my bones, the second our eyes locked, that she was going to be the biggest love I've ever had.

Ruby hums out a little sigh, nuzzles deeper into my neck to place painfully soft kisses along my skin, and I know, *I know* tomorrow's going to hurt like hell.

3

RUBY

I watch Morgan as she sleeps.

She's curled up on her side, her face just a few inches from mine, with my arm currently going numb under her head. There's a hint of a smile on her face, and I hope this means she's having good dreams. She should. She deserves them.

I want this moment to last forever, to stretch it out all the way until it snaps, but I know that soon an alarm will go off on her phone. Morgan will stretch sleepily and then hit snooze like she always does. If I'm lucky, she'll slide back down and burrow against me, grabbing my arms to wrap them around her herself because she never thinks I'm fast enough.

Today, I plan to be fast enough.

Because I know what will happen after that. After that, exactly eight minutes later, her phone alarm will go off again.

This will be the time she pushes herself up to sitting and starts her day. She never hits snooze twice.

I can already picture it: Morgan will stretch and sigh. She'll look at me with her big sad eyes and force a smile, and then . . . she'll climb out of our nice warm bed and begin the business of leaving me behind. It will be the last time I wake up next to her for a long time, a thought that makes me want to scream if I think about it too hard. So I don't. Or at least I try not to.

I try not to think at all—at least not about anything outside of the gentle sound of her breaths or the way her eyes shift under the delicate skin of her eyelids. Oh, it's going to kill me when she leaves.

Sometimes I almost resent her for this.

Not for the going-away-to-school thing—that's important and we both recognize it. Even if it wasn't the ideal school for her (it is), she would have been crazy to give up all the track scholarships. Yeah, her future has always been big and bright, and it starts right now with all the connections she's making and clubs she's already been able to join—who knew there were so many college clubs centered around service and politics? I don't know how she even has time for all of that, but then again, Morgan's never been one to let anything stand in the way of something she wants.

So yeah, I would never, ever resent her for going away to school. I'm proud of her for that. Just like I'm proud of myself for my own schooling and the awards that make this community college here the absolute perfect fit for me. If all goes right, I'll graduate with my associate's degree in occupational studies, specializing in automotive technical sciences, in a year and a half. Last semester was all about engines and automotive electricity, along with a stupid math class I had to take. But this semester I get to take Passenger Car Chassis 1 *and* an automotive welding class that I'm really excited about.

I have a clear and definite leg up on things from working with Billy for so long, and it's been really nice to suddenly be the respected one for once. Sure, I had to show up a bunch of the guys in the beginning to earn their respect—I'm the only woman in the class—but it was kinda fun. Most of them are actually pretty cool now, and even the ones who aren't still come to me for help sometimes.

No, school is good, for her *and for me*. That's not what I resent at all.

I resent the other stuff. The stuff we have to *lose*, even temporarily. Like the fact that I've spent our winter break re-memorizing the exact weight of her head on my arm and cataloging how long it takes my fingers to go all pins and needles from it. And the fact that I know she's always going to say she doesn't want extra fries at the diner but then steals half of mine when hers are gone. The fact that everybody at the apartment complex began leaving my spot in the parking lot free when they started seeing my car again all the time, and soon someone else will take it over. The fact that tomorrow, when I go get coffee, I'll only have to order one. The ten thousand little things that make life so much better and that I would never, ever have even known about had I not met her.

Morgan shifts closer, sending fresh sparks of electricity careening down my wrist and hand, which have long since gone numb. I flex my fingers and wiggle my hand instinctively, regretting it when the tiny motions accidentally coax my girlfriend awake. She blinks up at me sleepily, breathing in and out deeply as she shimmies closer, grabbing my free arm and tugging it around her as she settles under my chin. I sigh, pressing a smiling kiss to the top of her head.

Too slow again.

"What time is it?" she grumbles into my chest.

"Too early to start the day," I say, even though I know her alarm will go off any second. It feels like the truth, though, because even if it were eight o'clock at night, it would feel too early to start *this* day.

Morgan huffs out a laugh, snaking her hands under my shirt to rub tiny patterns against my back. I hold her as tight as I can, ignoring the fact that my one arm is still definitely at least semi-offline.

Worth it.

As expected, the alarm on her phone starts blaring a few moments later—obnoxious submarine sonar noises that drive me up a wall. Second to the actual siren setting, it's *the* most brutal way to wake up. Morgan stretches one of her arms out behind her, nearly knocking over her lamp while trying to find her phone without breaking our hug. I take pity on her, grabbing it myself and hitting snooze. I might squish her a little in the process, but neither of us are complaining.

The second time the alarm goes off, I get the regretful hum and the sitting up that I've been dreading since about four a.m.

There she goes, pushing that first domino down.

After that, the morning slides together, a choreographed dance of taking turns showering, eating the bagels from her favorite shop that her brother surprises us with, and packing up the last few things she needs from her room.

Before I know it, we're loading the car.

"Why do you have to leave?" I whine, helping her carry out the bags of groceries and toiletries her parents got her the day before.

"The sooner I leave, the sooner I get back," she says, her eyes as red-rimmed as mine. "At least that's what I keep telling myself. I just . . . Are you going to be okay here without me again?"

I'm fucking this up, I realize, as fresh tears spill down her cheeks. *I'm making this harder on her.*

I set her bags in the trunk and shut it hard before leaning my hip against the side of the car. I tug her closer, wiping her tears away with the pad of my thumb.

"I'm gonna be fine, just like I was last time, and so are you! All those clubs you joined aren't going to run themselves! And you're right, the sooner you leave, the sooner we get to go to DC," I say, smiling at her with my most natural pageant smile. I pray she can't tell the difference even though I'm sure she can. It doesn't matter. I need her to know I mean it. I need her to understand that I've got her back as much as she's got mine.

Last time she left, I think she was worried that I would go back to how I used to be: shut down, walled off, and all those other words people use when they're trying to avoid admitting they're just scared. But that didn't account for the fact that Morgan had made me realize that sometimes the best things can come out of being scared but ditching your comfort zone anyway. I really took that lesson to heart, grabbing on to school last semester with both hands and kicking ass, just like her. But still . . . that doesn't mean standing here, knowing she's about to leave, doesn't feel like an ice pick to the heart right about now.

"We'll FaceTime every day," Morgan says, her tears picking up again as her brother steps outside, locking the door behind him.

I can't breathe.

These moments, these last moments, they're the absolute fucking worst, but I also wouldn't trade them for anything. I can take it. I can do this. *I can be strong for her.*

"We'll text constantly too," I remind her, wishing my voice weren't wavering, wishing I were braver, stronger, tougher, more of a rock.

"We'll work out the whole DC itinerary," she says, wiping her nose. "Starting tonight. Every exhibit you want to see, every tour and meeting I want to go on. Everything. It'll be perfect."

I smile again, and this time it's genuine—I'm so fucking full of love for this gremlin standing here in a hoodie she stole from me. So fucking grateful that she burrowed her way into my life when I least expected it.

I lean forward and kiss her lips, chasing the salt from her tears. I don't even care that her brother is right there, getting into the very car I'm leaning against.

Right now, only me and Morgan matter. Only we exist.

"Yeah," I say, pressing our foreheads together one last time before letting her go. "It'll be perfect."

"You sure you need that coffee?" Everly asks as she drops down into the diner booth across from me. "It's almost three p.m."

I smile, soaking up the comfort of having my best friend home for an extra day. Thank god for staggered spring starts. "I'm sure. I still have to teach the littles at the dance studio tonight, and I've been up since four a.m."

"Why?" she asks, tucking her braids behind her ear as she picks up the menu—as if she's not going to order her usual side of fries with a vanilla shake for dipping.

"Couldn't sleep last night."

"Because of Morgan leaving?" She flicks her eyes up to meet mine. "You okay?"

"No, I just couldn't sleep. I'm fine."

"There you go, trying to be a hard-ass again. It's okay not to be okay," she says, quoting the poster in our old guidance counselor's office unironically for probably the first time.

"'It's okay not to be okay'? You're spending too much time with woo-woo hippie art students, aren't you?"

She snorts. "I can't help it! Everybody in the photography program is super white with way, way too much time and money on their hands. If the girl that runs the photography equipment sign-out tries to teach me about crystals one more time, I swear to god . . ."

"I thought you liked her!"

"I do! She's not bad, other than the crystal thing." She laughs. "I guess that's part of the whole college experience, though, you know?"

"Hmm," I say, tapping my chin. "I'll remind myself of that the next time my forty-five-year-old roommate forgets to replace the toilet paper roll. 'It's just part of the college experience,' I'll say."

"Hey, at least he doesn't steal your last tampon. That gets messy real fast, literally and figuratively."

I burst out laughing right as the waitress comes to take our order. Thankfully, Everly knows my order as well as she knows her own. She handles it for me as I wipe the tears from laughing so hard from my eyes. Only . . . they don't stop coming.

Jesus. Get a grip.

I think about running to the bathroom until I get control of myself, but that just reminds me of the time Morgan followed me in there before we were even dating. I forgot my mascara on the counter, and she drove all the way to the Miss Tulip pageant just to give it back to me.

What would have happened if she hadn't done that?

"Hey," Everly says, realizing something is up. "Seriously, you good?"

"Yeah," I say, taking a deep breath as I try to pull it together.

"I don't know why you torture yourself. When Marcus left for his school the other day, I just gave him a quick kiss and went in my house. I bet you stood there watching her drive away today, didn't you? You coulda got in your car and left before she did."

“I wanted every second I could have,” I mumble like the lovesick idiot I am. “Plus, if I watched her leave, that meant she didn’t have to be the one to watch me.”

Everly grabs her heart dramatically and falls back against her seat. “That is the most romantic thing I’ve ever heard. Marcus better be saying that same shit right now.”

Unlikely. We both know that he probably just left early to get back to his video games and frat parties sooner, even if she won’t admit it. While my relationship with Morgan has only gotten more intense after a semester apart, Everly and Marcus’s seems to have faded. I’m not surprised—they were off and on the whole semester, but it figures that they’re on again, just in time to leave. Sometimes I think with them it’s less about loving each other, and more about not wanting each other to date anyone else.

“I’m not doing it to be romantic,” I say. “I’m doing it to be practical. If I can make shit easier on her, I want to. She does the same for me. Remember how she came home in the middle of my finals week? I was freaking out about it. Not only did she help me prep every night, but she was also waiting outside every day with a coffee, a muffin, and a hug the second I was done. We have each other’s backs; we’re solid.” I look up and notice Everly’s grinning at me. “What?” I ask.

“Loving and being loved looks good on you.”

“Oh, shut up,” I say, flicking a napkin at her. “It looks good on everybody.”

“Yeah, but I never got to see it on you before you moved in with Billy.”

My phone buzzes on the table before I can reply. I flick my eyes over, in case it's Morgan, but it's not. It's my mother again, just like last night. I flip it over with a frown.

"Your mom still trying to get ahold of you?" Everly asks, the smile slipping off her face.

"All day, every day," I say. "She even stopped by Billy's a few times."

Everly clicks her tongue. "You asked her for space; you deserve space."

"I guess she thinks I've had enough," I say bitterly.

Like I need one more thing to feel down about today.

"You ever think about answering her?"

"All day, every day," I sigh. "I mean, she's my mom. For the longest time, it was just us against the world, you know. It's hard to . . . to not have that anymore. I know she's probably just calling because she and Chuck are fighting again, or to try to convince me to sign up for one of the pageants she keeps texting me about, and not because she's magically become a loving, accepting person, but I don't know. A part of me misses her. A part of me hates her. A part of me is scared to find out exactly what she wants to say."

"Yeah, I get it," Everly says. "I don't know what I would do in your shoes, honestly. I just hope you know that there's not a wrong choice here—answer or don't; do what you need to do to be happy. Just don't ever let her disrespect you again."

"Yeah," I say as the waitress drops off our food.

I could argue that her refusing to give me space is already a sign she *won't* be doing that, but I get what Everly means.

Fuck.

"All right, enough deep shit," Everly says. "Are we watching the game tonight after work or a movie?"

"A movie," I say, because I already feel a headache forming, and if I have to listen to the squeak of basketball shoes, I might honestly explode. "But nothing sappy."

"Fine, we'll do scary. Again. But nothing with Mia Goth this time. Please, I'm begging here. I'm really trying not to judge this little crush you have, but if you want a scream queen, what the hell is wrong with Maika Monroe? She's, like, right there! And a million times hotter!"

"They're both hot." I laugh, and she shakes her head.

Since I officially came out as queer to Everly last spring, she's been almost overly supportive. As in, constantly talking about girl crushes with me and even making her parents hang a pride flag on their house. I think they thought *she* was queer at first. I try not to read into the fact that they looked relieved to find out it wasn't her, it was *me*.

"Fine, you pick," I say. "Anything you want, as long as it's not a romance or something that will make me cry."

"Deal," she says, holding out her hand to shake on it, as my phone buzzes again.

4

MORGAN

My alarm blares entirely too early, and I drag my tired, aching body out of bed. I stumble around the room as quietly as I can, trying to find my gear for my six a.m. track practice without waking up my roommate, Megan, and pissing her off even more.

I get it. I wouldn't like to be woken up at the crack of dawn for no reason either, something I hadn't considered when I begged to be put in the freshman dorms instead of the apartment-style athlete quarters the school provides for all recruited athletes.

I know, I know, never look a gift horse in the mouth, but I wanted to get a real freshman experience. I didn't think I'd get it living with upperclassman runners. I don't want to get all special snowflake about it, but student athletes tend to be dialed in all the time—if not about competitions, then about making up all the work they missed while *at* competitions . . . I guess I just wanted some time to not be just Morgan the runner but also Morgan the first-year college student having fun. Although, if you listen to Mika, I'm not really doing that either.

I can't help that I'm homesick, or, well, Ruby-sick, I guess, if I'm being honest. I miss her so much when I'm here. I hate it.

Which, speaking of Ruby, the athlete quarters also don't allow overnight guests, so. Yes, Ruby only made it out once last semester—her class schedule was as intense as mine, plus she had to borrow Dylan's car—but still, she couldn't have visited at all if I weren't in the freshman dorms.

I bump into my desk chair reaching for Ruby's hoodie, which sends the chair squeaking across the cheap linoleum floor. Oof. I freeze, waiting for Megan to flip.

"Shut the fuck up," she groans before grabbing one of her pillows and throwing it in what I guess she assumes is my direction. She misses by a wide margin, but given that she still has a sleep mask covering her eyes, I'm kind of impressed.

I resist the urge to make a joke about throw pillows and opt for the apology angle instead.

"Sorry, sorry," I settle on, grabbing my toothbrush and heading to get ready. The harsh automatic fluorescent lights blind me as soon as I step into the Jack-and-Jill bathroom we share with the room next to us. *You wanted this freshman experience,* I remind myself. *Just be glad you didn't land on a floor with shared public bathrooms only.*

The bathroom is blessedly empty, though, allowing me to

brush my teeth and finish waking up in peace. I make quick work of the rest of my morning routine and shove a protein bar in my mouth as I jog down the stairs, surprised to see my track captain waiting for me outside.

Mika Hosseini, or Captain Mika as she signs her emails to the team, is a senior this year on the premed track. She's a third-generation Iranian American originally from Long Island, and her family moved upstate—only about forty minutes from where I live—the second she graduated from the swanky private school her grandfather insisted on her attending.

Mika's a lesbian like me and had somehow actually heard about the lawsuit my family filed against my own private academy last year—back when my school gave me the choice of leaving or being expelled after finding out I was gay. What Mika didn't know was that it had jeopardized all my D-I college track offers, including the one here, and had almost bankrupted my family with legal fees, so regrettably we eventually had to agree to drop the suit in exchange for them not contesting my running reinstatement.

Having my new track captain shake my hand and tell me I had "infinite aura" for suing, even if it didn't end up the way I wanted it to, was kind of a mind-blowing start to my time here. She's basically taken me under her wing since then, always looking out for me and encouraging me. If I'm being honest, she's pretty much the only person I'd consider a close friend, even though I pretend I have tons to everyone back home.

"Hey, freshie," Mika says, shoving off the ledge she was sitting on and trotting over to me. While we do hang out fairly regularly, this is the first time she's ever walked me to practice, and for a second, I worry this is going to be some sort of weird hazing thing, even though my team isn't really like that. At all. In fact, we have the highest overall GPA of any of the teams on campus. We're more likely to be setting up study sessions than pranking one another.

"Hey, what's going on?" I ask as we start walking toward the indoor track where we'll have practice today. I hate indoor. It makes me miss cross-country season even more. The mud, the woods, the peacefulness . . . it definitely beats running in circles inside a loud, echoing arena.

She shrugs, passing me a tube of GU, the energy and electrolyte supplement she swears by on competition days, before pulling her straight black hair into a tight pony. All little tells that mean she's got something hard planned for captain's practice today. "I remember how much it sucked to come back after my first winter break," she says. "So I thought I should check on our resident infant."

I shake my head, rolling my eyes as I fight off a smile. "I'm barely three years younger than you."

"Ah," she says, "but it might as well be three hundred in life experience terms."

"Mmm," I hum, because if there's one thing I'm lacking after last year, it's not life experience. Between moving schools, handling the lawsuit, working at the center, and creating my own nonprofit, not to mention everything with Ruby, I got a pretty healthy dose of it.

"Seriously, though," she says, putting on her best mom

face, "are you okay? I know how hard it was to leave Kennedy after winter break that first year. This long-distance stuff is garbage."

We both ignore the fact that Kennedy—her girlfriend of five years—visits constantly and that they're planning to get an apartment together right after graduation in a few months. Although, as my mom loved to say when I was debating staying closer for college, it's just as easy to break up at the same school as it is to stay together long-distance.

I'm not totally sure that's true, but either way, Mika is the only one on the team with a relationship longer than mine. I'm willing to take any advice she wants to throw my way.

"It sucks, yeah." I shrug, trying to make the best of it. Sure, we FaceTimed for two hours after my class last night, but it's not the same. Plus, with Ruby's classes starting today, time is going to get even tighter. "We're planning a big trip to DC for spring break, though," I say, as if that isn't forever away still. "So there's that."

"Is she coming out again before?"

"I don't know. Her class schedule is wild again this semester. With track practices ramping back up and my class schedule running from morning to night, I don't even know that it'd be worth it. Maybe for a long weekend or something? It's hard with her car."

Mika bounces her head from side to side a little, eyes narrowed like she's thinking. "I vote yes for a weekend visit. You should see if she can catch a ride with your brother to some of our meets too. I still think you need to integrate more into campus life, but if you're serious about making it work with this girl, I know you need to take advantage of any time you can get—without messing up your grades or missing practices, of course." She smiles. "Especially not the practice part."

I shake my head with a little snort. "Thanks for the tip."

"Anytime," she says, tossing our wrappers in the garbage before breaking into a jog. "Last one there has to collect towels after showers."

"Not fair," I call after her, lamenting her head start. Normally I love not being the fastest girl in school anymore—it's great to have people better and faster than me to help me set goals and push my pace—but moments like this, I miss it. Towel duty sucks.

Mika laughs over her shoulder and picks up her speed, even though we both know we've got a grueling practice ahead of us. Still, I know what she's doing. Mika's like me; she needs to run out her feelings. I suspect that's exactly what she's making me do right now.

"Thanks," I say when my second sprint burst, coupled with her lowering her pace, has me jogging beside her again.

"You're welcome, freshie," she says, with a wink.

I slide into a front-row seat for my Philosophy of Public Policy class twenty minutes before I even need to be here. I'm exhausted from practice, but too excited that I got into this, my most anticipated class, so early in my school career to wait another single second to arrive. Freshmen are last in line registration-wise, but athletes get early registration *and* a dedicated academic adviser, which is how I squeaked in. The professor who created this course, Professor Dunner, is legendary, having been a part of several big-deal movements before she settled down into a life of teaching.

The classroom is blissfully empty. I'm the only one obsessed enough to get here this early, I guess. I relish the quiet, though, after several hours of Mika shouting and blowing her whistle at us. In addition to our regular workout, Mika also put us through a bunch of 1Ks at tempo pace with only a thirty-second recovery between reps, my least-favorite thing of all. Did I say Mika was my closest friend? I meant power-hungry supervillain. Even if she did share her GU with me today.

I take my time opening up my note-taking app on my iPad and getting myself settled, savoring the moment of peace and reminding myself not to get all starstruck and quiet when the professor comes in. I know that to make my mark here, I need to really impress her. Professor Dunner has every connection I could ever hope for, and a reputation for helping her top students land research grants and internships.

I'm halfway through making a pros and cons list in my head of the best ways to make a great first impression on Professor Dunner when a girl slides into the spot next to me—despite the fact that we're still the only ones here. I glance her way. She's cute. Button nose, dark hair, pale skin, and tattoos, a couple piercings in her cheeks like she's dying for attention. As evolved as I try to be, I still can't help the way my eyes trail over her body, my annoyance from her sitting next to me replaced instead with curiosity. When my eyes shoot back up to her face, I realize she's caught me looking.

She grins like the cat that got the canary and then goes back to searching through her bag. "Shit," she says, pouting her lips out at me. "Do you have a pen? I forgot one."

"Yeah, sure," I say, reaching into my bag quickly, desperate to have something else to focus on. "I'm using an app anyway."

"I'm old-school." She shrugs, her fingers brushing against mine as she takes the pen. She flips open her notebook—a black leather Moleskine, because of course—and starts doodling little hearts on the blank page.

Subtle.

"You're here very early," I say, pointedly scanning the rows of empty seats behind us and raising my eyebrow as she follows my gaze. "Were there no other seats?"

"Nope," she says. "None that will let me adequately size up the competition."

I snort. "'The competition'?"

"Mm-hmm," she says, tilting her head like I'm the weirdo here. "I thought there'd be more of you, not that I'm complaining." She smirks. "Besides, the class is full, and the waiting list is miles long. If I don't sit here, someone else will. This way we can at least push each other."

"What makes me 'the competition'?" I ask, making air quotes and rolling my eyes. She's cute, I'll give her that, but *very* strange.

"Let's see," she says. "You're here incredibly early and have that faint lost look in your eye. Are you a freshman?" she asks. I nod, and she narrows her eyes. "I knew it."

"Knew that I was a freshman?"

A few more students shuffle in before she can answer, and the girl leans forward conspiratorially. To anyone else, we probably look like a couple of friends talking quietly, and not like she's a complete and utter stranger dead set on invading my personal space. The girl's so close now that I catch the faint scent of perfume on her neck, something unfamiliar and spicy, toned down like it's from yesterday.

I take a deeper breath, trying to place it, but startle when she whispers, "No, I knew that you were an overprepared, ass-kissing overachiever . . . just like me. I'm a freshman too. I was led to believe that I would be the only one in this class, but it's fine. This will be more fun. I bet you were sitting here all alone thinking about how to make the *perfect* first impression on Professor Dunner."

"No," I say, even though I definitely was.

"Don't lie," she says in a singsong voice. Her perfectly straight white teeth flash beneath a smile that's just this side of mean. I'm marveling at the fact that this eat-you-alive thing kind of works for her when she adds, "Besides, I'd be super disappointed if you weren't."

More and more students shuffle into the room, and the girl goes back to doodling in her notebook like nothing ever happened, while I'm left still leaning in my seat, swallowing hard, so far out of my element it hurts. I just keep watching her, too knocked off my game to look away.

Disappointed? Why?

She's so rude, so confident, and god, I want to say

something brilliant right now, something to match her energy, something to knock her off *her* game, but my mind blanks out, and now too much time has passed. Anything I say will feel forced and deliberate, instead of effortlessly witty.

Eventually, when her silence gets to me and the clock is ticking too close to the start of class, I mumble out a basic "Why would you be disappointed?"

I know it's what she wants me to ask. I'm not stupid. But as much as I don't want to feed into whatever this game is, I also don't want to be obsessing over it when Dunner actually gets here.

She sighs as if it's something she's told me a million times, even though we just met five seconds ago. "Because," she says, looking up from her notebook, "my brother always says girls can't be hot *and* brilliant, and I'd hate for you to prove him right."

"Oh, screw that. Besides, you already disprove that narrative, right?" I'm so annoyed by her brother's sexism that I don't even realize what I've just said, or what she has—in a roundabout way, we've both just called each other hot.

She stops drawing mid-heart, a faint shade of pink dusting her cheeks as she meets my eyes and holds out her hand. "Yeah, I do, actually." She laughs. "I'm Mackenzie, by the way, but you can call me Mac."

"Morgan," I answer, grinning before I catch myself as I shake her hand.

The girl—Mac, I remind myself—bites her overly glossed lip. I can't help but study the motion, my eyes trained to home in on shiny things, to covet them—a practically Pavlovian response after being with Ruby for so long.

Ruby.

Shit. What am I doing?

I take my hand back, guilt seeping out of my pores, although Mac doesn't seem to notice.

"Nice to meet you, Morgan," Mac says, tapping the pen twice against my arm before going back to doodling. "I have a feeling we're going to get along *very* well."

That shouldn't send a tiny thrill down my spine—it absolutely shouldn't—so I pretend that I've just caught a chill or that it's misplaced excitement about the class.

Oh god, what is wrong with me?

Before I can reply, before I can tell her that I have a girlfriend, that I *love* my girlfriend, that I need to move my seat or switch classes or run all the way back home to Dylan's, Professor Dunner comes into the room carrying a stack of papers. It's weird, the way she sets her coffee on the lectern, like she's a regular person and not the main reason I applied here in the first place. (Well, her *and* the track coach, but still.) It's surreal.

"All right, class," Professor Dunner says, giving me a warm smile as she steps forward to hand me a stack of papers. "I'm passing back the syllabus, but you can also find it in the classroom portal online."

Mac and I are still the only ones in the front row, so I dutifully pass her a copy before sending the rest of the stack behind me. Her perfume drifts back to me as she takes it.

5

RUBY

Usually when I stay after class, it's to experiment with some of the school's newer and more specialized tools. Billy's shop definitely needs an upgrade, but even though money is a little steadier now, it's not quite buy-the-latest-technology level of steady. My instructor for the Chassis 1 lab, who cringes when we call him Mr. Taylor and insists we call him Ben, says I'm welcome to do a little recon if I want. (Probably because he *also* uses the tools after class hours to work on his own projects.) We've had this deal since last semester, when I had him for Automotive Electricity.

That very generous invitation / way for my professor to be sure I don't rat him out is why I'm here today, killing the hour before I need to meet Billy for our regular Thursday-night dinner. Currently, I'm trying to use the digital torque wrench to make some adjustments on a brake caliper. Dealing with stuff like that has been the bane of my existence lately, and if the digital wrench actually helps, I'm going to beg Billy to add one to our shop.

Generally, if I'm in "try before you buy" mode here after class, I'm alone. Or worst case, Ben is here trying to see what his "star student" is up to or tinkering on something of his own. Yes, it *is* weird to be a star student after a lifetime of barely scraping by, and yes, it's kind of a mindfuck, but no, I'm not complaining. Except tonight. Tonight, I *am* complaining a little, because Ben told the new student he could stay in the lab too.

From what I've seen so far, this guy's a mess of a dude, really, just as likely to knock over an oil pan as to fill it—*and he isn't supposed to be changing oil in this class anyway!* I think it just might be the only thing he knows how to do. Seriously, he managed to strip three different bolts in class today. I don't even know how that's possible.

He wasn't in any of my classes last semester, which is curious because I thought this was a set program, with each class building on the last. When he came flying into the room on Tuesday, ten minutes late, motorcycle jacket flapping open, helmet flying out of his hands as his foot caught on the corner of his chair, I was equal parts intrigued and embarrassed.

Billy used to be really into bikes before he married my mom, but he stopped once he took on the role of stepdad. I didn't realize it at the time—I thought he was just sick of it—

but now I know it's because he wanted to be around for me. Kinda wild to think about someone giving up something they love to be responsible for someone else.

Billy never lost that wistful look in his eye when he heard a bike rumble by, though, and in the two minutes it took the kid—Shiloh, I think his name is—to check in with our instructor and take the seat next to me, I had imagined a whole scenario of hiring him as a bike mechanic in Billy's shop. It would be good to have someone solely focused on that as we expand the business even more. I was also thinking I could ask this guy for advice on if I should get Billy a bike of his own again someday, when my cash flow's better. Like to pay him back for how much he's done for me.

Of course, I realize now, after spending a couple classes with Shiloh, that he's got no business trying to fix anything mechanical. He might look good riding his bike in—something just about every person into dudes on this campus seems to have noticed—but that's where it ends. He's clearly just a rider. Why he's trying to cross over now is beyond me, and I haven't bothered talking to him enough to find out.

"Goddammit," he yelps from somewhere behind me.

Speak of the devil and all.

I spin around to see him clutching his hand to his chest, eyes squeezed shut in pain.

"You okay over there?" I ask, because I'm not a total monster.

"Do you really care?" he snaps, shaking out his hand.

I raise my eyebrows, caught off guard by his rudeness. "What's that supposed to mean?"

"Oh, does the class pet finally deign to talk to the giant fuckup?" He rolls his eyes. "You've been an asshole to me since I started."

"I have literally no idea what you're talking about." I shrug, walking over to where he's struggling with his . . . What even is that? Or what *was* that, I guess would be a fairer question.

I pick up what I think used to be part of an intake valve and start looking around for the rest of it. Shiloh watches me as he sucks on the freshly forming blood blister under his nail and frowns.

"Come on, you practically glare at my bike anytime I see you on campus! You ignored me when I asked you what your thoughts were on cruisers versus crotch rockets earlier. I'm pretty sure this is the first time you've said more than two words to me all week, and I sit right next to you in two different classes!"

I finally spy the valve spring where it rolled to on the floor a few tables away and hold it up triumphantly when I crawl back out. "I wasn't glaring at your bike; I was checking it out. I just have resting bitch face. And I def would have remembered you asking me about cruisers versus crotch rockets if I had heard you, because it's obviously cruisers and I could write an entire essay on the reasons why. Also, I don't talk to anyone here; you're not special. So see, I'm not an asshole."

He raises his eyebrows. "Right, because saying someone *isn't special* isn't being an asshole at all. I stand corrected."

I shrug, getting to work cleaning and reassembling the part. "I'm sorry, did you *want* to be the most hated of all my peers?"

"No," he says with a mischievous glint in his eye. "But maybe I'd like you to call me special."

And is he flirting? Oh god, I think he's flirting. Panic alarms go off in my head. *Abort, abort!*

"I have a girlfriend," I blurt out, turning bright red.

"Oh." He looks surprised, and I bristle when he adds on an incredulous "Really?"

"What? Are you homophobic or something?" I ask, starting to *undo* the work that I just did for him.

"Shit, stop, stop, stop, stop," he yells, jumping forward to put his hands over mine. "Please, I need that fixed to be able to drive home. I'm not homophobic. You just seem very . . . straight for a lesbian. That's all. You just give off a real bitchy pick-me kind of vibe, you know?"

"Oh, not homophobic, then. Biphobic. And misogynistic on top of that, got it. Cool." I flick his hands off mine and go back to messing with the valve. "Lesbians aren't the only ones with girlfriends, dude. And calling someone a 'bitchy pick-me.' Yikes."

"No, I know! I'm not any of that! Jesus, how could I be?" he says, blushing furiously and talking so fast I can barely keep up. "I'm fucking bi too. So technically, that makes you the biphobic one. Which you'd have realized if you'd ever bothered to say hi back to me!"

I arch my eyebrows. "In what universe does not saying hi back make *me* the biphobic one? You're the one who assumed I was a lesbian because I have a girlfriend! Also, while we're judging each other on the asshole scale, you're an eleven out of ten for calling me a bitchy pick-me."

"It's . . . biphobic . . . because you're being mean to a fellow bi?" He winces, his voice lilting up like it's a question. "I'm sorry for the pick-me comment. I love women, seriously. I'm literally raising one! Well, she's not a woman yet, but someday. Girl power and all that! I'm not a misogynist. I'm just frustrated that you know everything, and I don't. I'm sorry, okay?"

I scrunch my face up and then shake my head, leaning back against the desk. "No."

"No, what?" he asks. "No, you won't accept my apology?"

I look him up and down, reshaping my opinion of him with the context that he's a fellow queer kid in a program mostly made up of macho assholes. I had assumed Shiloh was one of them.

"No, that doesn't make me biphobic, but . . ." I trail off, narrowing my eyes.

"But?" he asks.

"But I guess you being bi too does make you *maybe* five percent more special than the rest of the class. For now. TBD on the misogyny front, though."

He beams like I just told him I hit the lotto and was signing it all over to him. "That's a start, at least. Now, please, help a fellow queer out. If I don't fix my bike, I'm gonna be walking home."

I'm about to offer him a ride when I flash back to last year, when Morgan tried to walk home in the rain and I had to beg her to get into my car. A wave of guilt washes over me. I know I wouldn't be doing anything wrong by giving him a ride if he truly was stuck, but still, it feels . . . intimate. Like something I shouldn't do. A can of worms not to be opened. Or maybe I just feel bad over the little zap of dopamine I'm getting from him looking at me like I'm a god.

I clear my throat and finish making my adjustment. "If you really needed this to work out, then why did you tear it all apart?"

He slides closer to watch what I'm doing. "It was making a weird sound on my way in this morning."

"Weird how?"

"It was going like *screeeeeeeech* when I stopped at red lights."

I burst out laughing. "So you decided to rip the valves out of your engine?"

"Y-yes?" he says, looking suddenly unsure. "Engine makes it go vroom, right?"

"Yeah, but it doesn't make it go squeak-squeak." I snort. "Where's your bike?"

"In the parking lot," he says, like I'm not holding his fucking valve train in the shop right now.

"In the parking lot?" I yelp. "You tore your engine apart in the parking lot because your bike squeaked at red lights, and left it out there all day?!"

"What was I supposed to do?"

"You were supposed to leave it alone until a professional could look at it, but second best would have been at least to wheel it into this garage bay before scrapping it for parts."

"Hey, I *am* a professional. I'm in this class, aren't I?"

"Yeah, no," I snort, following him outside and down the short walk to the main parking lot in back.

"Sorry, some of us weren't born with Chilton repair manuals in our grubby paws," he says, leading me to the end of one of the aisles, where his bike—or what's left of it—sits.

"I wasn't born with it; I work hard at it," I say. "Something you should do too if you want to pass this unit."

"I don't."

"What?"

"I don't want to pass the unit. Or I do, but I can't. I suck at this shit. Come on, we both know it."

"Then why are you here?" I ask, incredulous, because yeah, it may seem like a shitty automotive program to him, but it's actually well respected and something I'm proud of.

Shiloh winks. "That's way too complicated for our first date."

I nearly drop the intake valve. "This isn't a date. I told you, I have a girlfriend."

"Damn, it was a joke," he says, looking mildly horrified. "Sorry. I thought that was obvious."

"Well, it wasn't, and you shouldn't joke about that."

"You on thin ice with your girl or something?" he asks.

"What? No. Of course not, things are good. We're good," I say, reassuring myself as much as him. Because they are good, truthfully, even if it fucking blows to only be able to see her on FaceTime for now. "I just take it seriously, okay? Morgan's not up for discussion."

He opens his mouth as if he's going to make another smart-ass comment but then shuts it quick when I shoot him a glare. "Got it," he says, sitting on the ground next to me and passing me a screwdriver. “You got a picture of your girl?”

I roll my eyes. “Seriously? Why, so you can jerk off to the idea of us making out later?”

“No,” he says, pulling his phone out and pulling up a photo of . . . a toddler?

“That better not be your girlfriend,” I say, and he frowns at my bad joke.

“That’s fucked up. It’s my daughter, Stella Jane, and she’s not for joking about either. She’s also the reason I’m taking this course. I gotta give her a good life.”

“Where’s her mom?” I ask, even though I shouldn’t.

He scoffs. “God only knows. I hooked up with her a few times when I was in high school, but then she moved. I didn’t even know I had a kid until about four months ago, when Stella Jane’s grandma called and said her mama took off and they were going to turn her over to child protective services. Got the DNA test to be sure, then I picked her up and decided I needed to be a grown-up now. No more fucking around working at an arcade for minimum wage.”

“Honorable.”

“I guess. I don’t know. She’s worth it, though. I’m crashing in my aunt and uncle’s basement while I get on my feet. That’s why I need a job or a career, or both, really,” he says. “This was one of the only certificate programs with immediate openings, and I stupidly thought, *How hard could it be?*”

“Hard,” I snort, getting back to work. “You put your kid on this bike?”

“Nah,” he says. “I don’t have a car, so my uncle lets me use his bike to get to school and shit. I was trying to do him a solid by fixing the squeak, but—"

"Yeah, please don't ever do a solid for me." I laugh. He goes quiet, and I worry I insulted him. I awkwardly yank my phone out and flip the lock screen to him as an apology. "Shiloh, meet Morgan. Morgan, meet Shiloh."

"Hi, Morgan," he says, grinning at the picture before letting me get back to work. "She's pretty."

"Does she have a pick-me vibe too?"

"Can she also reassemble a bike in forty-five seconds?" he asks, watching me slot everything back into place on his motorcycle.

"No," I answer. "But she can save the world, so it's a fair trade-off. She's away at a university right now to make sure of it. She had a rough time in high school and is trying to make sure no one else does, thanks to her poli-sci degree."

"Cool . . ." he says slowly.

"What, you have a problem with humanities now too?"

"Nah," he says. "I just hope I'm a good enough mechanic eventually that Stella Jane can get an underwater-basket-weaving degree from a fancy-pants school someday like your girl. I sure as shit don't have the luxury."

"No rich parents to fund it?" I ask, even though the answer seems clear. I noticed right away when he said he was crashing with his aunt and uncle and not his mom and dad. I can't help but pry, though, curious to find out just how alike we really are.

"Uh, no," he says. "My dad's long gone, and it's very, *very* complicated with my mom." He shrugs, fiddling with his sleeve like he's embarrassed or, worse, ashamed.

"Same," I say, giving him a little shove to get him out of his head. Curiosity's one thing, but I didn't mean to poke a bruise. I know how slow wounds like that are to heal, if they ever really do.

He meets my eyes, opening his mouth like he's about to keep this impromptu therapy session going, but I can't. Not with the echoes of unanswered phone calls from my own mom still rattling around in my skull.

"My girlfriend grew up kind of loaded," I say, trying to move the conversation away from our own parents. "It's so funny, sometimes she doesn't even realize it. Like before she went back to school, she was asking my opinion on which running shoes to buy for the spring season, and they were all like three hundred bucks. I was like, *uhh.* I thought her parents would flip when she sent them the screenshot to have them transfer the money, but they were just like 'Okay, honey!'" I laugh. "Meanwhile, in my head, I'm like, 'You could pay the electrical bill for a couple months with that, and you're going to *step* on it?'"

"That's like five jumbo boxes of Pampers! That would last months!" He raises his eyebrows. "And your girl's parents don't care that she's dating someone like . . ." He trails off, the mood going heavy again despite my best efforts.

"Like?" I prod, my hackles up, even though I was just starting to warm up to him.

"Like *us*, I guess," he says.

I swallow hard, glancing at him long enough to see he's

moved on from fiddling with his sleeve to picking at his nails, before going back to work on his bike. It's not often that I feel the difference between me and Morgan anymore, but this is one of those times. Shiloh gets it in a way that Morgan doesn't, could never. What it's like to work your way up from nothing. He gets what it's like to live in someone's spare room, to not be born with that solid footing that it seems almost everyone else is.

I shrug and let his words hang in the air until I snap the last part into place and wipe my hands on my jeans. "You should be all set now," I say. "And if you need help on the unit, I usually stay after on Tuesdays and Thursdays till at least five."

"Thanks," he says, hopping on the bike.

"Oh, and a tip, Shiloh?" I add. "Next time your bike squeaks at a red light, check to see if your brakes are wet. Or better yet, don't ride your bike in the goddamn rain."

"Got it," he says, before riding off with a friendly wave.

I head back to the bay, shaking my head. This kid is a mess, sure, but maybe I can help. I don't plan to change the world the way Morgan wants to, but maybe I could change a life. Two, if you count his daughter.

And later, when we're halfway through dinner at Mike's Hot Dogs and Billy has to stop flirting with Shelby so she can get back to work, I tell Billy all about Shiloh and how he's a single dad like him. Billy thinks for a second, and then says we might need someone to organize the shop, since we don't have time anymore. Not great pay, but steady work, if I happen to know anyone looking. I snap my head up and smile, because yeah, I think I might know a guy.

6

MORGAN

I'm lying across a set of bleachers, gulping down water after a particularly grueling practice, when my backpack starts to buzz beneath my head. My first class is only an hour after practice, so on mornings like this, I have to hit the gym showers and get ready in our shared locker room. Usually, when I have short gaps between practice and class like this, I head over early, maybe grab a cup of coffee for a minute . . . but Coach really put us through the wringer today. I figured it wouldn't hurt to lie here and play dead for a while instead.

Especially since I know it's snowing again today, meaning I want to head outside even less. As it stands now, I have about twenty minutes before the start of class, and a ten-minute walk of icy misery until I get there. God, I hate winter.

Whoever is trying to call me is clearly not giving up, so reluctantly I force my aching muscles to pull my phone out of my bag. I grin when I see it's a FaceTime from Ruby—I didn't expect to hear from her until tonight. I click accept as fast as I can, my heartbeat picking up a little at the spinning circle that finally loads and reveals Ruby's face.

Did she get hotter?

"Looks like I did actually guess right," Ruby says, arching her eyebrow a little smugly. "Good morning, sunshine."

"Guess right about what?" I ask, adjusting the backpack under my head and holding the phone up above me so we can still see each other. I wiggle a little more to get comfortable—well, as comfortable as I can get on the crappy bleachers around our indoor track. It's really just painted lanes on a regular old gym floor, but if you close your eyes and wish real hard . . . no, it still sucks, even then.

"I was missing you, so I checked your forecast. I saw the snow and figured you'd be hiding out in the gym alone for as long as humanly possible. Wanted to sneak in a quick call before you had class."

I swoon a little at her words and softly ask, "You really check my forecast?"

"Every day, sometimes more often than that if I'm homesick for you," she says with a soft smile. "I know you hate snow, so I need to know when to be a little extra nice to you."

I smirk up at her. "And how exactly are you going to be a little extra nice to me today?"

"You sure you want me to tell you when you're in

public?" Ruby asks with a mischievous glint in her eye.

Maybe I can push the envelope a *little* further. "No one else is here, so . . ."

"Well, in that case, shut your eyes and imagine my hand slowly pushing up the edge of your shirt, as I trail my tongue—"

"Okay!" I say, jumping up to sitting as blush spreads hot from my ears to my toes. "Got it."

Ruby laughs on-screen—a wild, flushed, bright thing that makes my head spin. "I knew you were too chicken."

"Apparently, you know a lot of things about me." I giggle.

"I do," she says earnestly. "But it's the secret things I like best."

"You always did love your secrets," I reply.

I mean for it to land lightly, to keep the joking and flirting and banter going, but Ruby goes a little quiet. I hope I didn't go too far. I really, *really* don't want her thinking about last year when we got into our big fight. Back when I was ready to let the world know about us, and she wasn't. I angrily shouted, "I don't have a girlfriend. I just have a secret," and stormed out of the room.

I will always feel awful about that, even though we've obviously moved past it. Still, I don't want that in either of our heads right now. Not when we're separated by hours and miles, and we can't loop our pinkies or tangle our hands until we both feel whole and solid again.

"Anyway," she says, the moment clearly over, "I just wanted to check in before I have to head to class."

"You're early, no?" I ask, because I know things about her too. Things like the fact that her class is only a twenty-minute drive across town from Billy's house, and it doesn't start for over an hour.

"Yeah." She shrugs. "But I have to pick up this kid on the way. He's only got a motorcycle, and it's supposed to snow here today too."

"Is he in your program?" I ask, slightly wondering why this is the first I'm hearing of this guy—especially if they're close enough for her to be giving him rides to school. I know I shouldn't get that little twist of jealousy, but I do. I want to be the one riding in her car every day. I want to be the one keeping her company.

"Kinda," she says. "He sucks at it, but he's in a rough place right now, so I'm trying to help him out. Billy even found a little work for him to do around the shop. He's our age, and he's got a kid. Can you imagine having a kid right now? I would rather die."

"Kids love you," I point out, feeling instantly better knowing this guy has a family. If he's got a girlfriend and a baby, he's definitely not going to be a threat to my relationship. The second I think that, I'm annoyed with myself. I know people of any gender can be friends; I'm not going to get all caveman about her hanging out with a guy while I'm away.

What kind of girlfriend would I be, if I wasn't happy she made a new friend?

"Yeah, and I wish they didn't," Ruby says. "Hard no if he ever asks me to babysit. No diapers for me, thank you very much."

"Does that mean we won't have any little Ruby and Morgan babies running around someday?"

She's sipping from a mug when I say that—coffee, I realize, when it comes spitting out of her mouth like a cartoon. A little bit even splatters on the phone camera, painting her in a watery brown color. "You . . . We . . ."

"Calm down." I grin, getting up to head to my class. "I just wanted to see your face. Besides, I needed to get you back for teasing me earlier."

"Wow," she says. She still looks petrified, which makes me let out another giggle.

"Believe me, if we ever have the kids talk, it's not going to be anytime soon. You'll have to make do with your friend's rugrat for now."

She shakes her head, some of the tension leaving her body.

I smile, changing the angle of the phone so she can watch the snow as I trudge down the path to my classroom. "Is it supposed to snow this bad at home?" I ask, and when I flip the phone back, she has a dreamy look on her face that kicks up the butterflies all over again. "What's got that look on your face, Ruby Gold?"

"Nothing. I just *really* love hearing you call this place home. When your brother said he had to drive you back home last week and he meant your school, I literally wanted to tape his mouth shut."

"You're my home, Ruby. You know that," I say, loving the way that makes her whole face light up.

"I better be."

"You know how much I love—" My words cut off as a snowball smashes into the side of my face. "What the hell?"

"Morgan, are you all right? Who did that?" Ruby's tinny voice calls out from the speaker as I lower my phone to look around.

Suddenly, I spy her: Mac, the girl from class. The girl who made my stomach swoop when it really, *really* shouldn't have. *Ugh.* I was definitely hoping she would drop the class so I never had to see her again. Okay, that's dramatic, but I just want to do my work and get back to Ruby. I don't need any strange girls distracting me, even if they are semi-cute and stomach-swoop-able.

Maybe she'll leave if I ignore her.

Unfortunately, the second I look away, Mac tosses another snowball toward me, this one hitting me in the hip.

"Cut it out!" I say as she comes over, grinning.

"C'mon, we don't have snow in Cali. Let me experience the winter wonderland that is New England in January."

"You can enjoy it without me," I say pointedly as she slings her arm around me like we're old friends instead of people who met one class ago and shared a pen. "I hate winter."

"How can you hate winter? Don't you know how lucky you are to live in a place with *seasons*? I have to drive way, way north to get that back home."

Before I can even reply with my standard "seasons are overrated" speech, Mac points to the iPhone in my hand.

"Oh shit, sorry, are you on the phone?" she asks, like I wasn't obviously FaceTiming someone when she hit me with that first snowball.

Guilt slices through me even more than the cold does as I

yank my hand back up to my face. Of course, this only serves to frame Mac's arm around me in the screen for Ruby. I shrug it off.

"Oh shit, sorry, she is," Ruby says sarcastically, clearly having heard everything.

"Cool," Mac says, waving her fingers into the camera in Ruby's direction. "Hi, friend from back home, Morgan needs to get to class now before she's late. Talk later, bye!" Mac reaches forward and hits the end button before I can stop her.

"What is wrong with you?" I snap, scrolling back to Ruby's number.

"Nothing." She shrugs, walking faster toward the building. "I just always think it's sad when people are so hung up on their old lives they forget to start their new ones."

"Starting new lives doesn't mean you have to leave everyone else behind. It's *sad* that you think that," I argue, even though I did kind of have to leave my entire old life behind when I started living with my brother. Still, that doesn't mean everyone has to every time, right?

"Is it sad?" Mac asks with a laugh. "Or is it strategic?"

I roll my eyes. "Now you sound more like a tech bro than a poli-sci major."

"I am from California." She winks, falling back into step beside me.

"You should go back there, then," I snort. "If you'll excuse me, I have someone to call back and apologize to."

"You're excused," she says, jogging off with a quick wave. "Enjoy your sad little call."

I resist the urge to flip Mac off or, I don't know, pelt *her* in the side of the head with a snowball. Preferably an icy one. But I can't. Class will start soon, and I'm already halfway to the building. If I don't call Ruby back now, I won't be able to until the three-hour lecture gets out.

I absolutely don't want to wait that long.

I'm relieved when Ruby picks up after a couple rings. "Hey, sorry," I say at the same time as she asks, "Who was that?"

"Just a girl from one of my classes. Mac."

"You never mentioned Mac before," Ruby says, tilting her head.

"I just met her last week. It's a lecture class, only meets Tuesdays. Today's only the second time I've seen her in my life."

"She seemed super fucking friendly with you for someone you just met."

"Yeah, I know, right?" I shrug. "Maybe it's a California thing?"

"Maybe," Ruby says, her posture stiffer than it was before. Wait a minute . . .

"Hey," I say, a little softer. "Are you . . . jealous?"

Ruby rubs the back of her neck and looks away. "No. Of what? Why would I be?"

"It's okay if you are," I say. "If I'm being completely honest, I'm a little jealous too about you giving some guy a ride. At least I was until you told me he had a kid. If his girlfriend or wife or whatever doesn't care, then why should I?" Ruby opens her mouth to say something, but I cut her off. "I know, I know, it's stupid! Guys and girls can definitely be friends and blah blah blah. It's not that. It's just, I want to be the one in your car. I hate being apart."

"And I want to be the one pelting you in the face with snowballs," Ruby says finally. "And putting my arm around you . . . I get it."

"How many days until our spring break trip?"

"Seventy-three and a half, I think," Ruby says, a light blush dancing across her cheeks.

"Seventy-three and a half." I chuckle. "Did you make one of those countdown things like Everly has on her phone or something?"

"Everly *might* have helped me make one before she left for school herself." She scrunches her face up a little, tipping her head to the side, and I never really considered cute aggression a real thing until this moment, when I would give anything to crawl through the phone and squish her.

"That's the most adorable thing I've ever heard," I say. I'm kind of surprised that the snow isn't melting around me because of how warm and loved I feel from the idea that Ruby asked Everly to help her count down the days until we can be together. "I literally can't handle how that cute that is."

"Yeah, yeah, don't let it go to your head," she mumbles.

"Hard not to," I answer, and she makes a little pouty face.

"Don't you have a class starting soon?"

"Unfortunately." I groan. "I'd rather stay on the phone with you, though."

"Same," she says. "I can't wait for these seventy-three and a half days to be done. I really fucking miss you, Morgan."

"I miss you too, Ruby. Send me some of those sweet Smithsonian links when you have a chance. You know how they really . . . get my engine . . . revving?" I wince.

On the screen, Ruby has dissolved into a puddle of laughter. "Wow. Your innuendo really needs work. But yeah, I'll send you something to *get your engine revving* if you want."

"I'm never going to live this down, am I?"

"No," she says, blowing me a kiss before ending our call.

A few minutes later, just as I'm settling into my seat, my phone buzzes with a text: **Thought you might like this better than Smithsonian links** 😜

It's followed quickly by a picture of Ruby in her mechanic jumpsuit—the front of which she has unzipped deliciously low. I suck my lips into my mouth and close the app, blushing down to my toes. I accidentally shove my chair back too, interrupting my professor's class greeting with a giant screech. Professor Dunner gives me a weird look but then thankfully keeps talking.

Mac turns to look at me. *You okay?* she mouths, her eyes shifting around my face. I wonder if she can tell how absolutely giddy I feel right now.

I nod and give her a thumbs-up, because yes. Yes, I'm more than okay right now.

7

RUBY

Maybe I knew that full-on sexting wouldn't be Morgan's vibe, and it's really not mine either. Say what you want about my mom, but she did instill in me the fear of texting something you can't take back. But I have to say, I'm pleasantly surprised to see the flirty texts and slightly revealing photos have amped up ever since our talk last week.

While I'm dying for a flash of nipple, I know that's not happening. I'm definitely happy to make do with the collarbone and hint-of-hip pics she sent. Yesterday, she sent me a close-up of a bead of sweat trailing down her neck after practice. I almost exploded right as all the little kids were streaming into the classroom for a makeup tutorial that my old pageant coach had bribed me to do after my regular dance class.

One of them actually asked, "Miss Ruby, why is your face so red?"

Awkward.

After that, I make sure my phone is left safely in my backpack whenever I'm working.

Which is why I don't notice the three missed calls from my mother until right now, as I'm slinging my backpack over my shoulder and heading to my car to get back to Billy's in time for our weekly TV date. We declared Thursday nights our "family night," after we both discovered that we were secretly watching *Abbott Elementary* and *Mastermind Mechanics* on our own. Now we order in Chinese food and set up our little trays side by side on the couch. Dinner and a movie. Something like that, at least.

I sigh and shove my phone into my pocket. I'm still dodging her, even though I probably should pick up someday. I know answering is the right thing to do, like, objectively. What am I going to do, avoid her forever? *She's my mom.* She's the one who took care of me my whole life, who kept me fed and housed even when that meant she had to work too many hours and didn't get enough food herself. And yes, I get now that I don't owe her my life for that, but don't I kind of owe her *something*?

It's all so complicated, and honestly, I don't want to be thinking about any of it right now, but shouldn't I? Maybe I should call Morgan and ask her what she thinks. She always has the best advice. I open our location sharing and sigh when I see that she's at the library.

I won't bother her, then. She's been tied up for the last week researching some big project she's got coming up in this class she's obsessed with—something about philosophy and policy or whatever. She tried to explain it to me, but I won't lie, I kinda blanked out. It's not that I didn't understand—I'm not stupid or anything—it's just that for the first time . . . I really didn't care.

I know, I know, that sounds really shitty, and it *is* really shitty of me. Like, I fully and truly understand that, but I had just been to class all day and then worked at Billy's garage for five hours when she was telling me about it. It was eleven at night, and I was exhausted.

Every once in a while—not often, mind you, but very, very occasionally—when Morgan gets so caught up in the theoretical saving of the world or humanity or whatever you want to call it, I want to remind her that all her little theories don't mean anything if they aren't really making a difference for the people out there with their hands covered in grease like mine.

Sometimes this theoretical stuff she's learning now just sounds like bullshit to me.

Don't get me wrong, I support her *actual* work. I think I was as excited about the Rainbow Athlete Coalition as she was. Not to mention the fact that I even volunteered with her at the center this summer when I was off work. That stuff makes a difference. Hell, even some of the lobbying stuff she's talking about doing on our DC spring break trip makes sense to me. Like, yes, they're just meeting with her as a courtesy because she's a kid, but these are people who are fighting hard to make sure we don't lose the rights we already have. Or at least, they're supposed to be.

The other night, though, Morgan was going on and on about thought experiments and made-up scenarios, and it was just *a lot*. Maybe that will all have regular, real-world implications someday—I don't doubt she's getting something valuable from them in her own way. That alone should be enough to keep my ears perked up, but instead, I started wondering if she was somehow getting off track, buying into everything she's learning at her fancy expensive college and forgetting her privilege.

I don't know.

Maybe I'm just feeling a little jealous, a little *woe is me*, because yeah, as much as I love my family nights with Billy, sometimes it sucks to be the one still living at home when all your friends and your girlfriend are off on new adventures . . .

Determined not to let myself get too deep into my pity party, I flick over to my contacts and punch up Everly's number. I plug my phone into the stereo that I modified to install CarPlay. I hate that it's not authentic to 1970, but Billy told me if he caught me driving and holding my phone one more time, he was gonna disassemble my car in a way I could never put back together.

If anyone could follow through on a threat like that, it would be him. The guy's taught me everything I know.

Thankfully, Everly picks up on the second ring. "Hey, Ruby!" she says, sounding extra excited to hear from me. It's possible I may have been neglecting her lately, between class, work, and helping Shiloh not fail out.

"Hey, Ev," I say, trying to match her energy and failing spectacularly. *I guess seeing those missed calls from my mom rattled me more than I thought.*

"You good?" she asks, and yeah, it takes a true best friend to be able to tell your mood from a simple hello. She's too good to me.

"Yeah," I say. "Just homesick, I guess."

She hums, as if considering my words. "Your mom call again?"

"Yeah, but that's not what I mean, really. I think I just feel lonely. Like I miss you being here, and even Marcus, shockingly. I miss us all eating at the diner or driving in my car or sitting in your basement."

"Me too," she says. "But aren't you forgetting somebody on your list?"

"I thought it went without saying that I miss Morgan too," I say, pointing my car toward Billy's as I drive.

"Are things okay with you guys?"

"Yeah, they're great," I say. "I think. On paper, anyway. I have no reason to actually believe otherwise, so . . . yeah. Probably?"

"Ouch," Everly says. "You want to talk about what that means?"

"I didn't call just to complain, Ev, seriously. I miss you and want to hear about what's going on with you too."

"You will, believe me," she teases. "We haven't had an honest-to-god phone call since I went back to school. I'm not giving that all up just to listen to you the whole time."

I laugh, realizing I missed her bluntness even more than I thought.

"Let's start with what's bothering you first," she says. "Then I'll tell you all the shit that's driving me nuts, and then we both can talk about the good stuff to end on a high note. Deal?"

"Deal," I say.

And so we do. I tell her about how I'm terrified there's a distance growing between me and Morgan sometimes, even though we don't want there to be. How she seems like she might be changing a little bit, but maybe I am too. How we both love and miss each other, but that sometimes I just don't want to hear about another thought experiment or hypothetical situation. Everly puts me in my place, as I deserve, saying that I can't expect Morgan to be out doing the real work from the jump when she's a freshman like us. It helps, in that blunt way that only Everly can pull off.

And then she tells me about her latest drama. That Marcus posted a Snap of him dancing with another girl at a party, and how she ended it for real last night and isn't even mad. How she's in her independent woman era, and that entails going out to all the parties this weekend that Marcus tried to keep her from.

Then she tells me how she hates her 3D art class but shockingly loves her ceramics class almost as much as her true love, photography. That she might get on the teaching track as a backup, and that her mom is encouraging her to do so. She talks about it like it's a gift she hadn't considered before, not an indictment of her talent or judgment of her ability to make it as a pro photographer. She says it like it's an exciting thing, a great thing, and hearing the happiness in her voice makes me so happy.

I tell her she would be the best damn teacher a kid could ever hope for, and we get sappy for a minute. She admits that she was scared to tell me, because she thought I would take it as her giving up on her dreams instead of finding a new one, and I reassure her that she's being smart and isn't closing any doors, just opening even more.

We end the call as I get back to Billy's, both promising at least weekly phone calls because texts just aren't enough. And she's right, they aren't.

I sit in my car a little while longer, glancing at the little dot on my phone that shows that Morgan is still at the library and reframing my ideas about what she should or shouldn't be doing. *This is just the first step for her; the big stuff comes later.* Then I watch through the window as Billy sets up our little trays in the living room, putting the extra fortune cookie on mine, because we always buy so much food they assume it's for three.

I pull up Morgan's name and fire off a quick **Proud of you** text to her, just as much to make her smile as to remind myself that I truly am. I even add a screenshot of the countdown to spring break that Everly put on my phone before she left. It still feels like it's going to be forever, but I know every day is one day closer.

Morgan writes back immediately—a string of smiley faces with hearts around them—and I know, then, that sending the text was the right thing to do. I feel lighter somehow as I rub my finger over the hearts. I wish I could feel Morgan through the screen instead of just glass, but it has to be enough.

I take a deep breath and head inside to the warmth of the living room, the warmth of my home, feeling better already.

And the extra fortune cookie doesn't hurt either.

8

MORGAN

I'm sitting in the dining hall with Mika, both of us choking down frankly inedible slices of pizza that taste like they were made seven hours ago and have been reheated dozens of times since then. Somehow, they're both chewy and pasty, with way, way too much flour and not enough sauce. If you can even call it sauce at this point, when it's been dehydrated into essentially a glorified grainy red sand.

Mika is texting away with her girlfriend, who's coming to visit this weekend. She's over the moon about it, and her excitement seems to kick up a cloud of jealousy in my head. I actually contemplated asking my brother to come get me today too—homesickness is hitting me hard right now—but I know it would be a major pain for him. I'm sure he's already booked up with clients, plus Ruby always works weekends anyway. It would probably just end up being a huge hassle with very little reward.

When I told that to Mika, though, she brought up for the thousandth time that I really need to "integrate into campus more." I think this is code for going to one of the many parties that happen here every weekend, or even worse, one of the student morale things—the other day, she was going on and on about how I should go to the snowman-making competition on the main quad and make some friends.

Look, I'm not saying she's wrong on *all* counts. I'm just saying it's not really my thing, and in the very limited time I have, when I'm not at practice or studying or in class or writing my billionth paper or troubleshooting things with the Rainbow Athlete Coalition, I'd rather spend it FaceTiming Ruby than freezing my butt off with a bunch of strangers. When I pointed out to Mika how much time *she* spends talking to her girlfriend, Kennedy, she said it was "all about balance." As if any freshman in the history of ever has mastered the art of balance, especially one who's a student athlete.

Luckily, or unluckily, really, before I can get lost too deeply down that rabbit hole of misery, a hand appears in front of my face, waving a paper. I reach for it, but it gets tugged back before quickly being slammed down onto the table, barely missing my plate. I flick my eyes over to Mika, who looks equally confused, and then turn my attention to the hand, or rather the person the hand is connected to: Mac. Of course it is.

"Was pelting me in the face with snowballs last week not enough?" I groan. "Now you have to ruin my perfectly good lunch too?"

Mac scrunches up her face as she eyes my half-eaten pizza. "You call that 'perfectly good'? I weep for your standards."

"What do you want, Mac?"

"Did you see this?" she asks, waving the paper in my face again. It makes an annoying thwapping sound that sets my teeth on edge.

I yank it from her hands, smoothing out the wrinkles as I study the page. I don't know what I expected it to be, but definitely not a printed-out email from Professor Dunner. I scan the page, trying to absorb what she's sent us.

Apparently, one of her former students has requested she send recommendations and applications for their company's annual legislative internship. It's set in DC, from May until the end of July. I skip over the backstory of the business and down to the list of duties and expectations, which includes assisting with research, monitoring the legislative sessions in person until they break in mid-June, and producing a weekly newsletter for their clients updating them on the status of the bills they're pushing for. Then mid-June on—what they call the offseason—will be filled with research, administrative assisting, and other tasks "as mutually agreed upon." Apparently, students recommended by Professor Dunner generally move to the top of the pile. She says while she is very selective with her recommendations, anyone is welcome to apply.

I'm almost positive she'll recommend me if I ask.

"Where'd you get this?" I ask, snapping my head up to look at Mac.

"From my email. She sent it like a half hour ago already. Do you seriously not have email alerts set up?"

"Oh no, I guess not. Why? Does everybody do that?" I glance at Mika, who shrugs and gives me a curious look. "Anyway, thanks for bringing it to my attention."

"Thanks?" Mac says, snatching the paper back with a little huff. "I was just trying to gloat. Obviously, the internship is going to be mine. I just wanted to show you what you were missing out on."

I roll my eyes. "Why would she recommend you for the position? You barely even talk in class!"

"I talk when I have something important to say. One could argue that she wouldn't recommend you, because you never shut up. Do you honestly not see the light dying in her eyes every time you start spouting your opinions on theoretical morality and its role in the lobbying industry? Because it does. It dies. She looks like a zombie by the end of the class." Mac punctuates this by sticking her arms out straight and groaning, which I assume is supposed to be her impression of Dunner after listening to me.

I should be offended, but somehow, it's just goofy enough to be . . . charming?

I laugh and shake my head. "You're half-right," I admit. "But it's because of the dumbass guys in our class, not because of my mouth."

"Hmm," Mac says, narrowing her eyes and suddenly leaning closer across the table. "I'm willing to concede that your mouth itself may not be the problem." She flicks her eyes down to my lips and then back to my eyes, the corner of her mouth pulling up into a crooked smile. "If only the words coming out of it weren't so *fucking boring*."

I lean forward even more, matching her cocky energy. "That's funny, because you don't look all that bored when you're in your seat next to me, hanging on my every word." I pull the paper out of her hand. "Dumb move showing me this if you didn't want me to apply."

"Ever considered that maybe I want you to?"

"Why? So you can spend your summer hissing at the sun or whatever it is you do back in California, while I'm living my best DC life? There's no way she's recommending someone else over me."

"We'll see. May the best man win and all that."

"There's no way a man is winning this." I laugh.

Mika kicks my foot under the table, snapping my attention back to her. She flicks her eyes to Mac and then to me with a look that, if I'm reading it right, means some combination of *What the hell is happening?* and *Who is this strange woman?*

"Sorry, I'm being rude," I say, looking at Mika. "This very weird woman is Mac. She's in Dunner's class with me. Also, she sucks."

Mac snorts and holds out her hand. "And you are?" she asks, looking at Mika.

"Her track captain," Mika says, instead of her name. "But we're kind of in the middle of something here, so . . ." Mika uses her fingers to mime someone running away.

I crinkle my forehead, because we weren't in the middle of *anything*, but who am I to question my captain?

"You heard her." I shrug. "Buh-bye, now."

"Cool, cool, I love it when jocks close rank," Mac says, looking irritated. "Enjoy running in circles, or talking about running in circles, or whatever you were doing. I'm going to go start working on my application." With that, she grabs the paper from me, shoving it in her pocket as she walks away.

I can't help but watch her a little too long. I'm not sure if it's because I'm intrigued or because she annoys the ever-loving shit out of me. But I can't say I mind having her in class anymore, though—just like in track, I thrive with some healthy competition.

"What was that about?" Mika asks, as soon as Mac is out of sight.

"What? The email? It's about an internship opportunity that Professor Dunner can potentially get us into."

"No, I gathered that, but . . . you guys were flirting," she says slowly, narrowing her eyes.

"Hardly." I groan. "We can barely stand each other."

"Um, no," Mika says, abandoning her shitty pizza again to study my face. "She was one hundred percent flirting with you, and you seemed into it too."

"She was bringing me an internship opportunity at best, being an annoying troll at worst. You would do that for another premed student, right?"

"If you're asking me if I would print out an email that you already have in your own inbox and then search through campus, even paying for a shitty dining pass, just to pretend that I didn't want you to apply, while eye-fucking the shit out of you, then the answer is no. No, I wouldn't, because I have a girlfriend, but also more importantly because I'm not a creepy-ass stalker."

Okay. So maybe Mika had a point on some of it, but . . .

"I wasn't flirting back, though."

Mika scrunches up her nose and wiggles her hand back and forth like she doesn't quite believe me. "Let's call it a gray zone, then. Maybe you weren't fully flirting back, but you were definitely encouraging it."

"Oh my god, no, I wasn't!"

"You're getting awfully defensive for someone who feels A-OK with that interaction. I'm sorry, I'm just telling you how it looked. From my side of the booth, you seemed like an equal participant. Maybe I'm wrong, but all the smiling and talking about her hanging on your every word and stuff didn't seem like a conversation I would have with someone I hate.

"If Kennedy were leaning in and smiling all coy like you two were, I would probably wonder what the hell was going on with my girlfriend." She holds up her hand when I go to interrupt. "Maybe it's innocent and I misread it, but if I didn't, then that's really not a path you want to go down for your relationship's sake. Trust me."

"What do you mean?" I ask, a tendril of guilt sweeping over my skin.

"You're not the first person to get a crush on someone who *isn't* their long-distance partner."

"I don't have a crush."

"Okay," she says, picking at her crust. "A little advice, though?"

"Sure," I say, cleaning up the table and getting ready to head out. *I've had about all the shitty pizza and awkward conversations I can handle for one afternoon.* "I'm all ears."

"I'm not the enemy here." Mika sighs. "I'm just saying, if

it is a crush, or has the potential to be a crush, I would either squash it now before it's anything real, or hit pause on your relationship with Ruby. It's not fair otherwise."

My eyes go wide. "I'm not breaking up with Ruby just because I . . ."

"Just because you what?" Mika asks, raising her eyebrows and twisting her lips in a way that tells me she really thinks she's got me cornered.

"Just because I have a captain who reads into things too much," I say, picking up my tray and heading for the trash cans. "I'll see you next practice."

"See you then," she says, picking up her phone to no doubt go back to texting her girlfriend.

Her girlfriend, who she obviously has never had any doubts about in the history of ever.

Suddenly, it feels like I can't breathe, because I don't have doubts either. Do I? *Wait, do I?*

Sure, Ruby seems a little distant sometimes when I'm going on and on about class, but that's not a big deal. Sometimes I zone out when she's talking about car parts. She *does* seem to be becoming pretty good friends with that guy, though . . . But he has a *family*. I don't have anything to be jealous of there, right?

Right.

Still, I burst through the dining hall doors and out into the cold winter air, gulping down breaths as if I were just underwater. Because I wasn't flirting. I wasn't. I love Ruby. I *love* Ruby. I might be too young to be thinking about forever, and she might run off in a panic at the mere mention of it, but when it comes down to it, I can't picture anyone else beside me, ever. I need to just put this stupid crush—not that it's even a crush—out of my head. I need to trust our relationship.

I need to not picture her flirting with that guy she gives rides to.

I yank my phone out of my pocket and hit Ruby's name before I can stop myself, feeling like I'm on the verge of spiraling out. I love Ruby, and Ruby's not here, and I hate that. I hate how much I miss her all the time. I . . .

"Morgan? Is everything okay?" Ruby asks the second she picks up.

"Why wouldn't it be?" I snap.

"Whoa," she says, clearly taken aback by my tone.

I shake my head, watching my breath make a little cloud in front of me from the cold air. "I'm sorry. I just . . . I really needed to hear your voice."

"What's going on?" she asks softly. I can tell she's moving somewhere away from the sound of power tools. *Oh no, she's in class. I knew she was in class. Why did I call? Why did she even pick up?*

"Morgan?" she says, this time more urgently.

"I'm sorry," I say again, my eyes growing hot with tears. "I just . . . I miss you, and I hate this, and I don't want to ever do anything to hurt you or us, and—"

"Baby, slow down. What happened?"

"Nothing. Nothing!" I say. "It's just that Mika was, like, saying that girl from my class was flirting with me, and I was like, *No,* and she was like, *I know what I saw, and if my girl-*

friend . . . and I just . . . Ruby, I love you. I wouldn't do that."

"Oh," she says, sounding measured. "Oh."

Shit.

"I shouldn't have said anything. Sorry, I'm not trying to dump my feelings all over you. I just—"

"No, you absolutely should have told me. Do you . . . Did you want her to be flirting with you?" Ruby asks, hurt creeping into her words.

"No! Absolutely not!"

Ruby lets out a huge breath. "Okay, then no harm, no foul. I have a hot girlfriend. People will hit on her. I get it. As long as you only hit on me, we're golden."

"I will. I am, I mean . . ." I stumble over my words. "I wish I were hitting on you right now."

She laughs, and it's like I can hear the tension bleeding out of her body in real time. "I'm not stopping you."

"Oh, well, in that case, you come here often?"

Another laugh. *Good. Excellent, even!* I latch on to the sound as if it's proof that I'm a good person, a good girlfriend, and that I absolutely did not stare when Mac's tongue darted across her lips right before she left.

What is wrong with me?

"Scratch that," Ruby says. "If you're using lines like that, I don't have to worry even if you *are* flirting back."

"I'm not," I say again, and I don't even know if I'm trying to prove it to her anymore or to myself.

"I know," she says. "I trust you."

"I trust you too," I say, meaning it with my whole heart.

"I have to get back," Ruby says, and I can almost hear the wince in her tone, like she's as reluctant to get off the phone as I am.

"I know," I whine, even though I wish we could both skip and stay on the phone with each other for the rest of the night, her voice slipping around mine, the sound of our breathing lulling both of us to sleep.

"But, hey, I found some cool places to stay in DC when we go," she says, sounding way more cheerful. I know she's just trying to make me smile, and even though that's the last thing I feel like doing right now, I decide to play along.

"Oh yeah?" I say, forcing the doom and gloom out of my voice. I was aiming for excitement and probably fell short of it, but it's the best I could do.

"Yeah! Billy said he'd reserve them for us and everything, so we can get around the whole making-hotel-reservations-without-being-twenty-one thing. I'll send them over as soon as I'm out of school, okay? It'll be here before you know it."

"Yeah, I can't wait," I say, clinging to her voice like a lifeline. "I love you."

"I know," she says. *Freakin' Han Solo. I should have never made her watch that.*

"You better," I say, and I hear her laugh just before the call disconnects.

9

RUBY

In the middle of the Chassis 1 lab, my professor gets a text that leaves him grinning and tells all of us to take five. By now, we all know this is code for him needing to duck out and make a phone call (and get paid to do it).

I don't care; I'm working on cleaning up a power steering pump and having a good time doing it. While Ben said it was for display only, I have a sneaking suspicion that he's actually started using me to repair the old Dodge he's trying to restore. If I had to guess, the damage to this pump didn't happen this decade, and probably not the last one either.

Shiloh, however, is currently assigned to cleaning a pile of lug nuts that I'm pretty sure Ben nabbed from AutoZone on his way to class and then rubbed in oil to give Shiloh something to do. I suspect Ben has finally figured out what Billy and

I already know: Shiloh is a lost cause when it comes to cars.

Hopefully Shiloh figures it out soon too.

Speaking of, he looks over to me from the station beside mine and shrugs. "What do you think that's all about?"

"No clue," I say, glancing at him to see he's only halfway done with his task.

"Think he'll be gone awhile?" Shiloh yawns, putting down a clean lug nut and leaning his head against the workbench. I don't bother pointing out that he just dropped his head into a spot of grease, because yes, I *am* that big of an asshole. And because I'm curious how long it will take him to notice. (See point one.)

"Probably not long enough to take a nap and finish your work all before he gets back," I say, because while I'm willing to agree that I'm being an asshole, I'm not so big of an asshole that I want him to get in trouble. Shiloh shifts his head to the side, and yep, there's the oil spot right on his forehead. My satisfied smirk dies when I study his face and realize just how utterly exhausted he looks. "Are you okay? No offense, but you kind of look like shit."

"Thanks for that." He groans, sliding his hands up like a pillow before dropping his head back down. Hey, at least his forehead absorbed the grease and spared his hoodie, right?

"You want to talk about it?"

He shrugs, not bothering to look up. "Stella Jane's barely sleeping lately. I don't know if it's a growth spurt or molars coming in or she just misses me or maybe she just wants to ruin my life, but she keeps getting up and wanting to play. I couldn't even get her down last night until like one a.m., and then she was up at five, miserable."

"That sucks," I say, fully out of my element here. While I don't, like, fully hate kids, I've never had to live with one full-time or even babysit one overnight. I'm definitely not the person to go to for that advice.

I *have* had a lot of sleepless nights, though, worrying about random stuff like did my mom pay the lot rent this month, so on that front, I can hook him up.

"Try a splash of Mountain Dew in your coffee. Oh, and the caffeine pills at the gas station near Aldi are cheaper than the drugstore."

"I'm trying to get her to sleep, not stay up forever, Ruby," he whines.

I thwap him on the back of his head, which earns me a scowl. "I meant for you, dumbass."

It's been nice having shit parents in common with someone—well, as nice as something like that can be, I guess. Maybe *easy* is the better word. Last week, his mom called in the middle of one of our tutoring sessions, and I couldn't help but overhear the way she was tearing into him—there wasn't even any rhyme or reason. One second, she was accusing him of freeloading off his aunt and treating her terribly, and the next she was accusing him of loving his aunt more than her.

Some of the things she said could have come straight from my mom's own mouth. Is there, like, a guide somewhere? A script for toxic mothers? Do they stock it at bookstores right next to *What to Expect: The Toddler Years*—the book Shiloh's been obsessively poring over during every break?

He looked like a kicked dog by the time he got off the phone, but worse than that, he looked embarrassed that I had heard it all. Next thing I know, we're swapping shitty mom stories and trading strategies to survive them—although lately, my strategy has continued to just be avoidance.

"Oh yeah." He yawns again. "Thanks, I might need to if this keeps up. My aunt's theory is that she just really misses me and that eventually she'll adjust, but I don't know."

"Misses you?" I ask, wondering if he's ditching his kid the way my dad did me. I narrow my eyes, instantly suspicious, but then shove that thought right out of my head.

Somewhere along the way, I accidentally started considering Shiloh a good friend. And I know, I *know*, he wouldn't flake on his daughter. It has to be something else.

Shiloh frowns. "Yeah. I mean, I took time off when she first came to live with me, to, like, get her settled and stuff. But now I'm in this program all day, and then I've been picking up as many hours as Billy will give me the last week or two because Stella Jane keeps literally growing out of all of her clothes and I need the money. I haven't really had enough quality time with her, I guess. Sometimes she's asleep before I even get back . . . or she used to be, before she gave it up entirely. Don't laugh, but I really miss just hanging out with her. I feel like all the time I spend with her now is me trying to get her back to sleep or rush her through breakfast so I'm not late for school."

"I would never laugh at that, Shiloh. It means you're a

good dad," I say. "If you need to work less, Billy will totally understand."

"I can't afford to work less." He sighs. "My aunt and uncle aren't charging me for rent or watching Stella Jane, which is awesome, but they both work second shift—which means I need a babysitter whenever I'm at Billy's, because nobody's home. My aunt found somebody from her church willing to do it for cheap, but even cheap is way too expensive. I wish I could just, like, turn the lift at Billy's into a Jumperoo for her or something and bring her with me to work."

He laughs, clearly joking, but . . .

"You probably could," I say, raising my eyebrows. "Well, not the lift thing, obviously, but I wouldn't mind keeping an eye on her at the garage, and god knows Billy loves babies. It's not like we're doing a lot of heavy work when you're there anyway. We're mostly in the office listing parts on eBay as you go through each box. I bet we could baby-gate the room or something. There are no tools or anything in it. You'd just have to clean it up a little, and babyproof it or whatever. I don't think Billy would mind, honestly."

"Wait, really?" Shiloh asks, suddenly perking up.

I glance at the door and see that our instructor is still happily chatting on the phone, so I figure it's safe to fire off a text to Billy. His reply comes almost immediately that of course it's fine, and he might even still have some baby gates from the time one of my mom's dogs got sick.

I forgot all about that. It was like five years ago. I had told him about how worried I was about the dog because my mom kept forgetting to take care of it and it wasn't doing well. Billy basically kidnapped it until it got better so he could make sure it got its medicine on time. It didn't occur me until much later that he did that for me, so I would have one less thing to worry about.

My mom couldn't even take care of a sick dog. I wonder how well the pack is faring now that I've been gone for almost a year.

My mood drops considerably at the reminder of my mom, guilt gnawing away at my stomach over the fact that I'm still ignoring her calls . . . and that I've left the dogs to their own devices. I really should at least reply to a text or something, if not for her, then at least to make sure she's remembering to feed her pets. I shove my phone in my pocket, and try to shove that thought out of my head too, before getting back to work . . . Shiloh's gone back to cleaning his lug nuts, but I don't miss the way he keeps sneaking hopeful peeks over at me.

"Billy said it's fine. He might even have a baby gate already," I say, after I've taken a second to recalibrate my brain. It's amazing how much the mere thought of my mother can mess with me.

Shiloh's face splits open into the biggest grin, and before I clock what he's doing, he's jumped over and wrapped me in a hug. I tilt my head, not sure how to react, as the scent of his cologne invades my nose. It smells shockingly good for a dude whose wardrobe seems to consist of two hoodies and a ratty pair of jeans. It kind of reminds me of Tyler, my former friend with benefits from the pre-Morgan days, and I lean in a little to take another deep breath, freezing when I realize how this must look to the rest of the class.

Shiloh seems to register my lack of reciprocation. "Sorry,

sorry," he says, looking genuinely apologetic. "You're not a hugger, are you?" I shake my head no, and he winces, stumbling over his words. "Sorry, it just means a lot. Thank you. I love you." My face screws up in horror, and he immediately looks even more embarrassed. "I don't mean, like, *I love you.* I mean, like, as in *thank you, I love you for doing that, for asking Billy*. Not like I'm *in* . . . Never mind. You did me a huge solid. That's all I meant. If there's ever anything—"

Thankfully our instructor walks back in before either of us can make things any more awkward than they already are.

"Exciting news, class," Ben says, doing a slow jog to the front of the garage bay. "My old friend Matty just called. You might have heard of him—he's from a little show called *Mastermind Mechanics*."

My eyes go wide. "Holy shit."

Mastermind Mechanics isn't just a good show; it's the *best* show. It's a weekly automotive series that's one part restoration program and one part competition. Matty always opens with a short segment updating viewers on the progress he's made on a restoration in his own commercial garage. Then he tells us where we're headed for the episode, which is my favorite part.

He travels to different towns, highlighting small mom-and-pop shops like Billy's, selecting two at a time to do a related challenge against each other. I've been obsessed with it for years. It's even become part of my weekly family nights with Billy. We constantly talk about how cool it would be if Matty ever came here. Billy's going to die when he finds out my instructor actually knows him.

"What? Who is he?" Shiloh whispers, clearly not getting the significance of our instructor being on the actual phone with *the* Matty Masterson.

I can't even explain it to him. Even if I wanted to, my brain is basically crashing as it tries and fails to process the fact that my instructor knows him. That means I've been only one swinging door away from Matty Masterson and didn't even know it. *Basically.* If you squint. I mean, I don't really fangirl the way Morgan does—except, I guess maybe this is the exception.

This is big. Huge. And I don't know what to do. I don't know what to think. I don't even know . . . what Ben is saying right now, I realize, jerking my focus back to our instructor at the front of the room.

". . . student competition episode. Think like the *Jeopardy!* College Championship," Ben says, his eyes settling on me.

Damn, I'm glad I decided to tune back in before he caught me.

Ben shifts his weight from foot to foot, telegraphing his excitement. "Matty wanted to know if I had any potential candidates in any of my courses."

It feels like little sparks start shooting out of my ears at the idea that I could potentially be recommended for a spot. *I probably will be.* I mean, I'm arguably the best in the class, despite being the youngest. Well, I guess, technically, Shiloh is two months younger than me, but . . . Holy shit. *Holy shit!*

"Come talk to me this week if this sounds like something that interests you, and we can talk about throwing your name in the hat. I don't have all the details yet, but I do know it would film over spring break, so you wouldn't even fall behind on anything here. If that was a concern for you, it wouldn't need to be." Ben smiles directly at me, and I wonder if that's another nudge. He knows from previous conversations that finishing this program before my scholarship runs out is important. I can't help but think he's saying it directly for my benefit. That the universe has tailor-made this opportunity just for me.

I have to text Morgan; she's going to flip.

Ben heads over to his office in the corner of the bay and shuts the door, no doubt going to gush to someone about the call he just had. I'm about to grab my phone and join him in a collective squeal when it hits me.

Morgan.

I have a literal app on my phone counting down the days until we can spend spring break together. I can't blow that off, right? I mean, as much as I want to do this show . . . Morgan should come first. I think, anyway? I don't really know how this long-distance-relationship thing works, but I do know that even when we lived in the same town she would get pissed if I blew off our plans.

So, no, I can't.

I shouldn't.

I don't want to.

That last one's a lie, obviously, but what am I supposed to do? Morgan's been off lately, ever since she called me all upset that day to tell me that she was *not* flirting. Which, if I'm being real, sounds like something you'd say when you *were*. It's like every conversation since then has been her trying to prove how in love we are and how much we'll be able to reconnect on our trip. And her calls are way more constant now, not that I mind, but yeah.

At first, I thought she was worried that I was feeling insecure about her and that girl in the class, but the longer it goes on, the more I feel like maybe it's actually for her somehow. I don't know. Doesn't really matter. It'll get figured out. We love each other, don't we? We'll be there for each other always.

And that's exactly why I can't blow her off.

I slide my phone back into my pocket with a sigh. I catch Shiloh watching me, his head tilted like a puppy. "Why do you look miserable right now?! This is great news, isn't it?" he asks. "Obviously, you're a shoo-in for the recommendation. Matthew Mechanic, or whatever his name is, would be deranged not to cast you."

I shrug, not answering.

"Okay, what's happening right now?"

Could he be any nosier? Jesus. Just let me wallow in peace.

"Nothing you need to worry about," I mumble, going back to work.

"Um, excuse you," he says, coming to lean against my workbench. "You let me snot all over your sweatshirt when I was crying about my mom. If you're upset about something, I—"

"I have plans that week," I answer, trying not to sound as disappointed about it as I actually am—because I know I *shouldn't* be. "That's all. And you didn't really snot on me, did you? I thought that shoulder looked a little goopy after you left."

"You have to cancel them," he says, absolutely incredulous and one hundred percent ignoring my attempt to change the subject.

"I can't. I wouldn't want to, even if I could," I say, trying hard to make myself believe that.

Ben steps out of his office then and makes a beeline for my station. I avoid his eye, tinkering with the power steering pump that's definitely for his Dodge.

Apparently not one to take a hint, he knocks his knuckles on my workbench. "Make sure you stop by my office, Ruby, all right?" he says, and then turns to look at Shiloh. Shiloh smiles at him smugly, which I know is about him feeling validated for saying I was definitely in the running. Ben seems to think he's waiting for the same directive, though, and shoots him back a pained smile. "Hi, Shiloh," he adds, looking him up and down. "You have something on your face."

Shiloh flashes me a betrayed look as I start to laugh. I'd almost forgotten about the grease on his forehead in the midst of my mental meltdown over spring break. "Yeah, sorry, you have a little smudge right about . . ." I trail off, gesturing to my own forehead as Ben moves on to another group of students.

Shiloh sneers at me as he grabs a towel and grinds it into his forehead. This really only works to spread it around. Maybe I'll let him know the stain on his skin won't come off without water and Gojo . . . *after* he's done trying to sand it all off.

"How long have I had this *little smudge*, Ruby?" he growls.

"Who's to say?" I shrug, biting the inside of my cheek now to keep from laughing again.

Shiloh dramatically mimes pulling a knife out of his back before snapping his rag against my hip. A startled gasp escapes my lips, and a few of our classmates turn to look at us.

"I'm gonna kill you for that," he says through his teeth, snapping the rag again.

"I'd like to see you try," I yelp, dodging it and then grabbing his hand and pinning it behind his back, just the way Billy taught me. Billy insisted I learn after I told him a guy tried to get handsy with me when he was picking up his car. I never saw the guy, or his car, at the shop again . . . but I did notice the shiner the guy was sporting when I saw him in town a few days later—and I definitely noticed the way he scurried to get away from me.

"Hey!" Shiloh says, struggling against me.

I lean forward a little, keeping his arm locked in place as I whisper in his ear. "And don't forget you need me to keep buttering up Billy so your kid can come to the shop." (He really doesn't. Billy loves Shiloh and would probably bend over backward to help him, but Shiloh doesn't know that yet.)

"You fight dirty," he grumbles, tipping his head back and resting it against my shoulder to peek at me out of the corner of his eye.

I shrug. "You're not the first boy who's said that about me."

"I don't care if I'm your first anything as long as I'm your last," he teases.

At least, I think he's teasing? The shock of his words loosens my grip.

He wiggles out of my hold with a grin. "Gotcha," he says.

I look away, my cheeks burning. *Embarrassment,* I tell myself. *For getting distracted. I'm not blushing. I'm* not *blushing.*

Thankfully, Shiloh gets back to work after that, and I follow suit, content to get done what I need to do so I can get out of here. Unfortunately, I can still feel Shiloh's eyes on me.

The third time I catch him making a pathetic frowny face at me again, I crack. "What now, Shiloh?"

"Nothing," he says.

"Something," I snap. "Just say it. Get it over with."

"I just, I seriously think whatever you've got going on during spring break can't be as important as this."

I take a deep breath, trying not to lose it. "Leave it, Shi," I say, angling my body away from him to hopefully signal that this line of questioning is definitely over.

Because it has to be. I need it to be.

So why don't I want it to be?

10

MORGAN

I've just stepped off the track at a college two hours south of mine, and I need water and to lie down. I PRed in the 800, which means I set a new personal speed record for the race, which I'm attributing to my stellar training and not to the fact that I always run better when I'm on an actual track and not on a painted gym floor.

Coach was happy enough with today's performance that she's not making us take the bus back. This means that my plan to get dinner with my friends has turned into an impromptu sleepover at their dorms. Because, yeah, that college two hours south of mine I just ran at? It's where Aaron and Lydia, two of my very best friends from high school, both ended up—Aaron as a sociology major and Lydia undecided.

They didn't coordinate it or anything. It just happened

that way. Since they *weren't* really friends with each other in school, I took it upon myself to basically set up playdates for them all summer so they could both start the semester knowing someone. In my defense, I know that can be super annoying to do to people, but it *wasn't* really one of those situations where I wanted them to hang out just because of future proximity. It's because I genuinely thought they would get along if they weren't too stubbornly locked into their respective social circles to appreciate it. By the way, I was right.

Like me, Aaron was very out and proud in high school. He was one of the first friends I made last year after I moved in with my brother. Aaron's the one who made me feel welcome at our high school pride club and also got me into working at the local LGBTQ center. The Rainbow Athlete Coalition would probably never have been started if he hadn't decided to take me under his wing.

Meanwhile, Lydia spent high school as the queen of "don't ask, don't tell," even though she's bi and was madly in love with our other best friend, Allie.

No one was more shocked than me when, shortly after graduation last summer, Lydia finally confessed her feelings to Allie after telling me she never, ever would. Allie was weirded out at first, sure, but shockingly decided to give it a shot with Lydia, despite the fact that she had constantly told me she was straight as a nail up until that moment.

Hey, we all figure ourselves out at our own rates; I don't judge.

This means that they've only been together a few months less than Ruby and me. I'm so excited to hear all about how they're doing and if they have any tips for making the whole long-distance thing work better. They make the four hours between me and Ruby seem like small potatoes. Allie has to *fly* home for breaks—they are a miserable fourteen-hour drive apart. I can't imagine.

I honestly haven't really had a chance to talk to Lydia that much since I got back to school this semester, so I'm looking forward to catching up. It's possible that I've been skipping out on more than just social activities at school; I've been neglecting everybody. All my time has been used up on schoolwork, studying, training, and oh yeah, the multi-essay three-page-long application for the internship that Professor Dunner emailed our class about. Not to mention my favorite way to pass the time always—FaceTiming Ruby twenty-four seven, every second I can.

My *former* roommate even got so fed up with my early-morning practices and constant conversations with Ruby that she decided to move in with one of her friends after their roommate dropped out three days into the new semester from homesickness. So, if nothing else, at least now I don't have to deal with that. *Good riddance, honestly.* Maybe next time Lydia and Aaron can come to my school and crash at my dorm, since it's a single now.

The second my coach lets us all leave, I'm following the pin Lydia dropped to a diner just off campus. I've barely walked in before she rushes over to hug me. A laughing Aaron slides out of one of the booths in the back and stands beside it. Once Lydia is done tackling me, we make our way over to him, and I start my hugging-your-bestie-that-you've-desperately-missed thing all over again—only this time my eyes sting a little. I can't help it. Aaron has been there for me through a lot in the year-ish we've been friends. He's the absolute best friend a girl could hope for.

Once we've all finally gotten the hugs and happy tears out of our systems, we race through the standard catch-up questions like "God, how are you?" (good), "How was the race?" (great, since you decided to only run club, so I didn't have to worry about you beating me), and the ever-important "Did you pack an overnight bag?" (no, but I'll just borrow Lydia's pajama pants and wear the hoodie I bought today).

As silly as it sounds, it's kind of awesome. If I close my eyes and take in the smell of pancakes and sticky syrup and the sound of Lydia and Aaron chatting across from me, it almost feels like home... with only one very important thing missing, of course.

Ruby.

I was supposed to call her after the meet on my walk over, and I completely forgot to in my excitement to meet up with Aaron and Lydia—ironic considering she's the one I'm usually blowing people off for. I fire off a quick text apologizing and asking if I can FaceTime her after we order so she can say hi to everyone.

Ruby immediately agrees, probably more excited to talk to Aaron, who once upon a time was her neighbor and childhood playmate, than she is about Lydia, but still. Ruby and Aaron were able to reconnect last summer, and it was awesome to see. The more Ruby let her walls fall, the more I realized how much she had missed having that connection with him.

Ruby and Lydia made a lot of strides toward at least tolerating each other last summer too, but in that case, it definitely *was* only because of me. Otherwise, I think they would have happily gone on with their lives like strangers.

I get it.

There's *a lot* of history there. Ruby wasn't exactly the nicest to Lydia growing up, and vice versa, which sucks, because if they would let it go, I honestly think they would hit it off too. While Lydia wasn't *fully* in the closet last year, she was pretty damn close. She and Ruby have kind of been on parallel paths in terms of making peace with their queerness.

You'd think they'd have a lot to talk about, but whatever. You can lead a horse to water . . .

"Sorry," I say when I realize they've both stopped talking. "I just wanted to see if I could FaceTime Ruby for a proper reunion." I grin. "She said to call her once we're done ordering."

"Sweet," Aaron says. "How's all that going?"

"Great. Well, pretty great. It's hard being apart, but we're figuring it out." I give Lydia a soft smile, switching my attention to her. "You get it. It sucks to be apart, but you make it work. We're in it and committed as much as you and Allie are."

Aaron sucks in a breath as Lydia's face falls.

"I certainly hope you're in it more than Allie was, since she dumped me."

"What?" I ask, totally shocked. We all hung out a few times over winter break, and I honestly don't think they could have cuddled any closer unless they had been surgically attached. "How? Why? Wait, when?"

"I think you're only missing who and where, and you'd have hit them all," Aaron says, no doubt trying to lighten the mood.

"I know who and presumably when, since you guys were glued to each other all break. It happened when you got back here?" I ask, not willing to let this go.

I know *forever* is a cliché thing to think about your high school crush, but I thought it for them, maybe. They seemed as solid as, well, as Ruby and me.

How could they fall apart so soon?

"Yeah, she called me a couple days ago out of the blue and ended things." Lydia shrugs like it's no big deal, but I can tell she's trying not to cry.

I flick my eyes to Aaron, whose face is now painted with concern.

"Lydia, I'm so sorry," I say.

"Don't be," she says, wiping at her eyes. "It was dumb to fall in love with her anyway. I just wish she hadn't let me make a fool of myself all break. She obviously had been planning it for a while."

"No way. Allie seemed genuine whenever I saw you guys together. There's no way she already had it planned."

"She's got a new boyfriend already, Morgan," Aaron says, sliding closer to Lydia so that he can put his arm around her. "Allie posted pics of them together the day after she broke up with Lyds. He's been on her Insta before too. Always in a group of friends, but—"

"But she was next to him in every single picture, every single time. When I asked who he was, she was super vague, always saying he was just a guy from class. Obviously, he was more than that. I *really* could have done without the mindfuck of having what I thought was a perfect month home with my devoted girlfriend, only to find out she was probably cheating all last semester," Lydia says, sounding more mad than sad now.

Good. If what she's saying is true, then I'm mad too.

"I don't get it," I groan. "What is wrong with her?"

I pull out my phone and click over to see the Insta posts myself, sure that they have to be misinterpreting whatever posts they're talking about . . . but my eyes widen when I'm greeted with a selfie of Allie kissing someone who looks almost like Tyler—the captain of the lacrosse team at our high school senior year. Allie was in a situationship with him before she started dating Lydia . . . Ruby sort of was too, at one point, but that's neither here nor there.

Guess she has a type. This guy could practically be his clone.

"Damn," I say, closing the app. I'm not sure which part of things I'm more shocked about—the breakup, the cheating, or the fact that all of this was happening and I had no idea. That two of my closest friends didn't even think to call me when their relationship imploded. It makes me feel like I've been an even worse friend—and even less available—than I thought.

"Yeah," Lydia says, rolling her eyes. "Insult to injury, I just had to do a full panel of STI checks at the health center yesterday, because I have no idea how much of an overlap there was between me and him—or anyone else, for that matter."

"I would like to say none, but . . ." I trail off, shaking my head. "I'm sorry, Lyds, I really didn't think she was like that. This is blowing my mind."

“You and me both,” Lydia says, draining the last of her water when the waitress walks up to take our orders. We make quick work of picking out several appetizers to share family-style—including my new favorite, fried pickle chips. Aaron and Lydia both protest this new addition, but I know they’ll love them once they try a few.

“Anyway,” Aaron says as soon as the waitress heads back to the kitchen to put in our order.

“What’s going on with you?” Lydia finishes for him, in case I didn’t pick up on Aaron’s obvious attempt to change the subject away from Lydia’s heartbreak.

“Nothing too wild,” I say. “Mostly just running and studying when I’m not in class. We’ve finally got a home meet coming up and then a few more travel ones. Ruby and I are doing good. We’re planning a huge spring break trip this year because we have the same week off. We’re heading down to DC, and she’s even got this little app on her phone counting down the days.” I cringe as soon as the words are out and decide to switch gears away from cute romance-y things for obvious reasons.

“Oh, and I’m trying to land an internship for the summer. It’s really competitive, though,” I add. “I have to write like three essays and get a recommendation from my professor before they even touch my résumé. There’s at least one other girl in my class, Mac, who’s also going for it.” I smile thinking about her incessant teasing since I told her I was definitely applying too. “She thinks she has a shot, but she doesn’t. When Mac gave me the application, she was all, ‘May the best man win.’” I roll my eyes with a laugh.

"She sounds . . . interesting," Allie says, glancing at Aaron.

"Yeah, she's ridiculous! You would die. She can't even ever remember to bring a pen to class. I keep extras in my bag now because I know she'll ask. Oh, and oh my god, back at the start of the semester, I was walking to class on FaceTime with Ruby, and Mac hit me *right in the face* with a snowball. In the face! I wanted to kill her! She said I couldn't because it was her first time seeing snow. Can you imagine that? Can you imagine never seeing snow? But yeah, anyway, she's way too immature to get an internship at an actual lobbyist firm."

Lydia pulls a face, and I'm not sure what it means until she says, "You seem super animated when it comes to this 'girl from class.'" She even makes air quotes with her hands.

I realize what she's getting at and frown. "I'm not Allie, Lydia. I wouldn't ever do something like that to Ruby. I love her with my whole heart. Mac really is just a girl from class."

"Didn't you tell me that your captain mentioned something about her too, when we were on the phone?" Aaron unhelpfully asks. "Something about flirting or whatever?"

"Yes," I say, sitting up a little straighter. "When I was venting to you because of how ridiculous and across the line she was for even flirting a little, right? But I didn't flirt back, anyway, *plus* I told Ruby about it right after."

"What did Ruby say?" Aaron asks.

"Nothing, really, because she knows she has nothing to worry about. Seriously, is this a reunion or an interrogation? Because I'm not cheating on Ruby. I would literally never freaking do that, and you're both acting awfully weird right now. Do you two really think I would cheat?"

"No, no," Lydia says quickly, reaching forward to grab my hand across the table. "I know. That's not what we're saying. I'm sorry, I shouldn't project my shit onto you. Obviously, we all have friends in our classes." She sighs like she's exasperated with herself. "I'm just sensitive about that kind of thing right now. I do *not* want you to feel like we're grilling you. This is supposed to be fun. I'm really happy you're here."

"Thank you," I say, glancing at Aaron, who then mouths his own apology . . . but I can't say I'm totally sure he's not still suspicious, for some reason.

"Now that that's settled," I say, pointedly looking at Aaron, as if what I'm about to say next will assuage any concerns. "Speaking of Ruby, we owe her a FaceTime. Do you still want to? If it's gonna bum you out or something, Lydia, I can just text her that we'll have to talk later."

"Yeah, no," Lydia says. "It won't. Besides, it wouldn't be an awkward diner visit without Ruby joining us, would it?"

Lydia grins a little too big for it to be real, but I hurry to press call on Ruby's name anyway, suddenly needing a little reassurance in my own head that, yeah, Ruby and I are good. That we're solid even though Allie and Lydia are not.

That it didn't also feel nice to talk about how much Mac teases me around campus.

That talking to Ruby will feel way, way better.

Ruby's smiling face fills the screen just as the waitress brings out our food. I position my phone carefully atop the napkin holder so Ruby can see all of us, plus the table.

"Aw, man, are you guys eating fried pickles without me?" Ruby gives us her biggest puppy-dog eyes, and Aaron and Lydia groan in unison.

"Babe, they think fried pickles are nasty. Tell them they have to try them!" I laugh, feeling a hundred tons lighter now that she's here. Well, sort of here, anyway.

"That's the saddest thing I ever heard." Ruby tsks, shaking her head. "I thought college was about organically expanding your horizons and trying new things. Yet here you two sit—"

"Are you really equating eating fried pickles with people expanding their horizons?" Aaron shakes his head.

"Are you saying it's not? Or just that you're too chickenshit to try one?" Ruby asks, clearly enjoying messing with her old friend—a dynamic they restarted almost immediately once they reconnected last year.

"Fine," he says, exasperated. He grabs a pickle chip off the plate and shoves it into his mouth. "Happy now?"

I watch him as he chews it, trying not to gloat as his expression goes from annoyed to pleased and then back to annoyed as he sighs and says, "Dammit, Lydia, they're right. These are good."

"I told you so! See, kids, peer pressure works," Ruby says, clearly enjoying herself.

"What happened to organically expanding my horizons?" Aaron yelps.

Ruby bites her lip, pretending to look apologetic. "It doesn't count as an organic expansion if your friends have to force you, sorry."

"Your girlfriend is a manipulative beast," Aaron says, eyeing me as he goes back in for another bite of the perfectly fried pickley goodness in front of us. I notice that Lydia opts for a french fry instead. Fine, more for me, I guess.

"Speaking of expanding your horizons," I say, "Ruby, remind me to tell you about this internship opportunity I'm applying for."

Yes, I *am* only bringing it up now to prove to everyone at the table that there are no secrets between me and Ruby—especially not girl-in-my-class-sized ones. I can tell by Lydia's and Aaron's expressions it might be having the opposite effect, though. Because, yeah, I probably should have told Ruby about the internship before I even sat down to write the essays, let alone before I started telling everyone else. But whatever, I'm doing it now. *Better late than never, right?*

"Oh, cool," Ruby says, pulling me from my thoughts. "Is it starting during spring break? Because I have this chance to—"

"No!" I say, scandalized. "I would never do that. I can't wait for our trip! I was just telling Aaron and Lydia about your countdown clock. That trip is sacred; I know we need that time together." I flick my eyes back to my other friends, but their incredulous expressions haven't really changed. *Oh god, is it coming off like I'm trying too hard?* Am *I trying too hard?*

"Oh," Ruby says, right before pasting fake smile number four hundred thirty-seven on her face. The perils of dating a former beauty queen. I'm about to ask her if everything is okay when a guy's voice cuts me off through the phone.

"You ready to go?" he asks her.

Ruby nods, angling the phone away before he comes fully into view. I catch a snippet of his motorcycle jacket when he leans in to flick the back of her head, and my eyes snag on the side of his very chiseled jaw.

Wait, this *is the guy in her class?*

"Sorry I gotta cut it short, baby," Ruby says, looking apologetic. "Call you back later?"

"Sure," I say, suddenly wondering why she's not introducing me to this random guy that she's been driving home from class lately. I mean, her phone camera is *right there.* Would a quick wave and hello kill him?

He's a dad, I remind myself. *His baby's mom is probably waiting for him every day. He has a family. It's nothing. It means nothing. People of different genders can be friends. I'm literally sitting with a boy right now! Pull it together, girl!*

"All right, then, bye, guys. Enjoy those pickles, Aaron. Love you, Morgan." She makes a kissy sound and then disconnects.

I sit there silently for a moment, staring down at my now-dark phone screen as I bite the inside of my cheek.

"Who was *that*?" Aaron asks.

"Who?" I say, barely paying attention to what Aaron is saying. I can't help it, not with my head spinning in a thousand directions ranging from panic to jealousy to possessiveness and every ugly idea in between.

"That guy," Aaron presses, clearly not ready to drop things just yet.

"A friend . . . from class," I mumble, setting my phone facedown.

Aaron raises his eyebrows, choosing to sip his soda instead of saying anything else.

Thank god.

Lydia flashes me a pitying glance and then nudges my arm. “All right,” she says, trying to look cheerful. “No more talking about friends from class, okay? Slide me that pickle plate. I’ve got horizons to expand.”

11

RUBY

Shiloh is sweeping behind me while I pretend to read an article about the latest advancements in suspension strut technology, but really, I'm just thinking about how weird Morgan has been the last few days. It's been going on for a while, but ever since that FaceTime at the diner, it's been impossible to ignore. Something is wrong between us. And I don't know what it is.

We're still talking and texting all the time, but it's like she has her guard up. Or maybe it's that I do. I'm still a tiny little bit stressed about missing this chance to be on *Mastermind Mechanics*, and it's weirding me out that I can't get over it. Shouldn't I be more excited about seeing my girlfriend for spring break than I am about going on some stupid show?

Besides, it's not a sure thing that I would get on, even if I threw my hat in the ring. It's just a *chance*. And that's not to mention all the complicated things that get stirred up in my skull whenever I think about performing again.

Sure, being on *Mastermind Mechanics* and showing off skills I love is a far cry from being forced to stand onstage and relive my mom's beauty queen dreams, but still. Like, it feels weird that I was so adamant that I was never going to perform for anyone ever again, and now here I am, sad that I can't *be on TV*. A little hypocritical, no?

I can't help but daydream about all the what-ifs, though. I already decided that if I *was* going to try to get on it—not that I would, but if I ever *did*—I would want to talk about the 1972 Chevy Camaro I found in one of the junkyards five or six months ago when I was scouring for parts for Billy. He helped me get it and bring it back to the shop, calling it a solid investment, and I've been working on it ever since. While nothing could ever replace my beloved 1970 Ford Torino—it's basically my car soulmate—this run-down Camaro I'm restoring *is* my current pride and joy.

A little fling, until Billy and I flip it after we finish the restoration. It should bring in a nice little chunk of change for the shop too.

Even my instructor seems to share my sentiment. The other day, when I stayed late to tinker with the Camaro's brake master cylinder, he came to see what I was up to. I couldn't help but gush about the car and how excited I was to get it running smoothly again. Ben grinned and said, "Wow, sounds like a made-for-TV moment."

He even threw in a little wink at the end, in case I didn't

pick up on what he *really* meant: that I needed to make a move on the show casting. He's been laying it on a little thick lately, especially as the clock ticks down to decision day. I know it's killing him that I'm one of the only people in class who *hasn't* swung by his office to ask to be considered for the show. It's honestly killing me a little too. But it is what it is.

I know, or hope, at least, that if I explained to Morgan what's going on, she would be fully supportive of me ditching our trip. I bet she would probably tell me to do it, maybe even agree to come here and cheer me on.

But I can't shake the way she said that she would never, ever put something ahead of our vacation, that it was sacred. It makes me feel like a monster to even suggest it. Like it's some unspeakable thing I shouldn't even be considering, that doing so would be showing cracks in our foundation that neither of us wants to be there.

Sacred. She said *sacred.* And I'm over here pouting about it. I'm such an asshole. I mean honestly, who feels frustrated because their girlfriend loves them so much?

Probably only people like me who flip-flop between clinginess from abandonment issues and getting claustrophobic when people express anything remotely close to caring about me. *What can I say, I'm a work in progress.*

But there's something else there too. Something a little worse than that, something new that's never been there before: *resentment.*

I know, I know. *Monster behavior* and all that.

I'm trying to deal with it. I'm trying not to make it a thing, but hearing Morgan so excited about her internship is really getting to me. If she gets it, it's all the way in DC, and even includes a per diem for living expenses on top of her hourly wage. DC. That's a way farther ride than her college—which has already been next to impossible to get to, between our schedules and transportation drama. Worst of all, it runs all the way until the end of July.

That only gives us a few weeks together next summer before Morgan starts school again. I was holding on to the idea of a nice long summer break together, and now it's just *poof,* gone. No prior discussion, no second thoughts. Morgan sure doesn't consider summer break *sacred,* not if she's making plans for almost all of it that don't include me.

I know it's selfish of me to begrudge her this opportunity. I know it is. And I know I definitely need to get over it, because I think with her Rainbow Athlete Coalition, she has a solid chance of getting it.

Morgan keeps promising that I can come stay with her for weeks at a time, but I need to be here working with Billy, so that's not true. I don't know how she doesn't get that. I don't know anyone who could just take off weeks of work to screw around with their girlfriend in another state. But when I reminded her of that, she looked so sad, so I just said I was sure we could figure it out . . . which I'm not at all sure of.

Still, I'm proud of her. Of course I am. It's not that. It's just . . .

I drop my head and groan, leaning back on my stool so just two legs are touching the ground. Billy catches my eye as he walks toward his office after finishing his jobs for the day. "Do I need to put on the angry-old-guy music you pretend not to love?" he asks.

"I'm not pretending, Peepaw," I scoff, just to get him riled up. The other day, he got an AARP card in the mail, despite him not even being fifty yet. As he raged about it to me later, I said, "Relax, Peepaw. You're clearly far too ancient to be getting this worked up." It's not my fault that Shelby was walking in to surprise him with some takeout at that exact moment.

Shelby may or may not have said, "Peepaw? Is that the name you're putting on your little senior citizens card thing?"

Much to Billy's chagrin, the nickname stuck with both of us after that. Now whenever we want to troll him, or he needs to be knocked down a peg or two, Shelby and I will just pull it out and dust it off.

The fact that Shelby jumped right onto the Peepaw thing with me makes me like her even more. I told Billy she could start coming over for our family TV dinner nights, but he shockingly said no. He said he wouldn't ever bring someone to that unless they were, like, marriage-level committed. That was *family time.*

I . . . I didn't know what to say to that, so I just walked to my room and lay on my bed for like an hour. I'm not used to people saying shit like that to me, acting like I matter, like I'm really, truly family. Even though there's been no shortage of positive affirmations and cheerleading since I moved in with Billy officially, him saying that felt different.

It's one thing for him to say I'm important, but it's another thing for him to actually put it into action by, like, prioritizing me or whatever. I don't know. My mother's house was always such a revolving door of men, and what *they* wanted always mattered more than whatever I did. *They* always came first. I never had to invite them to family nights because (a) we never had those and (b) my mom would have moved them in with us long before I was comfortable with it.

It never really occurred to me that it wasn't supposed to be like that until I was already old enough to understand that it was also never going to change.

"I'll give you Peepaw," Billy says, hooking his foot under one of the bars on the bottom of the stool. I have to jerk my body forward or risk falling flat on my back.

Billy laughs at the split second of panic on my face . . . which is when I realize that he has his hand out to catch me in case the chair really did tip too far.

"You're an asshole," I say. Shiloh starts laughing from beside a pile of boxes behind me. I shoot him a glare. "So are you."

Billy holds his hands up in surrender. "Hey, I had to get you back for starting the Peepaw thing. Shelby called me that the other night when we—"

"La, la, la, I don't want to know," I say, plugging my ears like a snot.

Billy crosses his arms and waits for me to unplug them before he finishes. "When we were looking up new recipes to try and I mentioned that garlic gives me heartburn."

Shiloh comes over, carrying a box of parts he must have just finished inventorying. He hands it to Billy, saying, "Okay, you can't blame Ruby for that one. Saying that to a girl you want to impress genuinely does give off Peepaw vibes. I'm with Shelby on that."

Billy looks at Shiloh, incredulous. "You want to keep working here, kid?"

Shiloh winces, making a big show of picking up a broom and starting to sweep, even though we both know Billy would never fire him. Collecting wayward teens is apparently kind of his thing. Wait, that sounds creepier than it is, I think. I just mean Billy would rather die than turn his back on someone who needs help.

It's not his fault that his shop became a safe haven for damaged kids, after he took in his ex-stepkid. (He hates when I say that, by the way, even though I argue that it's accurate. He's all "kids are forever" or whatever. If I had a therapist, we'd probably be working for years on how that hasn't historically been the case in my experience, but . . .) Once is a fluke, but twice—three times if you count Stella Jane, who is currently passed out in her Pack 'n Play in Billy's office—and you've got yourself a habit.

"What's eating at you?" Billy asks, looking slightly more serious now.

He's been a mother hen about my moods ever since he read a parenting article about how bi kids are at a higher risk of mental illness than most. That hypothetical therapist I mentioned? Billy's been trying to make it a little less hypothetical ever since I moved in—even more so lately.

"Nothing, just school stuff," I say, which isn't technically a lie. It *is* school-related. I could tell my instructor was disappointed when I packed up to leave immediately *yet again*, instead of coming to talk to him about the show. Hell, even Shiloh has thrown his hat in the ring by now. The deadline to be considered is coming up fast, and I feel like me and Ben are currently locked into a game of chicken over who will bring it up first.

"Everything going okay over there?" Billy asks. "If those assholes don't realize you're one of the best mechanics in town, then maybe I should go over and give them a piece of my—"

"No." I laugh. "They know."

"That's why they want her to go on the show," Shiloh pipes up, because he seems to be allergic to minding his own business tonight. "If Ruby would take two seconds to consider it, she'd have to admit she wants it too. That's why lately she's been such a . . ."

I swivel on my stool, and if looks could kill, Shiloh would be beyond dead. A pile of ash. A tiny sizzle and pop, a—

Billy looks between the two of us. "What show's he talking about, Ruby?"

"You didn't even *tell* Peepaw?" Shiloh asks as his eyebrows shoot toward his hairline. And I get it. He's been around enough by now to see the dynamic I have with Billy, and frankly, Shiloh's right to be surprised. I don't keep much from Billy, especially if it's something big.

Except this, apparently.

And only because I'm not doing it. Because it would be a selfish, asshole, bad-girlfriend move if I did, and I left that kind of shit in high school. I've evolved. I've matured. I . . .

I can tell Billy is more than a little confused and

concerned, because he hasn't even seemed to clock that Shiloh just called him Peepaw for the first time—which means the nickname has escaped containment even further now.

"I didn't tell Billy," I say to Shiloh through gritted teeth, "because there's nothing to tell. I'm not doing it."

"You're being so stupid about this," Shiloh snaps.

I scrunch up my face, surprised by his tone. "Like Billy said, you want to keep working here?"

"You can't fire me," he says. "You don't have the authority."

"Barring the fact that if you ever caused any *real* problems for Ruby, your ass would be on the sidewalk so fast you wouldn't even register my boot hitting it, I'd say I should give you a raise for finally spilling why she's been such a bear lately. Now, Ruby," Billy says, turning back to me, "since the cat's out of the bag, you might as well tell me the rest of it."

"Traitor," I grumble at Shiloh. "It's not a big deal," I say, trying to sound sincere. "You know that Chassis 1 lab I have?" Billy nods. "Well, the teacher happens to know the guy from *Mastermind Mechanics*, and—"

"*Mastermind Mechanics*? As in *our favorite show*? The one we joke about getting our shop on? The one we've seen every episode of at least a dozen times?"

I take a deep breath—lord, give me strength and all that. "Yeah, that one," I say as Shiloh walks over.

"Our instructor doesn't just know him; they're best friends," Shiloh interjects, no longer even pretending not to eavesdrop.

This is what I get for being nice to people. I should have let him keep thinking I hated him.

"He basically said that Matty Masterson wants him to recommend a few students for a college episode of the show. He's made it very, very obvious that he intends to put Ruby up for it—if she would get her head out of her ass and tell him she's interested. All she has to do is go sit down and talk with him about it, and she won't."

I look away, not able to take the expression on Billy's face anymore. Because, yeah, I've probably said a hundred times in passing I wanted to do the show someday. And I've definitely wished we could get them to Billy's shop too. But none of that matters right now. Because I'm not doing it. I can't.

Why does this room suddenly feel so hot? Can they both stop staring at me for five seconds? Can they—

"Ruby, Ruby," Billy says, putting his hands on my wrist like he used to when I was little and started freaking out. "Breathe."

What? Oh.

I'm almost hyperventilating. I need to get a grip.

I don't think this has happened to me since I was a little kid. There was like a month after Billy left my mom where it kept happening because I was so stressed out about how much worse things were going to get without him around. Why only a month? Because I didn't need to panic about it after that. Not because Billy still came by to check on me and let me spend weekends at his shop, but because everything *did actually get worse almost immediately*.

It sucked, yeah, but it was a relief too. You don't have to worry about it all going to shit once it already has. Why it just happened now, when things are arguably the best they've been in a while, I have no idea.

So glad it's back in rotation.

Shiloh pats my shoulder and then goes back to sweeping the corner of the garage. I appreciate him giving me space and pretend not to notice that he's still watching me worriedly as he does it.

I shut my eyes, taking a few deep breaths in and out until I feel more in control. "Sorry," I say, embarrassed.

"Don't be sorry. Has that been happening again?" Billy asks, concerned.

"No, it hasn't," I say, and I'm telling the truth. "Not since you and Mom were getting divorced, I swear on my car. I really don't know what just happened here."

"Me neither," he says, giving my wrist a gentle squeeze before he lets go.

"That was weird," I say, looking at him like maybe he's going to have all the answers, the way he did when I was seven.

"I know I'm beating a dead horse here, but I still wish you would go talk to someone, Ruby. I don't even care if you do that peer thing at the center Morgan used to do. You've been through a lot, and for whatever reason, it seems to all be getting stirred back up right now."

"Yeah, I know. I *know*," I say, taking another deep breath. "But can we *please* not get into all that this second?"

"Yeah, if you tell me why you don't want to do the show," he says, crossing his arms.

"I don't know, a lot of reasons." I turn away from him, running my fingers along my workbench. Anything to not have to meet his concerned eyes. "The timing is wrong, mainly. The filming is during spring break, and Morgan and I have that trip planned, and . . ." I trail off, not sure what else to say.

"I'm positive Morgan would understand," Billy says, deliberately stepping back into my line of vision. "That girl loves you."

"I know she would, but it doesn't feel right to even ask. She wouldn't ever ask me to miss it; she said it herself. And now she might have an internship this summer, and I'll barely even see her, and what the fuck am I supposed to do with that? So it's, like, spring break or *nothing*."

"Why did you agree to her summer job thing, then?"

"Internship," I correct him. "But she's hoping it will turn into a job someday. It's a huge opportunity. And we didn't really discuss it . . . It's more like she applied and excitedly told me about it."

Shiloh lets out a little shocked noise behind me but has the good sense to go back to sweeping by the time I turn around to flip him off.

"So she can excitedly apply to what she wants, but you need permission to do the same?" Billy asks, looking unimpressed.

"No, but we didn't have set summer plans. It's not the same thing as canceling on her."

Billy raises his eyebrows at me. "Ruby, you didn't know this would come up. You'd be crazy to walk away from this without even talking to her about it."

"I can't!" I insist, and oh, my eyes are starting to burn. *I will not cry over this. I. Will. Not. Cry. Over. This.* "You don't get it! I *can't*. She's too excited, and I'm not . . . I'm not . . . I won't hurt her."

"I'm not asking you to hurt her. I'm asking you to have a conversation with her. I know how much you two love each other, but if you can't even have a simple conversation, then maybe this isn't the—"

"Don't even finish that, please," I say, practically begging, because if he even implies that we aren't the right fit, something I've been scared of since the moment I fell for her, I'll shatter. "Besides, even if I did figure all the Morgan stuff out, then there's still the whole, like, other stuff."

"Other stuff?" Billy asks, scrunching up his face as he tries to keep up.

"Like about competing again or whatever. I did the whole being-on-TV-and-performing-for-people-and-fake-smiling thing on the beauty pageant circuit with my mom, and now everybody wants me to do it again? After I blew that up and told my mom I never would again! You know, she still texts me entry forms and reminds me of dates. Hell, half her texts and voicemails are about it. So I'm blowing her off, obviously, but now I'm supposed to just hop on TV and smile for the camera? I already feel awful for leaving her alone in the first place. Going back in front of lights and cameras feels like an even bigger betrayal. Like I'm rubbing her face in it. And I know it shouldn't bother me. Everybody expects me to want to do it no matter what, and—"

"Ruby," he says, his hands going back on mine. "You're doing it again. Breathe, just breathe. It's okay. You're okay. If you don't want to do this, no one is going to make you. You don't have to compete ever again or be on this show or anything else that doesn't feel right to you. It's fine. This is your life. You get to decide what you want to do with it. Hell, if you really want me to fire Shiloh for even mentioning it—"

"Hey, none of that," Shiloh calls out from the corner. I laugh—I can't help it—but Billy looks serious still.

"You're not anyone's dancing circus animal, Ruby," Billy says, ignoring Shiloh's outburst entirely. "You do what feels right to you, and fuck everyone else. You're supposed to make mistakes at this age; that's kinda the whole point, kid."

I sniffle, and shit, when did I start *actually* crying? I'm halfway to full mortification when his words hit me. "You think not doing the show would be a mistake?"

Billy twists his mouth as tight as it goes. "Dammit, I did sorta say that, didn't I? I'm not trying to put my opinion on any of this."

"What? No, seriously, tell me what you think."

"It's not about what I think," he says. "It's about what *you want*."

"I *want* your opinion," I say stubbornly. "I trust you. You're, like, one of the only people I can trust. Your opinion matters to me. A lot."

Billy rubs his eyes and then moves his hand to massage the back of his neck. I'm not sure I've ever seen Billy this fidgety and uncomfortable in my life.

"I don't know what to do here," he admits eventually.

"I'm asking for your opinion, so you give it, right? That's what parents do, I think?"

"Your mom has too many opinions on what you should do. I'm trying not to be like that."

I smile, relieved by how seriously he's taking this. "This isn't like Mom forcing her thoughts on me. I asked for yours. It would be . . . helpful."

I don't know if that's true, but I really hope it is, because I'm sick of feeling so messed up about things.

"I think," he says, pausing until I nod, urging him on. "I think you've talked about wanting to be on this show for years, and you shouldn't let a spring break trip, or your past, hold you back. If Morgan doesn't support that, or you feel like you can't even talk to her about it, then maybe that's something to think about too . . . because when you love someone, you're supposed to want the best for them. Above all, though, I think—no, I know—that no matter what, you'll be okay. Show or no show. Morgan or . . ." He trails off.

Or no Morgan, my brain finishes for him.

"Oh," I say, and I don't know what I expected him to say. Probably that, if I'm being honest. But imagining it and hearing it are two different things.

Billy thinks not doing the show would be a mistake.

Billy wants me to talk to Morgan about it.

A big part of me agrees, but . . .

"Did I make it worse?" he asks, looking miserable.

"No," I say, leaning forward to rest my head against him in a half-hearted hug. Billy freezes, but then seems to get the memo, putting his arms around me as he takes a step closer. It's rare that I need a hug, or rather, it's rare that I'm comfortable getting one, but I know he's good for it when I do.

"If it feels wrong for you, though, don't do it," he says, awkwardly patting me on the back. Neither of us is super good with this kind of thing, really.

"That's the problem," I mumble into his flannel shirt. He smells like grease and gasoline, *like home*, and why oh why do I feel ready to full-on sob?

"What is, Ruby?" he asks gently.

I lean back, wiping my eyes before meeting his. "Going after the show doesn't feel wrong for me at all. It feels completely right. I want to do it so bad, but is that selfish? Is that messed up?" I ask. "Because I also know Morgan wants to go on the trip so bad, and I know my mom wants me to do beauty competitions so bad, and now I'm thinking about doing some other competition, and making some other spring break plans. I'm letting everybody down. I don't want to be selfish, I don't—" My breath whooshes out of me as fresh tears spring into my eyes faster than I can keep up with them.

"No, Ruby, god no," he says, and this time it's him initiating the hug, pulling me in so tight that I swear he's the only thing holding me together. "That's not selfish at all. Not. At. All."

Suddenly, there's a weight on my other side, squeezing me just as tight.

"Shiloh?" I sniffle out.

"Yeah?" he says, his voice a little wobbly.

"What the hell are you doing?" I ask.

I glance up to see that Billy's expression is just as weirded out as mine.

"Hmm?" Shiloh says as all three of us separate. "Was this not a group-hug moment? You guys get all sappy father and daughter over here, and I'm supposed to keep sweeping instead of thinking about being there for *my* daughter? Of course I fucking burst into a puddle of dad feels and needed a hug too! Are you trying to shame me for that?! What kind of monsters are you?"

I shake my head, incredulous, and look back at Billy, who's . . . giggling. He's giggling? I didn't even think he *could* giggle. Laugh, sure, but giggle?

What is happening right now?

"All right, all right, Shiloh, I know how the 'dad feels' can sneak up on you. Next time just warn a guy, okay?" Billy holds his hand up in a fist, waiting for Shiloh to bump it.

"A fist pound isn't a hug, Bill," Shiloh says, widening his arms as if he really expects Billy to step into them. "There's only room for one emotionally constipated dickhead in this shop, and I'm sorry, but Ruby has cornered the market on that. That means you and I have to be the ones to hug it out."

Billy's mouth falls open as he looks at me. "What is wrong with this kid?" he asks.

I shrug, letting out my own laughter now.

"I think the phone's ringing in my office," Billy says, practically running out of the bay despite the fact that his cell phone's sticking out of his pocket and obviously off.

Shiloh turns his attention back to me once Billy's gone.

"Uh, I think my phone's ringing too," I say, spinning back to my station.

“Unbelievable,” Shiloh groans, giving up and going back to sweeping. “Monsters, like I said.”

A few minutes pass, and then I hear him fidgeting around the shop again, punctuating his movement with an occasional sigh. He does that in class sometimes when he’s really got something to say.

“Spit it out, Shiloh.” I brace myself, already regretting what will come next.

“It’s just . . . I think Billy’s right, for the record. It’s not selfish. I hope you absorb that, I guess. That’s all. I think he’s right about you being okay no matter what too. For whatever it’s worth.”

I nod, not trusting what I’ll say if I open my mouth.

12

MORGAN

I leave it all on the track, just like Coach expects.

Unfortunately, this means my family has to walk over to where I've flopped on the hard gym floor after my last race to collect me. Dylan nudges me with his foot, and I smack it away. He pretends it's to see if I'm alive, but I suspect it has something to do with how bad he wants to go to Raising Cane's for lunch after. They don't have those back home.

Ruby was supposed to hitch a ride with my brother, but she canceled last-minute, saying she got hung up on a work project for Billy. I don't know if I buy it. Things have been weird between us lately, distant, and it's not getting better.

At first I thought I was just reading into things after that diner call. I wondered if I was projecting on us the way Lydia was projecting on me. Then I decided it was my own fault.

Finding out that her new friend she's *still* driving everywhere is definitely cooler than your average dad really had jealousy worming its way through me for a while. I got a little clingy, sure, but who wouldn't?

It didn't help that I put up a little bit of a wall while I processed how to not feel like that anymore. By the time I realized what I was doing and tore it down, I think Ruby had already started to put up her own. I figured she might climb over hers too, but so far, she hasn't.

I push myself up to sitting, my heart swelling at the sight of my smiling family—they always make me feel better. I didn't have a chance to talk to them before the meet, so this is the first time I've seen them basically since the semester started . . . and I know I've been doing a crappy job of keeping in touch too. I jump up and hug each of them, even Dylan, who protests that I'm all sweaty and gross but hugs back tight anyway.

Mika jogs over to meet my parents and let me know that Coach said I was good to take off. I don't miss the way she scans my family, no doubt looking for my girlfriend and realizing she's not there. I quickly introduce her to everyone without leaving her time to ask questions, and then gather my stuff. Mom offers to let me go back to my room and shower, but I decline, wanting to soak up every minute they're here while I can.

We find ourselves in line for fried chicken and crinkle fries twenty minutes later. I grab one of the few remaining free tables while Dad waits for the food. As we eat, I field a lot of questions about the semester, my grades, if I want a single next year or to move off campus or if I'm reconsidering the athletic housing option. Then they dive into how my times are, my newest PRs, and just about everything else—except the elephant in the room. I'm grateful for them not bringing up the missing person on this visit.

I almost believe I'm going to get away with it, but inevitably Dylan decides he just can't let it slide. He was the one who was supposed to be carpooling with her, after all. He made a playlist and everything.

"What's the deal with you and Ruby?" he says, just like that. No tact or sugarcoating.

My dad gives him a pointed look, one that suggests that perhaps they discussed this during the meet and presumably agreed not to bring up how weird it was that Ruby didn't take a free ride to visit me for the day—even though we both desperately needed it.

I'm trying not to read into it, I really am, but...

"No deal. Things are fine, same as always," I lie.

"I'm surprised she didn't even try to FaceTime for the race."

Right, that. I was surprised by that too.

She always has my brother or parents FaceTime her when I run if they're here and she's not. Or at the very least she asks me to have someone take a video of it. *She didn't even text me after the official results posted to say good job.*

She's never completely blown off one of my race days like this, and I don't really know what to make of it.

"She was busier than she thought at the shop. Billy took some emergency work for somebody who needed it done immediately," I say, reciting the theory I've been desperately trying to convince myself is true. "I think it was Marcus's mom, actually."

Dylan shoves a fry in his mouth. "Really?"

I shrug, wishing he would at least not talk with his mouth full.

"Well, whatever is going on, I'm here for you," he adds. "If you ever want to talk. Having lived through Ruby round one, I'm uniquely qualified to deal with round two."

My mom opens her mouth to protest, but Dylan raises his eyebrows at her. It's true my mom is super involved in my life—we're very close—but also, Dylan's not wrong. He's practically had a front-row seat to the entire Ruby saga with me so far. I guess that *does* make him uniquely qualified.

Maybe confiding in them wouldn't be the worst...

"I don't know," I say after a little bit. "I guess things have been a little strange between us lately. I think she genuinely did have work to do today, though—I hope so, anyway."

Mom pats my hand. "Did something happen between you two?"

"No, not really."

"But kind of?" Dad asks.

I sigh. "Some of it is on me, I think, and she could probably make a case that the rest of it is my fault as well."

"Okay, Riddler. Can you just tell us what you mean?" Dylan shoves more of the delicious crinkle-cut fries in his mouth and chews loudly, clearly trying to get a rise out of me. "I don't have all day."

"You literally do," I say, because I know their whole plan is to spend as much time with me as possible until we all go our separate ways this evening.

Dylan leans forward, chewing with his mouth open like we're kids again. *Did I say I was glad our brother-sister dynamic is back? Because I lied.*

"You're gross," I snort, which just makes him grin.

Realizing that I'm not going to get out of this, I tell them all about Allie and Lydia breaking up, and about getting a glimpse of Ruby's friend from class (who Dylan says he hasn't noticed around town but he'll look for now that he knows the guy's working at Billy's too). How I got a little jealous and started calling and texting her even more. I pointedly do *not* tell them about Mac at all, but I do tell them about my internship, or rather my almost internship, since I haven't officially gotten it yet.

"I know it's going to eat up most of my summer this year," I say. "I'm worried she's upset about that. I thought she could just go with me, but she says she has to stay home and work."

"Then you need to talk to her about how important this could be for you. You're way too young to be putting her in front of your work," Mom says. "This is an opportunity for you to connect with people who might be able to give you a job after graduation. It would also be a wonderful résumé builder, even if it doesn't turn into a job offer."

"I don't know." Dylan shrugs. "I get it. If Ruby thought she had the whole summer together and Morgie made other plans without even talking to her, she has a right to be annoyed. That's kind of the whole point of a relationship; you're a team. You decide things together."

"She's a teenager!" Dad says, clearly not liking that answer. "It's not like they're going to get married! Morgan, don't listen to your brother. You absolutely should not be putting your relationship ahead of an opportunity like that."

His firm assertion that there's no way Ruby and I can be forever hurts my heart in a way that I'm not expecting. Yes, I get that high school romances don't usually stand the test of time, but having my dad sound *positive* that we won't kills me in an entirely new way.

"You really believe we won't make it?" I ask, my voice cracking. I'm sure to him I'm focusing on the wrong thing, but it's all I can think about. The idea of Ruby and me breaking up shatters me. I suppose I never really considered the implications of forever . . . Marriage? Is that something we'd even want someday? Do *I* even want that someday? But that doesn't mean I didn't think we even had a shot.

"Honey—" Dad says.

"Dad, stop," Dylan cuts him off. "Look, nobody can tell you if you guys will go the distance. That's on you two to figure out, but I promise that you definitely *won't* if you don't start communicating better. It sounds like you and Ruby seriously need to talk about what's going on. If she's upset about your possible summer plans, maybe you can talk it through or something. There could even be a work-around that neither of you have thought up yet!"

"Right," Dad says, reasserting his place in the parenting sphere. "Even if there isn't a work-around, though, you need to apply anyway—and if you get it, take it. Trust me. The only things you can be sure about are your own choices. You need to plan accordingly, and you need to know that no matter what happens between you and Ruby, it's not the end of the world."

It will sure feel *like the end of the world, though, I bet.*

"Your father's right, honey," Mom says when she catches the concerned look on my face. She reaches across the table and squeezes my hand. "Whatever the future holds, you've got us behind you. You'll be okay."

"Also, if you're that worried about this new guy she's hanging around with, for the love of god, talk to her about it instead of letting it fester any longer," Dylan says. "Remember last year when you two figured out that honest communication can solve just about anything? Don't throw that lesson out the window now, when you really need it."

I nod, taking it all in, because who knows? It's possible there is a way to compromise and make it all work. Or she might be upset about something completely different. Or I might be reading into things too much. I don't know, because I've been too busy trying to pretend everything's great whenever I can get her on the line. I need to woman up and talk to her about the hard things.

I'm sure we can get through this if we talk.

We can do this. We can.

I don't even want to consider the alternative.

"I'm picking you up in fifteen minutes. Mandatory team bonding," Mika says the second I pick up my phone. "Make sure you look cute."

"It's ten o'clock at night, and I'm in my pajamas," I say. "I'm tired."

"A college freshie should not be in their pajamas at ten p.m. on a Saturday night."

"We had a meet today! Plus, you *know* I was entertaining my parents all day! Can't we mandatory bond in the morning?"

"Negative." She laughs. "Do not make me come and drag you out, and trust me, you do *not* want to be in your pajamas where we're going."

"Wait, where are we going?" I ask. *Please don't say a house party, please don't say a house party, please don't say—*

"Clari's boyfriend's frat is having a thing. We're going. Get dressed."

Oh, so worse than a house party. A frat *party.*

"Isn't hazing illegal on our campus?" I ask, looking for an out. "I don't think you're allowed to—"

"Taking you to a party isn't hazing! You don't even have to drink. In fact, you can be the designated driver since you're not even twenty-one. So there you go. No drinking, no hazing, just a community event! For a charity, even. Get dressed."

"How is a frat party a charity?" I grumble, shoving back my covers, because fifteen minutes is *not* enough time, and my clothes aren't going to pick themselves.

"I don't know, but it's five dollars at the door, and Clari said they're donating it to something."

Yeah, their beer budget for the next party, I bet. The frats here are nothing like the sorority my brother's girlfriend is a part of.

"Okay, okay." I groan. "I'm getting ready."

"Perfect, because I'm already outside. Hurry up," Mika says before disconnecting.

I roll my eyes but pull on my clothes and slap on some mascara and lip gloss anyway. Maybe going out wouldn't be the worst thing. If nothing else, maybe it will get me out of my head, since Ruby said she didn't have time to FaceTime tonight. *Which I'm not going to dwell on or get insecure about. Right? Right.*

I'm totally lying, but...

Less than ten minutes later, I'm sitting in the passenger seat of Mika's car and noticing a distinct lack of other people. "I thought this was team bonding," I say, gesturing to the empty back seat. "Where's the team?"

"They're there already. Well, some of them, at least," she says, pulling away from the curb so I can't even make my escape.

"Really?" I ask.

Mika shrugs. "Well, Clari is. And I will be. Plus you. So, sure."

I raise my eyebrows, crossing my arms. "Okay, what's going on?"

"Fine, it's less mandatory team bonding and more mandatory *freshie needs to leave her room because she's starting to freak me out.* You can't just isolate yourself like you have been. It's your freshman year! You need to acclimate! You need to find friends—friends who aren't graduating in May," she says, pointing to herself.

"You really think I'll find friends at a frat party?"

"Stranger things have happened," she says, speeding up.

Okay, sure, stranger things probably have *happened, but they don't usually happen to me.*

Except this time, they kind of do—if by finding friends, what Mika really meant is bumping into Mac while desperately searching for a good place to hide for the night. It turns out we both separately decided to scope out a very much unheated back porch of the frat house. I think Mac is just as surprised to see me there as I am to see her.

"You're at a frat party?" I ask, pulling my coat tighter as I drop onto the steps beside her.

"You're at one too, aren't you?"

"I was dragged here," I grumble. "I only came out here to find a quiet place to wait for it to be over."

"What makes you think I wasn't?" Mac asks.

The moonlight reflecting in her eyes off the snow makes them look almost preternaturally pretty, and I look away before I start to stare. *Friends don't let friends gaze into each other's eyes. Not even on moonlit nights like this one.*

"I think Little Miss 'Embrace Life' doesn't have to be dragged anywhere," I mutter.

Mac huffs out a little laugh, her breath going foggy in the cold. "Just because I embrace life doesn't mean I don't have standards."

"You sure?"

"I have very, *very* high standards, thank you very much." And the way she smirks at me makes me feel like I'm missing the joke.

"Noted," I say dryly, just to move things along. "Still

doesn't explain why you're here, though."

"You want the truth now, or should we circle around it for a while, making increasingly horrible jokes?"

"Now," I say, rolling my eyes.

"Ugh, no fun. Okay, so the truth is that my entire suite is in there getting wasted, and I want to make sure they get back okay. Last time, two of them came back and left our fourth roommate here because she was drunk and didn't feel like leaving. Luckily, nothing happened in the time it took me to bring them on a forced winter walk back here to get our missing roommate . . . but that doesn't mean it couldn't have. I'm the designated babysitter tonight, for better or for worse. The noise started getting to me, though, so I came out here to get a break from it. Since I was honest with you, you have to be honest with me. Who dragged you here? And why?"

"I'm not going after all that." I wince. "Your story makes you sound like a hero, and mine is just embarrassing."

"I'm sitting on a freezing-cold porch alone at a frat party. Trust me, I'm embarrassing too."

"You're not alone anymore," I point out.

She smiles. "No, I guess I'm not."

"Okay, cards on the table." I sniff, the cold already making my nose run, and stare at the snow-covered lawn. "My track captain—Mika, the one you met at the dining hall—dragged me here. She said I needed to get out of my room more and quit moping or whatever. I accused her of trying to haze me, and now I'm her DD, so I can't even have a beer to ease my suffering."

"Ouch." Mac winces. "Why'd she have to drag you out of your room?"

"It's a long story."

Mac glances behind us just as the bass kicks in even louder. "Something tells me we have plenty of time."

I shake my head with a little laugh. "Can't I just send them an Uber later and head home?"

"Oh, so now *you're* breaking girl code?" Mac smacks my arm. "Face it, Morgan, we're too responsible for frat party life, but clearly *also* too hot to sit at home alone. We're destined for a life of back porches and babysitting our friends."

This time when I laugh, it's real.

"Look, I get homesick too, if that's what it is. I only pretend to be all hard and stuff because if I don't, I'll probably start freaking out that I'm on the opposite side of the country from everyone I know and love. I do like this school, though, don't get me wrong. The campus is beautiful, the professors next-level, and the company's not so bad either," she says, bumping her shoulder against mine.

"Aren't we supposed to be enemies or something, at least while we vie for the internship?" I ask.

"Nah, women hating women for their success is so boring," she says. "The way I see it, birds of a feather should stick together."

"Okay, Billie Eilish," I snort.

"No! I'm serious! Look, one of us *will* probably get the internship. I talked to a TA for one of Dunner's other classes, and he said that they almost always pick a freshman for it. I guess Dunner encourages it, wants to get us engaged with nonprofits before we end up getting an internship later working for, like, fracking or big tobacco or something. I don't know, makes sense, kinda. But it doesn't really matter which one of us gets it, because people like you and me . . . we're gonna do big things, internship or not."

"Yeah? How do you know?"

"I just do. That means that someday I'm going to be working for a senator or something, and you're going to be running a massive nonprofit or advocating for one, and we'll need to work together on a bill or a vote or—I don't know. So yeah, no use tearing each other down when it's inevitable we're going to end up friends in the end regardless. Well, if you keep leaving your room, anyway."

"Shut up." I laugh again, and it feels good. It feels good to sit here with someone who understands the future I daydream about just as much as I do. It feels good to be out here right now with her at all. Not worrying about Ruby or what it means when she says she's too busy to talk, or that I need to call home more, or that Dylan might be stalking Billy's shop to find out what that mystery guy's deal is.

I can finally just breathe—at least as much as the icy winter air lets me.

"Are you ready to tell me why you're moping yet?"

"No," I say. "I'd rather daydream about the future more."

"We can do that." She smiles, reaching behind her to pull an old wool blanket off the ratty couch someone thought would be a good idea to set next to the back door. It's gross, and we both wrinkle our noses at the smell of alcohol coming off it in waves, but . . . it's warm, and it's nice, and it's big enough for both of us to sit under.

"Okay, do you want to work for the senator this time?" she asks, leaning her head against the rail. "Or, ooh, you could *be* the senator."

"We could *both* be senators. Form some kind of subcommittee to . . ." I trail off.

"Make it impossible for private schools to discriminate against LGBTQ+ youth?"

I turn toward her. "That's . . . oddly specific."

Mac shrugs. "If you think researching the opposition isn't standard procedure, I'm not sure you'll make it on Capitol Hill after all, Morgan."

"Opposition? Whatever happened to women supporting women?"

"Oh, I'm all for that, like I said!" She grins. "Remember, I made *sure* you saw the email about the internship. Doesn't mean I don't want to know who I'm up against, though. Pretty impressive résumé you got there—starting your own non-profit right after high school and all."

"I guess I should Google you, then, so I can be impressed too."

"Are you implying that my ability to shut down dumb boys in class while *also* having a better snowball-throwing arm than half the people here on baseball scholarships isn't impressive enough?"

"Your snowball skills aren't bad. It would have been nice if you didn't aim for my head, though."

She leans closer. "You want to know a secret? I wasn't

aiming for your head. I was actually trying to make it land next to you so you'd turn around. I didn't mean to piss you off."

"But you said you had a better—"

"Everybody lies on their résumé," she says quietly, scooting closer so she can drop her head against my shoulder. "It is freezing out here," she mumbles, shivering as she snuggles in a little more. "Are you sure you want to go into politics? You seem awfully gullible."

"That's it, you're off my subcommittee," I say, subtly inching away. Her heat is nice along my side, but . . . it's the wrong body. The wrong girl. Everything feels off.

"You sure you want me off it?" Mac asks, snapping her head up to look at me. "You might need my cunning wit someday."

"Is that what you call 'lying' out in California? 'Cunning wit'?"

"Yeah, mostly." She shrugs. "You like?"

"No, not really," I tease, and gently press her shoulders back against the railing, the way she was sitting before. I tell myself it's because I miss Ruby, and I do, but a part of me is also scared that it's because I could get used to this—the banter, the dreams, the sitting so close . . . more than used to it, if I let myself.

But I'm not ready to let myself. I don't want anyone else.

Mac seems to take the hint, or at least figures the post is as good a place to rest as any, because she doesn't move back—even though I know we're both a little bit colder now.

Even though it would be infinitely more comfortable if I let her, and warmer still probably if I encouraged her.

And oh god, I really need to figure things out with Ruby.

13

RUBY

"We need to communicate better," Morgan says as soon as our FaceTime call connects.

She looks adorable in the flannel puppy-print pajamas I got her for Christmas, her hair piled up on her head in an oversized scrunchie that I make her wear these days. She's been insisting on sleeping in them lately, too exhausted to deal with her hair after long days of class and practice. She had been using little rubber bands and cheap hair bands—no doubt ripping half her hair out by morning—before I stopped her. This one is loose, the least damaging of all the options. It's comically big, and velvety soft, and I would trade almost anything to be able to reach through my phone and let her hair down.

She's been letting it grow out since last summer, and I love it—playing with her hair quickly became my favorite thing during winter break.

"Ruby," she says. And *oh. Oh shit.* I've just been staring at her longingly this whole time, haven't I? I suppose there are worse things, though.

"Sorry, sorry," I say, forcing my attention back onto her words. "I was distracted by this really hot girl on my screen. Maybe you know her—cute, cozy, has an obnoxiously big yet adorable scrunchie on top of her head?"

She smiles but looks away. "Ruby, I'm being serious."

"So am I," I say, covering my heart with one hand, holding the other one up like I'm taking an oath, and it almost feels like I am, if I'm being honest. My girlfriend *is* hot.

Her face falls, letting me know my joking is definitely missing the mark.

"What's up?" I ask.

Dread ties quick hard knots around my spine, making me sit higher, bracing for impact. Maybe this is it—the ending I've been worrying so much about. That I've been wrestling with as the distance grows between us, even as we both pretend that it's not.

No, she didn't say, "We need to talk." She said, "We need to communicate better." That's not necessarily a bad thing.

"I think there's some stuff that I haven't been totally honest about," she says, and suddenly that sense of dread is back with a vengeance. "I think there's a chance that you haven't been either."

My head rears back, instinctively going on the defense. "Like what?"

But then again, I guess she's not wrong. I haven't told her about the show. I haven't told her about how stressed I've been or anything else. *So how does she know? Does she even really know? Or is she just guessing?*

"Like this guy from class you're driving all around."

Wait, what?

"Shiloh?" I ask, utterly confused. "What about him?"

"Well, just, he's kind of . . . your type," she mumbles, picking at the fuzz on her pj's.

"My type? He's an absolute dumbass! Plus, he's so busy with his kid and class and working at Billy's—"

"Yeah, I was wondering about that too. How often is he at Billy's?"

I can't decide if I'm mad that she doesn't seem to trust me or frustrated that we never talked about this before. I honestly didn't realize it was bothering her at all. "A few evenings a week, and sometimes on the weekends. Since he can bring his daughter with him," I say, biting my lip.

"You didn't tell me all that."

I shrug. "I didn't really know his work schedule was a big deal."

"Why is his daughter there too? Where's his wife?"

"Wife?" I laugh, trying and failing to picture him standing in a tux, before I give up. "That dude does not have a wife."

"Girlfriend, then? The *mother*? Why doesn't she take the kid while he's at work so you and Billy don't have to deal with it?"

"Oh," I say. *Is that what she's getting at? Does she think Stella Jane's the reason I missed her meet, and not that we were just super backed up and Billy needed my help?* "Yeah, no, the mom dipped out. Shiloh takes care of her on his own. Well, he did before Billy started helping. You have *got* to hear Billy's baby voice, it's so creepy, but Stella Jane seems to—"

"So he's single?"

"Huh? No, Billy's still dating that woman from the hot dog place. I would tell you if they ended things."

Morgan rolls her eyes. "Not Billy, obviously. This Shiloh guy. He's single?"

"Yeah, why?" I ask, utterly confused about why she looks so pissed all of a sudden.

"Because you're spending a lot of time with this guy, playing happy family with him and Billy, and you haven't really mentioned it to me. I wouldn't even know his deal if I didn't keep pressing. Were you . . . hiding it?"

All right, now I'm *the one getting mad.*

"No more than you're hiding your snowball-throwing buddy who hung up on me. Did you know that Lydia even texted me to keep an eye on it after you hung out with her that day?" I ask, sounding a little meaner than I intend to. "I didn't tell you because I thought she was just shit-stirring and didn't know what she was talking about."

"She doesn't!" Morgan says.

"What about that time you called me freaking out about *not* flirting with her? Maybe we should both play the 'what don't I know' game now. Is Lydia right? Should I be keeping an eye on you? What would that even mean when you're hours away anyway?"

Morgan looks absolutely stricken when I say that, and oh, whoops, maybe I *do* have something to worry about here. *What. The. Fuck?*

"Ruby," she says softly.

"Why do you look so guilty right now?" I ask quietly, still stunned.

"I don't look guilty," Morgan says, but she doesn't sound sure.

Holy shit, I'm walking away from the opportunity of a lifetime for this girl, and, wow, Billy does always say people accuse you of what they themselves are doing. My stomach free-falls to my feet. *Please don't let him be right.*

"I'm not . . ." Morgan trails off, and it's not exactly reassuring.

I cross my arms. "You said we needed to communicate better—so let's do that. What's really going on?"

Morgan's eyes go glassy, and she shrugs. "Everything is weird between us lately. You have to feel it too. You didn't even come to my track meet when my brother offered to bring you."

"I was working," I shout, because she can imply that was an excuse all she wants, but this time, it was actually true.

"Are you mad at me for trying for that internship without talking to you? I feel like you are."

"Why are you changing the subject? We're talking about our 'friends' right now."

She shakes her head. "I don't know why Lydia texted you, but she shouldn't have. I guess I shouldn't be surprised, though. She made a comment to me when I was there visiting her and Aaron. Did you know they broke up?"

"I didn't know they were ever dating," I say. "Didn't she and Allie *just* break up?"

"No, not Lydia and Aaron, Lydia and Allie. Yeah, they did. Can you believe that?"

"Well, yeah, of course," I say, scrunching up my face. "That relationship had, like, *maybe* a three-month shelf life at most. I was honestly surprised they weren't done by Thanksgiving. They were never gonna work."

"Some people say that about us," Morgan says glumly.

"Who?"

"People," she says, looking away. "Allie and Lydia breaking up made me wonder if—I don't know . . ."

"We're not Allie and Lydia. At all. I don't care what people say or think, unless it's coming from you. Are you . . . are you having doubts?" I force myself to ask.

"No!" she says way too fast. It doesn't exactly make me feel better.

"Morgan, you're freaking me out here. Be honest, are you having doubts about us? Is there something going on with you and that girl?"

"I would never cheat on you, I swear." Morgan looks up at me, her eyes red-rimmed. "I just hate being so far apart. I hate feeling like an outsider in your life."

"You're not!"

"You got that guy a job at Billy's! You wouldn't even let anybody come to the shop until—"

"Until you," I finish for her, mentally kicking myself for not even considering how that might look. "But it's not the same at all! I brought you there so you could *know me*. The real me. I didn't hire you to sweep the floor!" I sigh. "I got Shiloh a job there because he was in a bind, and I wouldn't have made it as far as I have if people didn't give me a hand up. That's it."

Morgan looks away, wiping at her eyes. "Well, I can tell he's hot too—like, really hot, from the five seconds I saw him—and I started thinking about how Allie was already dating some guy at college before she even broke up with Lyds! What if you decide that this guy's easier and more convenient? Or maybe you've already decided. I don't know!"

"Where is this coming from?"

"Come on! He's like the boy version of you!"

"No, he's not!" I snap. "And you would know that if you got to know him instead of getting jealous! Like, sure, we have a lot in common, and he's easy to talk to, but he's a friend. *You're* the one I love."

"Yeah, well, it hasn't felt like it lately. You've been really hard to get ahold of sometimes, and . . ."

Shit, I guess I kind of have been, haven't I?

"What about my internship that you *clearly* don't want me to do over the summer? If you love me—"

"I never said that!"

"No, but every time I try to talk about it or get excited, you change the subject. I get it. We'd be apart for most of the summer, and that sucks, but I don't know why you aren't being supportive of me at all. Don't you see this is a huge opportunity for me? I have to go after it!"

"I know you do!"

"Then why are you being so weird about it? Sometimes I feel like you resent me or something!"

"Maybe I do!" I shout, before I can stop myself.

I regret it instantly as tears start spilling down Morgan's cheeks.

"You do?" She nods to herself, looking absolutely shattered. "Okay, then."

"No, not 'okay, then,'" I say. "I'm sorry, I shouldn't have said that."

"If it's how you feel—"

"It's not. Not really. And definitely not how I *want* to feel. Okay, let's rewind a second just to clear something up once and for all. I don't have feelings for Shiloh. He's cute, sure. I'm not going to lie and say I never noticed that, but I'm in this with you. *I am.*

"I have no feelings for him, and I would never, ever cheat on you. I hope you know me well enough to know I wouldn't; it hurts if you don't. I'm not the person I was a year ago. I don't care about easy and convenient anymore. I care about real and genuine—and that's you.

"If you want to FaceTime with him or whatever would make you feel better, like, he's definitely down to do that. I talk about you *a lot*. He would love to meet you. I promise. And yeah, I fucked up by not telling you more about him, or considering how it might look for me to have him with me at Billy's. I want to say that I'm just a dumbass, but maybe the truth is that I was scared you would think exactly what you ended up thinking anyway. Clearly, I don't always know what

I'm doing with relationship shit, but I do know I love you and I want the best for you, always. And I want to be supportive of this internship thing . . ."

"But . . . ?" she says quietly, urging me on as I struggle to find the right words.

"I *have* been keeping something big from you that's separate from all this stuff. And it's probably why you feel a little resentment and distance coming from my side." I meet her eyes, hating the fear and hurt I see there. *That I put there.* "I have the chance to possibly be on that show that I make you watch sometimes—*Mastermind Mechanics*."

"Oh my god," Morgan says, letting out a huge breath and looking suddenly relieved. "I thought you were going to say something bad! That's, like, your favorite thing! That's incredible! You gotta do it! Why didn't you tell me? Why would you ever feel weird about that?" She shifts closer to the screen. "How is this happening, or maybe happening? When will you know? Ahh, I'm crossing everything for you! This is so cool."

"It's a long story, but the gist is my instructor's been friends with the host since they were kids, and they want to do a college episode. My instructor kind of hinted that I'm the one he wants to recommend for it, if I give him the green light."

"Obviously, you're giving him the green light. Why wouldn't you?"

"Because it's on our *sacred* spring break."

She goes quiet then, absorbing my words. "Oh. That's very . . . um . . . yeah."

"Yeah. I know how much the DC trip means to you, and the internship too. It's not that I'm not proud of you or supportive; it's just that I'm a little bitter, I guess."

"I have all these meetings set up during our trip," Morgan says slowly. "It would be unprofessional of me to cancel them."

"I know," I say, so quiet I wonder if she can hear my heart breaking behind my ribs. "I'm not going to do it, don't worry, but that's why I've been a little down."

"You want to do it, though."

"Yeah, Morgan, are you fucking kidding? Of course I want to do it. But I'm not going to blow you off . . . even though you seem to have no problem making plans for the summer without telling me! It just stings a little, I guess. I would have wanted it to be more of a conversation than just a two-second thing *in front of our friends* where you're like 'Oh, hey, I'm doing this.' "

"I'm not making plans without you. I thought you would come with me and—"

"You know I have to work all summer! Billy needs help. I know it's, like, this weird situation, but at the end of the day, I'm his employee. I can't be running off all the time."

"Could you just stay with me for like the first half, and then after, go work the whole rest of the time? Or we could do a week on and a week off or something? You work all year! You're allowed to take a vacation if you want."

"Morgan! I have to pay for things! I have to pay for gas. I have to pay for whatever the scholarship doesn't cover. I'm not trying to get Billy stuck with every bill either," I say, because how does she *still* not get this? "I only work a few hours a week during school, and I took most of winter break off already. I need to work full-time over the summer. I can't afford to take a few weeks off, let alone a month. I don't have rich parents or—"

"Don't make this about money."

"Sometimes it *is* about money, though."

"Fine," she says, leaning back. "I won't apply. It's okay. There will be other internships. I probably wouldn't get it anyway." Her voice is almost monotone, robotic, like she's just going through the motions now of what she thinks I want to hear. I hate it.

I groan in frustration. "I don't want you to not apply!"

Morgan scoffs as fresh tears spill down her face. "You're giving up your show, but I'm still supposed to do the internship and then have you resent me for it? What happens next, Ruby? We break up? You date your hot guy, and I date my hot girl, and we just . . . That's it? That's what you want? No. No, I'm not doing that. Or . . . or what's the alternative? You do your show, and I do my internship, and we just never see each other and end up breaking up that way? I don't want to do that either! I refuse. I won't! The only chance we have is if neither of us apply to our—"

"Wait, what hot girl?" I ask, my tongue heavy as lead as I force the words out. It dawns on me now that while we just dissected my relationship with Shiloh, we never got into Morgan's new *friend*. "Snowball girl? *Do* you have a crush on her?"

Morgan shakes her head, looking away. "No, not a crush, but . . ."

"But you could, if you let yourself, right?"

She doesn't answer for a long time.

"Right?" I nudge.

"You couldn't on him?" she asks. "You couldn't ever fall for a down-on-his-luck guy with a sharp jawline and a cool motorcycle jacket? A great, responsible dad, apparently? You're telling me that not one time, ever, period, you felt even a single butterfly?"

I don't know if I'm madder that this means she clearly feels butterflies with the girl from her class, or that she's right about Shiloh. In a whole other timeline, we might have made sense together. But not in this one. Still, even though I squashed my butterflies, even though they're deader than dust, they existed for a second, in the beginning.

It would be hypocritical of me to hate her for the same thing.

"Thought so," she says, studying my face. "Ruby, I don't want to lose you."

"I don't want to lose you either!"

"Okay, then it's decided. I won't apply to mine, and you won't apply to yours. We'll have spring break and summer as planned, and it will be great. It'll be fair."

Is it decided? Then why do I still feel so awful?

Is this what being in a relationship is? Is it sacrifices for the greater good? Is it nobody getting what they really want? Or, shit, am I just repeating my mom's old patterns of throwing everything away for the person I love?

I don't know. Maybe Morgan's right. Maybe waiting for Morgan to get out of her meetings in DC will feel great. Maybe I won't think about filming the show at all because I'll be so happy to be with her. Maybe Morgan will feel great volunteering at the center while she waits for me to finish my forty hours a week at the shop, and she won't wish she's anywhere else. Maybe she'll like that more than working with lobbyists and doing what she loves. But, fair or not, I'm not so sure.

"Morgan—"

"I love you," she cuts me off. "I love us. Nothing and no one will ever change that." She says it firmly, like that's the end of the conversation, like everything is settled.

I can't help but wonder: *Is she trying to comfort me, or is she trying to convince herself?*

14

MORGAN

I push myself harder, my feet thundering through the trail in the woods, even though it's all mud and half-melted snow. It makes for sloppy, difficult conditions that have my muscles screaming, but I don't care. I don't care. I can't.

All I can think about is that I'm losing out on a huge opportunity and so is Ruby. I know it's the right thing, the *fair* thing, but it feels somehow so wrong. We decided, I remind myself. *I* decided.

There's nothing left to do but run it out.

I just have to run it out—to pretend the tears on my face are really rain. To pretend that this all makes sense and it's what I want, that it's easy and joyful. That Ruby and I aren't holding each other back—we can't be, because this is love. This is meant to be. We didn't fight so hard last year just to throw it all away. If it has to be like this, then it has to be like this.

It has to be.

It has to.

It . . .

What the hell am I doing? How can I walk away from a chance like this? How can I let myself? Why does it come down to walking away from this internship or walking away from Ruby, when I can't do either?

I use my shirt to wipe the sweat from my face, and I run. I run, and I run, and I run until I'm just a pile of meat and bones in motion. Nothing matters but the next breath, and the next step, and the next, and the next, and the next, and the next, and the . . .

15

RUBY

Everly is home visiting for a long weekend, and she couldn't have come at a better time. I'm currently flopped across her bed, torn between pretending this is any old sleepover and wanting to, like, I don't know, unburden my soul on her or whatever—especially after that phone call earlier with Morgan.

Hey, I never said I wasn't dramatic.

Tyler's home too, and while we haven't really stayed in contact, it was nice when we bumped into him at the little Starbucks inside of our Target and caught up for a minute. He and Everly shit-talked Marcus and Allie a bit, both of them glad to be rid of their exes . . . if you can even really call Allie his ex. I mean, I don't think I'm his ex, and we hooked up *way* more than they did once upon a time.

I was actually still mulling that over when their focus

shifted to me and what was going on in my life. I gave him a sugarcoated version, the same one I gave Everly. Tyler seemed genuinely happy to hear that I was kicking ass in school and still with Morgan. It honestly took all my willpower not to throw up my complicated feelings about those things all over him when he said that. But that's not what you do when you're making small talk. You tell people you're chill and everything's fine, and then you go about your day.

I think Everly knows something is up anyway. She can generally read me like a book. I wasn't surprised when she asked me to sleep over for a girls' night—I'm only surprised that she hasn't pressed me about things yet. I'm sure it's coming, though.

As if on cue, Everly steps back into her room with a plate of dino nuggets and mozzarella sticks. I raise an eyebrow, and she laughs. "My mom made these for us. I think she wants to pretend we're still seven."

I grab a nugget and bite the dinosaur's head off, chewing thoughtfully. "I'm not opposed," I say, watching her play with a gooey mozzarella stick.

I think she's going to ask me now, but instead she reaches for the remote. *Maybe she does just want a low-stakes girls' night.* Grateful for the reprieve, I follow her lead, and we both settle in to watch whatever she picked for tonight. Or rather, Everly settles in, while I do my best to pretend I'm not spiraling about everything going on in my life.

Generally, Everly declares her room a "no phone zone," and I'm happy to oblige, but tonight I can't stop checking my texts every few minutes. I don't know if I'm hoping or dreading hearing from Morgan—but the fact that she hasn't so much as sent me a meme since this afternoon probably says more than any text ever would.

I flop back against the pillow and stare at the screen. I've been so distracted, I didn't even realize she put on *ShopTalk*, Morgan's favorite rom-com. My heart flip-flops in my chest, and I almost wonder if Everly can hear it.

This is the movie Morgan tried to put on that very first time I was ever at her apartment. We had just had another little mishap with my car, resulting in Morgan twisting her ankle, so I had driven her home and made sure she put something cold on it. Morgan asked me to stay and watch, and god, I wanted to, but I didn't. At the time, I didn't think I should... I've watched this movie a hundred times with her since then to make up for leaving that day. Madelaine Petsch runs across the screen in front of me, and I feel my eyes stinging. Morgan insists this is the best opening of any rom-com ever, and I can't help but wish that she was here. Or that I was there. Or that she would at least text me so I know where things stand.

Everly glances at me and then quickly pauses the movie before rolling to her side so we're face-to-face. "Okay," she says gently. "I've tried to give you space to tell me whatever's bugging you, but now I'm calling you out on it, because I know you're not crying over some corny movie when we're barely ten minutes in. What's going on?"

"I'm sorry," I grumble, wiping at my eyes. "I feel like every time we're together or on the phone I'm relying on you to fix a problem or give advice. I don't want our friendship to just be about me."

Everly smiles, seeming genuinely touched by this. "It's not. How many hours did you sit on the phone and listen to me vent about Marcus? How many times have you fixed my car for free? You're my best friend, and whatever pity party you're having in your head, don't throw that into the mix. Sometimes I need you, and sometimes, like now, you need me. That's how it works. I know if I call you, you'll pick up. Every time. It's not about being equal; it's about being there. So let me be there for your dumb ass, the way you're always there for mine."

"Well, that's not gonna help me stop crying. Why are you so fucking nice?" I ask, choking out a wet laugh.

"Hey, sometimes you need it. Like right now, obvs. So spill, what's the deal? Did you and Morgan hit a rough patch or something? You having issues at school? Billy doing a one-eighty and kicking you out? Whatever it is, we'll figure it out."

"If Billy ever does a one-eighty, we should probably call a priest or something, because obviously he's been possessed or body-snatched."

"True." She laughs. "And school?"

"School's great."

"So are you and Morgan fighting?"

"Not exactly," I say. "But kind of? We're making the right choices for the relationship. At least, I think so? But they sort of feel like the wrong choices for us individually. Is that . . . I mean, is that what relationships are? Putting the other person first?"

Everly props her head up on one arm. "I think I need a little context before I answer that. It's, like, yes, but also no, if you get me."

"I don't," I say, banging my head gently on the headboard. "How can it be both?"

"It just is sometimes." She shrugs, like it's the easiest thing in the world, and slides her hand behind my head. "How about you tell me what's swirling around in this head instead of knocking any more of those brain cells loose."

I sigh and shimmy back down onto her pillows.

"People keep telling me that relationships are a lot of work, and you need to put each other first. So I do that, but then I just feel miserable the whole time. I'm supposed to be proud of myself, right? For finally being a good girlfriend or whatever? But instead I keep feeling bitter about having to give up things that I think would be really good for me.

"And then I start freaking out about my mom. My mom, who put literally everyone first *except* me. Nothing came before whatever man she was with that week. *Nothing.* And if that's what relationships are, if that's what they're supposed to be, then do I even fucking want one?"

"Your mom is not the example you want to use as a guide," Everly says. "Hell no."

"But then what does it mean when they say all that putting-the-other-person-first bullshit? I love Morgan so much, like, *so* much. I want the best for her. I want her to go do big things. I want to support her! But I want to do big things too."

"You are. You will!" Everly says.

"No, neither of us are now! Because we're putting the relationship first, just like everyone says you're supposed to. It doesn't make sense. How can it be good to put each other first if we totally lose ourselves in the process? If my mom hadn't put so many guys first, I bet her life would have been way better. Mine would have been too, for that matter."

"Hey, hey," Everly says, squeezing my shoulder. "You're getting yourself all worked up. Take a breath, seriously." She takes several deep, exaggerated breaths, motioning for me to follow her lead, like I need a map for something that other people find instinctual. Maybe I do. *What the hell is wrong with me?*

I take a beat to steady myself and then roll onto my side to face her again. "Sorry, I'm a mess. Let's watch the movie, okay? I don't feel like talking about it anymore."

"You're not your mom," Everly says. "I need to make sure you understand that."

"I do." I shrug. "Because if I were like her, then I wouldn't have any problem putting the other person first. She treated her boyfriends like gold."

Everly shakes her head. "No, she didn't. She just treated them better than you. Your mom was codependent and toxic as hell in every relationship, including yours. She was a terrible mom to you, and it wasn't your fault, and it *definitely* wasn't because she was being a good partner to them. It was because she had a lot of issues and decided to hide instead of dealing with them. That's not you."

"Jesus, Ev! Dropping nuclear truth bombs on me when I'm already upset? That's cold." I give Everly a watery smile so she knows I'm kidding . . . mostly.

"I got locked out of registering for a gen ed class I needed, so I took a psych elective about interpersonal relationships. You might want to do that too. Or better yet, get a therapist to unpack some of this stuff with."

"Okay, Billy," I snort.

"Billy wants you to go to therapy too? I did not think I could like him any more than I already do, and yet!" She laughs. "Seriously, though, Ruby, putting your relationship first means putting it before the rest of the world. It means prioritizing and cherishing it. It doesn't mean throwing yourself away in pursuit of it. It doesn't mean going against your own best interests, and it definitely doesn't mean getting dragged down or staying with someone you're not supposed to."

"How the hell do you know if you're with someone you're not supposed to be with? How do you know where the line is between watching out for yourself and being selfish?" I groan. "I wish there were some kind of book or something!"

Everly smiles. "There are millions of books that give relationship advice, but I don't think that's your problem."

"Then what is?" I practically shout.

"That's what I'm trying to find out," she says. "What *is* the problem here? Is she treating you like shit?" I shake my head. "Is she cheating?" I shake my head again. "Are you bored with her?" I shake my head again. "What do you mean about putting her first over your own interests, then? What is going on?"

I take a deep breath as Everly waits patiently for me to find my words. When I finally do, I tell her everything. I tell her about the show, Morgan's internship, her little snowball-throwing friend, and Shiloh, who I don't have a crush on but could have, maybe, if I hadn't let those feelings go in favor of making the first new solid friend I've picked up since I was little.

I tell her how I'm scared that these new friendships mean our relationship is doomed. What if we both found our better matches, people who are easier to understand, since they've lived our same lives? I tell her how confused I am about putting Morgan ahead of the show, and her putting me ahead of the internship. Is it any different from my mom putting her boyfriends ahead of me and her own best interests? And alternatively, if I do the show anyway, aren't I making Morgan live through something she doesn't want, the way Mom did to me with the pageants? And speaking of pageants. Speaking of pageants! How am I going to hate my mom for making me perform, and then turn around and smile for a camera all on my own?

"It's not the same at all," Everly says when I finally finish, dramatically pulling a pillow over my face to signal I'm done. "You're not like your mom, and none of this is anything like what she put you through. I almost wonder if talking to her would clear some of this up for you."

"You think I should talk to her again?" I ask, lifting a corner of the pillow so I can see.

"I didn't say that exactly," she says, peeling the pillow all the way off and smoothing back some of my hair. "That's way above the class I'm taking. I don't know if that would make you feel better or worse. I do know that it's been eating you up every time she calls. I know that you have a lot of mom stuff mixed up in everything you're saying, and I'm not sure it needs to be there. Maybe having an honest conversation with her would help—if you feel okay about that and think she's capable of it. If she sucks again, at least you'd know. Could give you closure, you know. Could also mess you up in the head more, though."

I bark out a shocked laugh. "You're *really* selling the idea, Ev."

"I'm not trying to sell you anything. In fact, I recommend talking to like a dozen therapists, or at the very least Billy, before doing it. I'm just winging it because she seems to be taking up way too much space in your brain."

"That's fair," I admit.

"Back to the Morgan stuff, though. You absolutely shouldn't be giving up the chance at *Mastermind Mechanics,* and she absolutely should be applying for that internship. You're not wrong about there being a point where putting the other person first, or putting the relationship first, is harmful. I'm not saying this is quite that, but it would be you two walking away from super-unique opportunities that could have a huge impact on your lives."

"Morgan has a huge impact on my life," I say, because I don't see how we could each pursue our dreams and have it all work out. Morgan herself had a list of reasons it wouldn't.

"Yeah, and that's why you shouldn't be blowing off her track meets to fix Marcus's mom's car," Everly says. "Her impact is a reason to show up for her, but that's not a reason to sacrifice an opportunity that could get you and Billy's shop on the map like it's done for so many others."

Now it's my turn to sit up. "Are you honestly saying you

think we should apply and then never be together again?"

Everly shakes her head. "No, so knock it off with that all-or-nothing mentality. I'm saying you don't even know if you'll both get the jobs, but you owe it to yourselves to try anyway. I think you guys need to be real with yourselves. You're college freshmen who've been together a year, not forty-five-year-olds with a mortgage and a bunch of kids. You need to be living your lives. If you can make it work, that's awesome; I want that for you! Just not at the expense of your future."

"Wait, are you telling me to cut my losses or something?" I ask, horrified.

"I didn't say that. That's for you two to decide. I just think there's no point in being together if you're going to hold each other back, you know? You're not gonna do big things if you're trying to keep each other in these stupid little high school boxes. *Evolve or fuck off.* That's my mentality after wasting my first semester still trying to make it work with Marcus."

"'Evolve or fuck off'? What does that even mean?"

"It means I'm not letting anyone hold me back anymore, and you shouldn't either. If you and Morgan can figure out how to stay together *and* let each other evolve, I'm all for it. But if not, then you both need to fuck off away from each other."

It kills me that what she's saying actually makes sense.

"I hate your psych professor," I say, throwing myself face-down on my one remaining pillow with a groan. I don't want to think about this anymore. I want to eat dino nuggies and watch bad movies—although not *ShopTalk*—with my best friend, and preferably not think about anything ever again, because the idea of Morgan and me having to "fuck off," as Everly so eloquently put it, if we can't figure this out is making me feel like my heart is clawing up my throat.

Everly rubs small circles along my back, and the fear and frustration drain right out of me. My mom used to do that when I was really sick. It was the only time she would. I used to pretend to be sick just to get her attention, to feel like I had a mom who loved me, who really cared. Who was doing her best to make me feel happy and safe.

Why does it always, always go back to my mother—the person I haven't talked to in a year. That I never want to talk to again, except . . . that's a lie. I do want to, with my whole heart. Or maybe I just want to be that little girl with the mother who brings her juice and takes her temperature and sits beside her on the bed. *Damn.*

Another hot tear slides down the edge of my nose and falls onto the pillow. If Everly notices, she's polite enough not to mention it. She gives me time to fall apart and pull myself back together, her hand never stopping its soothing pattern on my back.

I finally roll over to face her, feeling embarrassed. If I had any self-respect, I would run right out the sliding glass door and straight into the safety of my 1970 Ford Torino. I would let the growl of its engine make me feel strong and grounded the way it always used to. I would tell myself it's all I need and believe it.

Maybe I don't like this person I've turned into, actually. The one who lets people in and talks things out and doesn't run from the hard stuff. Maybe I just want to worry about myself again. Maybe it's for the best. Maybe I can still do big things without having to *feel* so damn much all the time. I don't know. Because maybe I *do* like this person I've been becoming. The one who's helpful and feels so much and . . . damn.

Is this what it means to evolve?

I hate that I've had to fast-forward through a lifetime of emotional learning just to try to catch up, because up until last year, I was too busy worrying about surviving and taking care of the person who was supposed to take care of me to have the space to worry about who I wanted to be and what that might look like.

I don't know which way is up right now, but I think Everly helped me figure out at least one thing.

"I'm going to email my instructor and tell him I'm interested," I say, pulling out my phone before I lose my nerve. "Then I think I'm going to go see Morgan tomorrow. I want to tell her in person that I'm applying for the show, and that she should apply for the internship. I don't think that's a FaceTime call, right?"

"That's a great plan," Everly says. "I'm really proud of you, Ruby. You know that, right? I know this is all so hard and confusing, but you *are* crushing it. Sincerely. You've got this."

I blush furiously, shaking my head. I don't think I'll ever get used to people saying those kinds of things about me. But you know what? I think I'm proud of myself too.

16

MORGAN

The library is blissfully empty today.

That's not totally unusual this time of year, long before everyone is panicking about midterms and finals and filling the library with their anxious chatter, and especially during long weekends like this one. Most kids went home for it and aren't back yet. I considered it myself, but since we still had practice this morning, it didn't seem worth it to make my brother drive all the way here and back twice.

Despite having my pick of tables, I take my usual spot in the far back corner where no one can really see me. It's peaceful back there, being surrounded by countless books and only the occasional sound of turning pages or books being shelved.

I've come here to work today. The silence of my bedroom, when I wished it was full of the sounds of Ruby FaceTiming me, got so loud that I couldn't bear it. I can handle the silence here, at least. Silence *belongs* here.

Ruby and I have barely talked since our argument—no, not an argument, really—since our . . . *decision* . . . to set aside both of our goals and focus on each other. I was the one who said we should. That means I should be happy or at least neutral about it, then, right?

Spoiler alert: I'm not.

I'm sad—sad that someone else will get a spot that feels like it was tailor-made for me. I'm jealous too. Angry, even, if I think about it too long. None of that is Ruby's fault—but I knew I would take it out on her if given the chance, because you can't yell at intangible things like ideas or relationships, but you can yell at the person you love.

I don't want to be like that, and I especially don't want to be like that to her. So instead of reaching out and risking saying something I'd regret when my emotions were still raw, I just haven't texted her at all, other than a good-morning text I make sure to send every day. I couldn't bear to skip it.

Ruby hasn't really texted me either—not outside a quick "thanks, you too," anyway.

Thanks, I hate it.

I tried to stay busy. I got caught up on homework, deep cleaned my room, and then spent the rest of the time staring off into space and letting the seconds tick by. I should have spent it writing my economics paper, which is due in two days, but wallowing took priority. Oh well, I'm doing it now.

At least, I'm pretending to. So far, I've mostly been taking up space at this big oak table in the back of the library and watching TikToks with my AirPods in. There are eight chairs around this table; it's one of the biggest. I might be kind of a jerk for using it instead of one of the individual study cubes dotting the walls, but whatever. I wanted to take up space today—needed to—since I won't be this summer.

It's not long before I find myself drifting over to pull up the website of the lobbyist group that's hosting the internship. There's nothing about it on their website—seems like they really are giving Professor Dunner advance notice and special preference. That's fine. There are a lot of other great students to recommend, I'm sure . . . like Mac, who I haven't talked to since the party and definitely shouldn't even be thinking about either.

Ruby and I are committed to each other. We *are*.

I click through to reread for the hundredth time the services they provide and the history of their company. I'm practically drooling at the thought of getting to work there. I let myself daydream for a minute about what it would be like and if they would ask me back summer after summer before offering me a job someday.

A swift kick to my chair leg wrenches me from that thought. I spin in my chair and see Mac, grinning behind me.

"I was hoping you were here, Senator," she says.

I click my laptop shut as she slides into the seat beside me. Clearly a deliberate choice given the abundance of chairs. Her leg presses along the side of mine—the heat of her thigh scorches through the layers of her leggings and mine. I curse myself for throwing on thin running pants instead of something solid, like denim or steel. I look over at her, expecting that she's going to shift away because she must feel it too, and am met with only a soft smile.

Is it because I haven't moved my leg away? That thought hits me like ice water.

I know we had an *almost* moment the other night, but even if I felt it too, I definitely shut it down by the time I went inside to find my friends and head back to our rooms.

I slide my chair over, letting the cool library air rush in between us, creating a fresh chasm of deliberately missed opportunities. A tiny divot appears between her eyebrows, and I look away.

I open my laptop, angled away from her, clicking over to open a clean document the second it lets me. *Essay, essay, I need to write the essay.*

"You're a strange one, Morgan," Mac says.

"Then why were you hoping I was here?" I ask, scanning the instructions that tell me I need to cite three sources and write a minimum of four pages double-spaced. Should be easy enough, or at least it would be, if Mac weren't sitting next to me making my brain feel like it's full of lightning bolts. It feels somehow wrong to be alone back here with her, especially when things are so fraught right now between me and Ruby.

"Are you grumpy today?" Mac pouts instead of answering.

"I'm not grumpy," I snap, not doing much to make my case. "I'm just wondering what you want."

"Whoa," she says. "No need to be a dick about it."

I pinch the bridge of my nose, trying to get my frustration

under control. It's not Mac's fault that I'm so upset right now. Taking it out on her wouldn't be any better than taking it out on my girlfriend. "Sorry," I grumble. "It's not you."

"You ready to tell me what has you moping so much lately?" she asks, her voice painfully sincere.

"Not really." I don't look up, not sure what my eyes will tell her if I do. I can only hope that she picks up on the fact that I need to be alone right now.

She doesn't.

"Oh no, are you pissy because you fully get it now? You're all, *Just bury me, I guess, because I know I'll never be as good as Mac*?" she teases, flicking my arm to get my attention. "I know I'm getting the internship, but like I said, we're gonna be subcommittee bros. It'll all work out."

"You'd never get it over me in a million years," I snort, not even caring that her winning the spot over me would technically solve all my problems.

"Sure, sure," she says. "You're almost cute when you're mad, you know? Like a little house cat pretending to be a lion."

"I'm a house cat?" I shake my head. "What does that make you, then?"

"Wouldn't you like to know." Mac winks and nudges her foot against mine . . . and shockingly leaves it there. I should move my foot away, just like I moved my leg—my entire chair, really—but it's kind of nice. I can almost, if only for a second, pretend that my life hasn't been a total disaster lately—that I'm just Morgan at College, instead of The Girl Who Got Kicked Out of High School or Ruby's Girlfriend (or, more accurately lately, Ruby's Potential Life Ruiner).

"I think you're grossly overestimating how much I want to know about you." I laugh, kicking her foot back . . . but then I keep our sneakers pressed together too.

Mac's eyes snap to mine with a heat that I recognize—I've seen it reflected in Ruby's a hundred times. My smart words and witty comebacks dry into dust in my mouth, and it suddenly feels like a neon sign flashing WRONG appears over her head. Wrong eyes giving me that look, on the wrong body, of the wrong girl.

"I know you like me," Mac says, leaning forward as if she considers my nervous lip-licking some sort of invitation. Her eyes go soft to match her smile, and before I can react, she scoots forward and presses her lips to mine.

I freeze, the neon sign turning into a blaring alarm in my head, all sirens going off as I try to get myself to shove her off. Except I'm sitting here pinned to my chair in shock, wondering how things got so off track so fast.

This isn't what I want.

Mac presses against me a bit more firmly, bringing her hand up to the side of my face as her tongue slips against my lips, begging for them to open. There is maybe a timeline that they would, in another universe entirely. But in this one, this one right now, all I can think of is Ruby, and how much I love her. How much I don't want someone else's hand on my cheek or lips kissing me.

My heart beats to her name—*Ruby, Ruby, Ruby*—as I struggle to bring my body back online.

Finally, I reach my hand up and press Mac back into her seat. It feels like I've been screaming in my head for an hour, but I know it was barely a few seconds.

Mac seems to think it's a joke at first, her face giving me that mischievous glint it does before she contradicts me in class. My panic must finally register, though, because that look turns to confusion and then embarrassment.

"I'm sorry, Mac." I shake my head. "I'm . . . I don't want that from you. We're friends, and I'd rather keep it that way."

Her face screws up in frustration, her eyes going wet. "You—"

"I'm sorry if I gave you the wrong idea."

"*If* you gave me the wrong idea? You've been flirting with me this whole semester!"

"I didn't mean to. I'm sorry, maybe I did blur the lines a little. I understand if you're upset. I swear I wasn't trying to mess with you or any—"

Suddenly, she's back, pressing herself against me like another kiss will change my mind. Only this time I'm not frozen, I'm *mad.*

I said no. It doesn't matter if I was flirting or not flirting; it doesn't matter if I gave her every mixed signal on earth in the past. I. Said. No. *NOW.* That's all that matters.

I'm about to shove her back, hard this time, when she's yanked back instead. Fear crosses her face as she realizes it's not me doing the removing.

"What the fuck? She told you no."

My eyes snap up to find Ruby, hard and angry and glaring at Mac. She has a white-knuckle grip on Mac's hoodie, her hands so tight they're shaking.

"Ruby?!"

"You okay?" she asks, her eyes locking on mine. All of her anger is still there, but a tempest of worry and fear swirls in her eyes. "Morgan? Answer me. Are you okay?"

And oh god, how is she here?

What did she see?

What does she think *she saw?*

17

RUBY

"Oh my god, Ruby, I didn't . . . I wasn't . . ." Morgan says, her eyes frantic. But I don't care what she did or didn't do before I got here. All I care about is that I heard her say no, and then this asshole squirming under my fist tried to kiss her anyway.

"It's okay," I say, even though it's not.

Either way, I'm sure any second one of those snooty-ass librarians from the front of the building is going to come and investigate why one of their students is practically hissing like a trapped feral cat. If somebody is getting in trouble for this, it probably won't be any of the enrolled students here. It'll be me.

No different from when the cops used to pull me over back home to see what I was up to.

I let go of Little Miss Can't Keep Her Hands to Herself, adding one final shove to get the point home.

"What the hell!" she grunts, fixing her sweatshirt.

"Have you ever heard of this little thing called consent?" I ask, placing myself between Morgan and this horrible girl. I don't know how they ended up here together, and I'm not sure I want to, but Morgan's no should have been a hard stop. I'm not about to let her have another chance to hurt her.

"She gave it," the girl says, raising her chin.

"Maybe," I say, as much as it kills me to even think she could have. "But then she clearly took it away. Consent's not permanent. She said no! I heard her."

"I'm right here," Morgan says, ripping my attention back to her. "You can both skip the alpha posturing and let me speak for myself."

I swallow hard and look down. I wasn't trying to talk over Morgan. I was trying to help.

I'm fucking this up, I think, before realizing by all accounts this was fucked up before I even got here.

"Who even are you? I'm calling campus security," the other girl rages.

Morgan must notice the panic winding its way through my veins, because she reaches out and links her finger with mine.

"Don't call them," Morgan says, standing up to face the other girl head-on. The roles instantly reversed as she protects *me.* I try to force a look of nonchalance onto my face so the girl with no boundaries can't tell how well her threat worked.

"Do you even know her? I've never seen her on campus in my life. You're gonna blow me off for some rando after you spent all semester—"

"She's my girlfriend," Morgan says, cutting off a sentence that I very much would like to hear the end of. "From back home."

Spent all semester . . . What? Kissing? No. No, Morgan wouldn't do that. Especially not after telling me about her own insecurities about Shiloh. But she did say . . .

"Hold on, this is snowball girl?" I ask. "Your *friend*?" I want to make sure that Morgan knows what I'm *really* asking, because I can't bring myself to say it out loud. *Is this the girl you hypothetically said you could have a crush on?*

It doesn't feel so hypothetical anymore.

"Oh, this is rich," the girl says. "You've had someone else the whole time and never said anything to me? Seriously? It sure sounds like you've talked to her about *us*, though. Hi." She holds out her hand to me. "I'm Mac. Nice to finally know you exist, girlfriend from back home."

I look at Morgan. *Did she really never even mention me? Or that she had a girlfriend at all? Not once?* Before I can say anything, Morgan starts shouting.

"Us?!" Morgan says, sounding shocked. "There is no *us*, Mac. What is wrong with you?!"

"Right," Mac says. "You kind of have to say that now, don't you?"

If I'm reading this girl right, her words sound more hurt than angry. I shouldn't feel a sick sense of satisfaction from that, but I do. I can't help it. Watching this boundary-stomping, consent-ignoring piece of shit realize that *she's* the one who's not good enough for Morgan, not me, soothes my soul.

Well, as long as I don't think about everything else—which is the stomach-churning realization that I've *become the secret this time.*

"Look, Mac," Morgan says, clearing her throat. "I've been with Ruby for almost a year, and I really like you as a friend, but—"

"Do you flirt with all your friends the way you flirted with me?" Mac asks, fixing her collar once more before taking a step back. "You know what? Forget it. I don't even care. If you want to go have your life ruined by some girl you banged in high school, be my guest." She flicks her eyes to mine. "Enjoy holding her back," Mac adds, slamming into my shoulder as she pushes past me.

Holding her back?

My stomach twists at having one of my worst fears about our relationship vocalized, followed quickly by a fresh wave of fury that she thinks I'd be the one to do that. I start to follow the girl, campus police be damned, but Morgan reaches for my hand, her fingers lacing between mine in a way that feels almost desperate. There are fresh tears welling in her eyes when I turn back to look at her.

"Ruby, I'm so sorry that you had to—" She sniffles, and I pull her into a tight hug before she can get anything else out.

"Shhh," I say, holding her as she nuzzles in even closer. I slide one of my hands up and cradle her head, my thumb skimming back and forth against her neck.

People have come to stare now, lured over by all the commotion—but let them. I don't even care. As long as she's in my arms, as long as she's safe. That's all that matters right now.

I'd scoop her up and drive her back to Billy's if I thought my car would make it, keep her far away from the world for as long as I can . . . but I know it won't. It barely made it all the way here, even *with* me stopping every so often to tinker with it. I know it needs at least a few hours to cool down before it'll take me anywhere.

Just like I know that the conversation I came here to have still needs to be had, only now with the added bonus layers of *What's with you and Mac* and *why am I a secret?*

Morgan pulls back, and a tinge of embarrassment creeps up my skin, heating my cheeks as it sinks in how overdramatic this probably seems to everyone else.

What are we doing to each other?

I watch as Morgan packs up her stuff one-handed and leads me out of the library, refusing to let go of where we're linked. She doesn't speak until we're far outside. Our path across the campus lawn is lit by little streetlamps, which seem to be dotted in random intervals—shadow and light existing side by side, like the opposing thoughts inside my head about what to do next.

"I didn't want her to kiss me," Morgan says, breaking the silence. "We're friends . . . or were. I wasn't— I didn't reciprocate. I wouldn't. Ever."

I wait until we're in darkness again, not wanting to see her face, to ask, "Did you want to?"

"No," she says, tugging us back into the light a little faster, squeezing my hand even harder.

And that's kind of her thing, isn't it? Holding on too tight? She did it the first time we got together. What if she's doing it again? I was so worried about repeating my mother's habits, I didn't once stop to wonder if Morgan was repeating her own.

"Ruby," she says, waiting until I finally force my eyes to hers. "Please believe me. I don't want her, or anyone but you. I didn't want her to kiss me tonight. I love you too much to ever do anything like that."

I nod, studying her face. Morgan always telegraphs her emotions so earnestly—and right now, I only see honesty and genuine concern. "Then why didn't you ever tell her about me?" I ask, dreading the answer.

Morgan looks down, her eyes squeezed shut as she shakes her head before looking back up at me. "There's no good explanation for that. I just . . . didn't. I think I just wanted someone to see me as strong and put together, like I used to be. Instead of as the girl who sits in her room, homesick and pining for her girlfriend every day. It wasn't because I was trying to cheat or hurt anyone. I just wanted to forget for five seconds how much it kills me to be away from you. That's not an excuse. It was messed up and I hurt you and—"

"Did it work?"

"What do you mean?"

"Did it work? Did she make you feel better? Did she make you . . . forget me?" I ask, the words clawing their way out of my throat so painfully. I don't want to know the answer, but I *need* to.

"No! Never! It just made it hurt more—I wanted it to be you sitting at the desk next to me or throwing snowballs. Not her. Never her. Please, *please*, Ruby." Morgan stops suddenly to pull me into another hug.

Her guilt-tinged tears burn against the skin of my neck as she clings to me. The worst part of it all is that I *know* she's telling the truth. *I do.* Because I've had moments like that with Shiloh, those glimpses of an imaginary life—an easier one, maybe—where he and I are together and I'm not pining for a girl four hours away who's doing the same. And yeah, it does make it worse.

"I didn't know it would be this hard," I whisper.

"What?" she asks, our breath making little clouds in the freezing-cold air as she pulls back and starts walking stiffly, as if she's bracing for something. I gently squeeze her fingers, chasing the heat that's suddenly gone missing from my chest. She squeezes back but still picks up the pace.

"Loving you," I say, and instantly regret it.

"Ouch." Her grip on my hand falters, and it breaks my heart.

"That came out wrong," I say, tugging her closer to me as she keeps trying to rush us down the path.

I have no idea where she's leading me—back to her dorm, I guess, but I can't be sure. I've only been here once. I wasn't planning to stay over tonight—now it seems kind of inevitable.

Morgan resists my attempts to slow us down at first but then finally settles in beside me. I stop walking when we're face-to-face under one of the streetlamps and let the rest of the campus fall away. Right now, it's just me and her, under this bright light. *Nothing else matters more.*

"Let me explain. I didn't mean . . ." I trail off, pleading with her with my eyes. *Why is everything going so wrong?*

"Okay," she says, a little breathless. Like she feels it too. She tucks some of my hair behind my ear with the saddest smile I've ever seen. "What did you come to tell me, Ruby?"

"You're not hard to love, Morgan," I say. "That's not what I meant just now, and I've *never* felt that way either. It's as easy as breathing. If I could spend the rest of my life doing nothing but loving you, it would be the simplest thing I've ever done." I shake my head, the admission bringing a fresh wave of heat to my skin.

"But you can't," she says, shaking her head. "Isn't that what you came all the way here to say?"

"I don't know," I answer honestly.

She drops my hand and takes off in an impossibly fast walk. I have to jog just to catch back up. When I finally do, I reach for her hand again. She shoves it in her pocket instead and somehow walks even faster.

"Morgan. Morgan! Stop."

"It's freezing out," she calls back to me, like that matters.

"I don't care! I'd rather freeze than have you run away from me."

Morgan turns toward me, her eyes flashing. "Well, I do care! I just had someone try to make out with me in the middle of the library. Please don't make me follow that up with being dumped in the middle of the square," she says, her breath hitching. "I've been enough of a public spectacle today. I can't do this right now. Not out here. *Please.*"

Please. The word sounds so broken coming from her lips. I stand there stunned, rooted to the spot by the devastation wrapped around those six little letters. She nods once and then turns back to walk.

"Morgan," I shout, chasing after her again. "I'm not trying to break up with you!"

For someone who doesn't want a public spectacle, she's not exactly making it easy to avoid one.

Morgan must realize the same thing because she *finally* stops, giving me a full chance to catch up.

"I'm not—"

She presses her fingers to my mouth. If that didn't shut me up, the fresh tears streaming down her cheeks certainly would.

"Can we just get to my room first?" she asks. "I want to take a shower or at least wash my face, and then we'll talk, okay? I promise. Are you able to stay that long?"

Shit. I should've realized. I'm making this all about me, and she's the one who just had someone— Double shit, I haven't answered her yet.

"I'll be here as long as you want me to be," I say, and she lets out a sad, small laugh that almost sounds like a whimper.

I raise my eyebrows at her reaction, and a clearly forced smile crosses her lips. "Then I guess you live here now."

I wrap my arm around her and pull her close while we walk. "C'mon, let's get you home."

"You're my home." Morgan sniffles.

I kiss her temple, squeezing her even tighter, pretending that we're solid, that we're strong—that she doesn't feel like water slipping through my fingers with every step.

18

MORGAN

I turn the shower up as hot as I can stand it, wishing it could wash away the mess I've made of things.

I know that Ruby is waiting in my room for me, and while I should probably be as quick as I can be getting back to her, I almost want to drag this out. It feels safe between the locked doors of my bathroom, the scent of my lavender Epsom salt body wash steaming up all around me.

I reach for the face wash, scrubbing at my skin like it will help me forget the feel of Mac kissing me. I can't help the bitter snarl of guilt inside of me, the one that whispers, *You were flirting, you were, and you liked it.*

God, everything is so twisted up right now, and I hate it.

I shut my eyes and stand under the stream. I would slip down the drain if I could. It would probably be a nicer end to my night than whatever had Ruby driving here out of the blue, putting so many miles on her beloved car. I can't hide from it forever, though, and even if I could, it would be wrong to.

Still, I very slowly and methodically go through the steps of the rest of my routine—shaving, hair treatments, anything to drag it out. When even that's finished, I stand still under the spray and let the heat sink into my skin.

Coward.

A knock on the door startles me a short time later, and I switch the water off. I can't tell if it came from my neighbor's room—someone wanting a turn in our shared bathroom—or if it's Ruby getting impatient. I'm honestly not sure which I should hope for.

"Morgan, you good in there?" Ruby asks, sealing my fate with a second knock.

I grab my towel off the hook and wrap it around myself as I step out of the shower. The ice-cold floor tiles send a shock from my feet to my brain, smacking me in the face with the fact that the little warm cocoon I just created for myself is long gone.

Time to face the music.

"I'm okay," I call out, much more cheerfully than I feel, as I grab my pink caddy from the shelf. It holds my lotions and hairbrushes, my makeup and hair ties and deodorant and everything in between. I grab my wet brush and am dragging it through my hair when I hear it—a subtle rustling against the door.

Is Ruby still standing there? Wait, is she worried?

I lean over quickly and flick the lock, pulling the door

open a little so she can see I'm fine. Ruby jerks back to prevent herself from falling in; she must have been leaning against it while she waited. The relief that washes over her face pushes my guilt up yet another notch.

I turn back to the mirror and go back to brushing my hair, still overwhelmed by the night's events.

Ruby comes up behind me, her hands hesitating instead of wrapping around me. "Can I touch you?" she asks.

I tip my head to the side. "You can always touch me, Ruby. You don't have to ask."

"That's not true at all," she says, stepping forward and slotting herself against my back. She hooks her chin over my shoulder and meets my eyes in the mirror. "Just because you let me before doesn't mean you have to *now*. I've been in situations like the library before, and I didn't . . . I wouldn't have been comfortable being touched after, even if it was someone that I loved. It's good to check in sometimes."

I spin around in her arms so that we're face-to-face. "Thank you for checking," I say, soaking in the sight of her. I tilt my head toward her, so close we're trading breaths now.

My heartbeat picks up into a steady thrum of her name, a happy sigh instead of the scream of before, and Ruby pulls her eyebrows together almost like she can hear it too. The hurt and worry in her eyes give way to desire as she licks her lips once and then twice—a nervous habit she only does when she wants a kiss but isn't sure if she should ask for it.

I smile at the familiar sight, sliding my hands into her hair with a little nod to urge her on. She closes the distance, our kiss steady and deep and full of so much love I can barely stand it. The kiss lingers for far too long and not long enough. My hair is damp against her skin as she trails fresh kisses along my jaw and her fingers dig into my hips—holding me like she's afraid to lose me—and, god, I almost hope it leaves a mark. I roll my head back and then tip it forward to catch her lips again with my own. Our kisses a heady mix of honoring and atoning . . .

"Morgan," she whispers as I slide my hand under the back of her shirt higher and higher.

Her movements become more frantic, more insistent, and then . . . and then they stop. She reaches behind her, covering my hands with her own, and slides her shirt back into place.

I lean back to look at her, utterly confused. She looks absolutely gone for me right now—her skin flushed, her pupils swallowing up her irises . . .

Why did she stop?

Ruby lets out a shaky breath and leans against the door. I stay pressed against the bathroom counter, watching her.

"Why are you all the way over there now?" I ask, the desperation evident in my voice even though I tried to shove it down. Ruby doesn't meet my eyes.

"I don't want to do that."

"Do what? Touch me? Or kiss me? Or both?" I ask, terrified of the answer because Ruby's never the one who hits pause. She doesn't say anything, and I search her face, my stomach twisting up inside me.

This is going to hurt.

She looks like she's torturing herself. Like she's one second away from completely falling apart. Any thoughts I had of making out with her slide down the drain as I push off the sink. I offer a hug, letting her choose if she wants even that—Ruby steps forward, dropping her head to my forehead as her arms hold me like a lifeline. I wait for her to speak, but she doesn't. Her tears soak into my skin, telling me more than words ever could.

Oh, Ruby.

I squeeze her tight until she collects herself, and then we head back into my room. She wipes her eyes as she drops onto my bed, clearly embarrassed. "Sorry," she mumbles.

Her hand tightens around mine when I try to step away.

I press a gentle kiss on her head, giving her a little smile when she looks up at me. "I left my pj's in the bathroom," I say. "I'm just going to throw them on quick, and then I'll be right back."

Ruby nods and reluctantly lets go, running her hand over her hair and letting it settle on the side of her neck—like she can't stand for it to be empty. I make quick work of throwing on my clothes and piling my wet hair into one of her oversized scrunchies. I flick the lock to the other room open in case they get home, and then shut and lock the door from my side so we won't get interrupted.

Ruby's hugging my pillow when I get back, looking as pitiful as I feel. I lie down beside her, tugging her over to rest her head on my chest. She's always loved listening to me breathe, always told me how it calmed her down. *I think we both could use a little calm right now.* She drags my hand up from the duvet to the top of her head, and I let out an amused little sigh and start running my fingers through her hair, scratching just how she likes. We're silent for a while, our bodies intertwined, her thumb tracing the sliver of exposed skin between my ratty sleep shirt and the bottoms from the puppy pajama set she gave me for Christmas this year.

"I hated seeing you like that," Ruby says, slicing through the charged silence of the room.

"I'm sorry," I say. "I wouldn't have liked to see that either. I would probably be pretty pissed."

"No, not the kiss—well, the kiss too—but I mean the other stuff. When you said no, and she didn't respect it. I was mad, but not at you. I don't care if you have an almost crush. I don't care if she's a better fit for you or if you were flirting or whatever she was talking about. I just . . . when she tried to kiss you . . . I just wanted you to be safe. I was so scared and so mad and—"

"She's not a better fit for me, Ruby," I say, smoothing out some of her hair. "I love *you*."

"Two things can be true. They don't have to cancel each other out."

"This time they do," I insist, and she squeezes her eyes shut like she doesn't believe me. "Why did you come here tonight? Really, why?"

"Because I'm going to apply for the show, and you *need* to apply for the internship."

"No," I say, shaking my head. "We decided we're not doing that. We need time with each other. We need—"

"Not to hold each other back."

"We're not."

"We are. Right now, we are."

I huff out a breath, feeling like I got punched in the throat. "You really *are* breaking up with me," I struggle to say. "I don't want to do that! I love you."

"I love you too, but what if that's not enough anymore?"

I gently shift her off me. I need to be sitting up for this. I need to not have her holding me like I'm precious as she throws me to the curb. "I'm not enough for you?"

"You're perfect," she says, reaching out to pull me back down beside her, but I don't go. "Morgan . . ."

"Where is this coming from? Why are you doing this to me? To us? This is what you want? This is really what you want?!" I'm shouting now, and I feel so out of control. First Mac, now this, and I . . .

"This is the last thing I want!" she says, pushing up to her elbow.

"Then stop!"

"Do you promise not to hold it against me if I get the show and skip DC?"

"We won't see each other!" I say, and here come the tears again. *God, I'm so sick of myself today.* "If we both get our things, we won't see each other for break *or* summer. We're already glorified pen pals now; I don't know what we'd be by then. I don't want this. I can't do this. Ruby, I love you. I fucking love you."

I'm breaking. I can't do this. I—

Ruby surges forward, wrapping me in a tight hug. "Okay," she says. "Okay, we'll figure something out. I love you too. I don't want to hurt you, Morgan. I don't. We'll figure it out. We will. Please, baby, just don't look so sad. You're killing me."

"But . . ."

"We'll figure it out," she says, over and over, like she's convincing both of us now.

I let her words lull me into a sense of calm, even though I know they probably aren't true. I'm too overwhelmed by the thought of losing her to even process everything else she's saying. She crawls under the covers and holds them open for me, until I settle against her, pretending it doesn't hurt that my track meet wasn't worth a drive, but dumping me is.

I'm being horrible—I know I am—but I'm so mad I can't stand it. I'm mad at the timing of everything. I'm mad at the universe. I'm mad that people don't think we'll make it, and now we're proving them right. I'm mad that her breath goes slow and deep as her eyes close, when I know I'm going to be up all night thinking about what happens next.

But mostly, I'm mad at myself, because as the hours tick by, I realize that she's *not* wrong. Telling her not to do the show was wrong. Offering to give up my internship sucked, but it wasn't the same. Not really. There are other internships; there's only one *Mastermind Mechanics.* This is a once-in-a-lifetime chance for her . . . and I tried to make her give it up.

How could I do that?

I roll back onto my pillow to watch her sleep. I love her so much it hurts, and if this is the last night we'll ever spend together, I'm not missing a second of it.

19

RUBY

I roll over and nuzzle back into Morgan's blankets at the quiet click of her door opening and her soft footsteps on the floor.

I take long, slow breaths, doing my best imitation of sleep, peeking out from between my lashes to watch her move around the room, and hoping she doesn't notice. I've been up since I heard her getting dressed for practice two hours ago, but I wanted to give her some space. I know Morgan didn't sleep much last night, if at all—her tossing and turning woke me up more than once. I figured the least I could do was let her have some time to herself this morning.

It's not like I was in a rush to deal with everything that we talked about last night anyway.

We agreed to figure something out—to find a solution that doesn't ruin us both or make us break up. And I'm fully aware that's going to mean a lot of emotionally draining talk today until we do. For now, though, I just want to soak up her presence.

Last night was so heavy.

I follow her around with my eyes—she's sweaty, her cheeks flushed, panting like she ran all the way back here. Maybe she did. I'm not sure if I should get up now or keep going. I've committed to the bit, but at what cost?

Morgan glances over at me, pausing before she narrows her eyes. *Ah, yes, I'm never as good of a faker as I think I am.* I slam my eyes shut, fighting off the smirk that's desperate to come out once I hear her drop her shoes on the floor.

She crawls up the comforter until she's lying right in front of me. I expect her to call me out on being awake, but she doesn't. Instead, Morgan stays perfectly still beside me.

What is she doing?

I wait until I can't bear it anymore—which is only about thirty seconds—and then crack one eye, just to see what she's up to.

"Ha!" she says, staring at my face. "I knew you were awake."

"Not true," I say, wrapping my arms around her. I swiftly roll onto my back, dragging her on top of me.

"I'm all sweaty right now," she says, like that doesn't make her a thousand times hotter.

"That's okay." I grin.

"I'm all gross from practice." She pouts.

"Now, that's definitely not true," I say, leaning in for a

quick kiss as she presses herself up onto her arms. "You're perfect."

"Unfortunately, we've already established you are a liar with the whole fake-sleeping thing," Morgan answers. "Which means anything you say is suspect."

"Not when it comes to you," I say.

She almost lets herself smile. *Almost.* But any levity we had between us disappears when she pushes herself back onto her knees and looks down at me, her eyes heavy, as if she's got the weight of the world locked inside of them.

Morgan swallows hard and starts to climb off, but I clamp a hand on her thigh, a silent plea for her to stay. Her skin is ice cold—her running shorts did nothing to keep her warm on the way from the gym to her dorm. Morgan's eyes flick down to my hand and then back to me, but she remains stubbornly silent.

I'm not the only one stalling this morning.

"What's happening in that head of yours?" I ask, when the silence starts to get to me.

"I don't know."

I push up to sitting, never breaking contact between us. "We could talk through it? You said we need good communication, yeah? It's the only way we're going to figure this out."

"With what time? I have to shower, and you have to go, right? Don't you have class today?"

We both know that her questions are just excuses in disguise. I wouldn't have made it to class even if I'd left when she got up for practice, given the distance. I made the conscious decision to skip when I didn't set an alarm last night. Maybe it wasn't a responsible choice or whatever, but some things are worth skipping for . . . *Morgan* is worth skipping for.

"I don't have to leave for a few more hours," I hedge.

"You shouldn't miss class because of me," she snaps. "We can't keep holding each other back, right?"

And oh. Oh. She's *mad*?

I filter through my memories of last night, trying to figure out how I could have pissed her off so bad in the five minutes since I've stopped pretending to sleep. We were going to figure it out; that's what we decided last night. Today was going to be hard, yeah—it always is when there's no clear answer—*but it wasn't meant to be a fight.*

Morgan sniffles, and my eyes snap back to her face. She's not even bothering to wipe her tears away, just letting them run down her cheeks in pathetic rivulets, and then I get it.

Not mad. Upset.

A crucial difference. And a huge one.

I slide forward and wrap my legs around her. I do my best to wipe her tears, but that just seems to make them come faster.

"Hey," I say, running my hands along the sides of her face. "Hey, talk to me. Please?"

Morgan shakes her head, and I kiss her temple, and she pitches forward and buries her face in my shoulder. I bring my hand up to her chin, gently coaxing her to look at me—she resists at first but finally sits back with a heavy sigh.

The sight of her face—her resigned look—knocks the wind out of my lungs. Her tear-drenched face is both devastatingly beautiful and beautifully devastated. I can see it in the tension of her body, the way her eyes slide to the wall instead of meeting mine.

Morgan slept on it . . . and she gave up hope.

"No, there's gotta be a way," I whisper.

"I can't think of one." Morgan gives a slow, sad, one-shoulder shrug before squeezing her eyes shut in frustration. I lean forward, pressing my lips to her eyelids, and then her cheeks. A sob rips its way out of her chest, and then she's there, surging forward, kissing me back.

Our hands scramble for purchase, clinging to each other like we're desperate, *and we are, aren't we?* Because if letting go now means letting go forever, then I never fucking will. I'll kiss her on this shitty extra-long twin bed until we both crumble into dust.

Fuck the car show and the internship and everyone who ever had an opinion about us. Fuck everyone who ever said it would be fine if we didn't work out. Fuck them all, because this is what matters.

This. Now. Her. Me. Us.

Morgan presses me back down on the bed, her body never leaving mine. I chase the salty taste of tears that won't stop falling—hers and mine, because I know that everything that matters is between my arms right now.

I roll her over, lacing our fingers and pressing them up as I kiss down her collarbone, reveling in the taste of her skin.

How could she think this wasn't beautiful?

My hand rucks up her shirt, tracing over her belly and sliding up to the edge of her sports bra. *If we just keep going, if we just don't stop, we don't have to think or talk. We can just be. Just be. As long as we . . .*

I pull my hand back like I've been burned, and her eyes shoot open, shock and confusion written all over them. I'm pulling back *again,* like I did last night. I'm making it worse, *again.* But I'm the worst either way, and I won't throw a year's growth out the window. I won't recycle the coping mechanism I threw away once Morgan showed me there was better.

"I don't want us to use each other to forget," I say. "I don't want to fuck as a stalling tactic. I don't want to use you as stress relief. I . . ."

She pulls me back down, and I let her—forever helpless against her. She scratches my head the way I like, keeping one leg hooked over mine, like she's afraid I'm going to run away even though I'm holding on to her just as tight.

"You're right. No, you're right," she says softly.

"I love you," I whisper.

"I love you too," she says, because she's too good to ever say *I know* like I sometimes do. She gets how much I need the words.

"But," she adds, "I think we should take a break."

My heart fractures into tiny shards. It's a critical hit to my most sensitive circuitry. I'm a Hemi V8 with no injectors, a Jeep Wrangler without 4 Low. I'm lost, flailing in my head, because why is there always a "but" when it comes to people loving me—an asterisk, an addendum, an added escape clause at the end of every single *I love you.*

Never with Morgan, though. Never.

Until today.

I roll off her, slamming my back against her mattress. To her credit, she doesn't try to stop me. We stare at the ceiling side by side, and I wonder if she's struggling just as hard as I am to figure out how to speak, how to live in the aftermath of our breakup.

"Yeah," I say eventually, sparing her the torment. "We should. I get it."

"Do you really?" she asks quietly. "Do you understand?"

I flick my eyes toward her at the sincerity in her voice. I take a deep breath instead of answering, because what am I supposed to say? *Yes, of course. Everyone always bails on me at the slightest inconvenience, or I bail on them. It's how life works. Right? For people like me?*

I'm already reinforcing my skull with steel and covering what's left of my heart, brick by brick. All of it stamped with tiny scribbles reminding me that nobody stays. That the only person you can count on is yourself. That I did this to myself for daring to believe any different.

"Mm-hmm," I say, letting myself go numb. "It's fine. It was kind of what I expected when I came here, right?"

Morgan's breath hitches. She's crying again, or still, I guess, but I'm done with all that. If we're going to follow through with this, if *I'm* going to follow through with this, then I need to keep a white-knuckle grip on my emotions, tight as I did on that girl's hoodie last night. Nothing good comes from letting go.

Nothing.

I school my features into something neutral as I push

myself up off the bed. "It's not like we'll see each other for months anyway. What's even the point?" I shrug, like saying that doesn't gut me.

Morgan reaches out for me, but I take a step back.

If she touches me, all bets are off. And they can't be. I need to get off this ride where she begs me and then I beg her and so on and so forth. You don't keep pressing the gas when your car's stuck in the mud.

Sometimes you have to go back a little to go forward.

Besides, acting like I'm not dying inside is probably the kindest thing I can do for her. Let her hate me—she'll get over me faster. It'll be easier on her.

I understand things like loss and grief in a way she doesn't yet. I've lived with it my whole life—it's a persistent thing, a ghost in the corner of your brain, a screw that never comes unstuck.

Morgan has her own history, trauma, and feelings, sure, but she doesn't get loss—not real loss. Not the kind that changes you forever.

I can carry that for her. I can set it right next to my feelings about my mother and the father I never knew. Right over the memory of Billy finally leaving my mom. I've got a whole filing system, and Morgan? She doesn't even have a folder.

Yeah, I'll carry this one. She's worth the weight.

"Could we . . ." Morgan starts. "Can we still be friends during all of this? I don't want to be like Allie and Lydia. I can't . . . I don't want to lose you."

Does she not realize I'm already lost? That I was lost the second I sat down in my car to come here?

I stare at the wall hard, trying to hold it all in, trying to be cool and aloof. "I don't know," I say finally. "Maybe they have the right idea."

"You don't mean that," Morgan says.

I can tell that I've twisted the knife by the anguish in her voice. I hate it, but I'm clumsy and new, and I've never had to dump anyone I've actually loved before. I think I'm allowed a little grace, a couple missteps here and there.

Morgan climbs over the bed to put herself right in my line of vision. I don't react, so she ups the ante. Her hand wraps around mine—the ultimate kill shot to send me toppling.

Mercy, I think, reminding me of wrestling with Everly as a little kid. She would always get the best of me, never letting me up until I said it. *Mercy, mercy, mercy. Morgan, please let me go.*

"You should hate me," I say pathetically, because I can't say the rest. "It'll be better."

"I could never," she says, squeezing me even tighter. "Ruby, I love you more than anyone, and I know you feel that way about me too. We're not taking a break because we don't love each other; we're taking a break because we *do*. It's not over—it doesn't have to be, not forever. It could just be for right now."

A record scratch replaces the alarms blaring in my head.

"Wait," I say, genuinely confused. "What the hell are you talking about? People are together or not. There's no such thing as breaks."

"Who says?" she asks, looking determined. "Breaks can definitely lead to breakups, but they don't have to. Not really."

What is she even saying?

"Then why are you crying so hard?"

"Oh, gee, I don't know, Ruby." She laughs bitterly. "Probably because it sucks to know that we can't figure this out? The idea of not talking to you every day kills me! You saying we're not friends kills me! This hurts, even knowing the door is still open for us when things calm down."

When things calm down? What the . . .

"I need you to tell me how you see 'breaks,' because I don't think we're working with the same definition here," I admit. "To me, it's just something you say to someone you don't want to be with but don't want to be a total asshole to. Like you say it and never talk to them again, and eventually they find someone else."

"Yikes," she says softly. "That's not how I meant it at all. To me, it means that we've mutually decided to hit pause for a minute. Like, we do our own thing and focus on ourselves, and then when things are a little different, we decide together if we're ready to . . . unpause."

"Are we kissing 'friends from school' during this *pause*, or—"

"I won't be," she says. "You have to decide that for yourself."

"So we're just, like, in limbo? Not together but not moving on? That sounds awful."

"I don't know, Ruby!" she cries. "I don't have all the answers! I just don't want to close the door on us forever. Do you? If you do, then—"

"No," I say, surprising myself. Limbo with a *maybe* sounds horrible, but forever with a *never* sounds worse.

"Okay," she says, nodding to herself. "Then it's settled."

"So we just, what? Go live our lives and . . ."

"We keep the door cracked a little. We'll have a chance to pursue things without guilt or worrying about each other and see how it feels. Maybe we find out we're okay apart—that we're different people after all. Or maybe we find out we don't want anyone else and end up back together in a few months when we have more time for each other. We're just catching our breath. That's all it has to be."

I nod, just glad that she's not crying anymore—and that I didn't even have to make her hate me. It feels like a win. A win *and* a loss—*the story of my life.*

"So can we be friends?" she asks hesitantly.

I look at her, not sure that I want to say yes but not willing to break her heart all over again by saying no.

"We can try," I settle on. "Yeah."

And the way her face breaks into a smile tells me I've definitely made the right choice.

Fuck, I love her.

20

MORGAN

Aaron and Danny shoot matching concerned looks my way through the MacBook screen, and I am once again regretting setting up this meeting as a Zoom instead of a phone call.

Technically, "Danny" is a fake name, which I suspected when he first started coming to the LGBTQ+ resource center a year ago. And even though he felt comfortable enough last summer to share with me and Aaron that his real name is Simon, he still prefers to be called Danny, since he's not fully out back home.

I do my best to ignore them, instead continuing through the meeting agenda that Danny, as secretary of the Rainbow Athlete Coalition, helpfully sent over. I've definitely been neglecting the nonprofit lately, and I want to fix that ASAP. Even though Danny agreed to be boots on the ground while I went away to school, it's still not right to leave so much on his shoulders.

Aaron doesn't even care about sports, but we desperately needed a treasurer, and he's, well, a great friend. Luckily, he also discovered, during the course of handing out flyers to teams at college this year, that while he definitely doesn't love sports, he *does* love athletic boys. I don't think he's in any rush to get off our board these days. Especially not after a guy on the club basketball team recently asked him out because of it.

Currently, we're discussing plans to provide rainbow tape to the local ice rinks back home. They both agreed to host Pride Night games, the way they do in the NHL, and donate a portion of the proceeds to our organization. I'm not totally sure that the boys are hearing anything I'm saying, though, as they're still staring at me like I'm a ticking time bomb about to explode.

I'm fine. I'm fine. *As long as I keep moving, that is.*

I clear my throat, hoping that snaps them out of it. "Do you have the numbers from our distributor to compare whether it's better to drop-ship the tape to the individual rinks or have it all sent to the center and then handed out that way? Izzy said this year's student mentors would be happy to help out with that," I say, pulling up the email that Izzy sent me—she's the director of the LGBTQ+ resource center in town where Aaron and I used to volunteer together.

Technically, our nonprofit isn't part of the center. We're our complete own thing, with an Employer Identification Number and a Certificate of Incorporation and everything. There's a lot of overlap in what we do, though, especially since Izzy inspired us to start it. She's basically our unofficial adviser, and we do a lot of fundraising for them as well. Izzy even hops on these board member calls whenever she can get free, so we get the benefit of her experience on top of our own.

"Uh, yeah," Aaron says, shuffling his papers around as if this wasn't the first thing on our list to discuss. "Hang on, I have it right here . . . if that's what you really want to talk about."

I hold up the agenda that I printed out at the library this afternoon. "You got a copy of this, right?" I ask, flicking my eyes to Danny. Danny is usually super on the ball, but I'm trying to give Aaron the benefit of the doubt that he's not just trying to derail our meeting with my personal problems.

"He definitely did," Danny says, looking slightly offended.

Aaron hesitates, and I can tell he wants to say something else.

"Whatever you want to say, Aaron, just say it." I sigh.

"Well, you haven't been replying to my texts about anything except board stuff, and . . . I'm worried. I've been talking to Ruby, and—"

"I don't really see how this is coalition business," I say, sitting a little straighter.

"I'm gonna just . . . I need to take my dog out?" Danny says, suddenly logging off.

Wait . . .

"Did you two plan this?" I ask, frustration welling up inside of me.

"No," Aaron says. "Good on Danny for reading the room, though. That kid's going places."

I know he's just trying to deflect my anger with humor, but I don't want to deal with it. At all. The whole point of me even setting up this meeting was to get my mind off things, actually!

"This is really unprofessional," I say, crossing my arms. I hope it looks mad, tough, even, and not like I'm trying to hold myself together, which is unfortunately closer to the truth.

"I agree," he says. "Or rather it was when Danny was still on the call. I'm sorry I made it awkward. I'll apologize to him later, but I'm not going to apologize for being worried about you and Ruby."

"What's going on with Ruby?" I ask, leaning closer to my screen. "Is she okay?"

"Ish," he says, waving his hand back and forth.

"What do you mean, 'ish'? What's wrong with her?" My heart whooshes in my ears. "Is she okay or not?"

The first week after Ruby left, *after we hit pause*, it was almost like nothing ever happened. We weren't FaceTiming or flirting, but we were still texting every day. It was a little awkward as we both kept bumping into new boundaries, but overall, it was nice.

This week, though, this week she's been slow to respond. *Really slow.* I finally asked her what was going on, and she said she might need a minute before we could pick back up as friends. I offered to text her less but said we didn't have to do full radio silence, and she agreed. *Ruby agreed.*

Except then she stopped responding entirely three days ago.

Three full days without talking.

It's the longest we've gone since we met. I've hated every

second, but I'm also trying not to push her. I still send one text each day—that same good-morning ritual I've done since we got together. I don't think that crosses any boundaries. I mean, *she agreed.*

Respecting boundaries might mean we don't text dozens of times a day anymore, but I don't think it means that I can't ask our mutual friend about her, casually and platonically, during our business meeting. Or rather, our former business meeting, since it doesn't look like Danny is ever coming back.

Aaron bites his lip and shrugs. "I don't know, man. Breakups are hard."

"We didn't break up," I say. "We're taking a break. There's a difference!"

"Is the difference that you guys make things as painful as possible? Because that's kind of how it looks from here."

"I'm sorry we don't hate each other like Allie and Lydia. We're mature about things."

"Allie and Lydia don't hate each other. They're just not pretending they can take a break and have nothing change."

"Ruby and I are friends! That is a *massive* change!"

"If you say so." He shrugs again.

"Why? What did she say? Does she not want to be friends? Is that why she hasn't replied in days?"

"I'm not betraying anyone's trust here," Aaron says. "I love both of you equally and would like to keep it that way. I'm not sharing anyone's business unless one of you specifically asks me to."

"Did she ask you to tell me anything?" I can't hide the hopeful lilt in my voice.

"No," he says, and I shove my tongue between my teeth, biting until it pinches so I have an excuse for the sting in my eyes. Whose eyes *don't* water when they bite their tongue? See, it's nature, not sadness.

"Okay, cool," I say, playing it off. "I was just checking."

He lets out a big sigh, and I know what that means. That's his "bad news" sigh. That's his "real talk" sigh. He only does it when he's about to eviscerate someone, usually me, with honesty. It's like he feels bad for whatever he's about to do, but knows he has to anyway, or something.

"Can I give you some advice, or should I mind my own business?"

"You should mind your own business," I say. "But I'm willing to concede that you do give the best advice, and since you've apparently been hearing both sides of this . . ."

"That's not really true," he says, putting his arms on his desk.

"Ruby's *not* talking to you?"

"No, *she* is, but you're not. Every time I ask how you are, you just say fine. Every time I try to talk to you about Ruby, you ignore my messages."

"Because I am fine!" I insist. "It was my idea to take a break! Remember?"

"Interesting. That's not exactly how she put it."

"She said it was hers? She might have brought some of it up first, but I was the one who—"

"Ruby said it was a mutual decision."

"Oh," I say, my rant effectively over. "I guess it was, technically. We decided to sleep on it, and then the next day we decided on the break idea. What else can we do? We wouldn't really see each other again until the end of July, at least. It just makes sense."

"This break is what you both want?"

"It's what we have to do. We never see each other, but somehow we keep getting in each other's way. I can't get held back, and neither can she!"

"Okay," he says, holding up his hands. "If that's true, then you're right; it's for the best you're not together. I'm just not totally convinced that keeping the door as wide open as you two have been is the best idea. It sounds more like torture to me."

"Did Ruby say that? And what do you mean, 'if that's true'? It's obviously true! I almost didn't apply for this internship! Ruby wasn't even going to try to get on *Mastermind Mechanics. Mastermind Mechanics*! Do you know what an epic mistake that would have been? It's her literal dream show."

"Yeah, I agree with you on that, but . . ."

"But what?"

"But it's clear you both still want to be together!" he says, raising his hands to really hammer the point home. I think he'd be shaking my shoulders if he could reach through the screen.

"She still wants to be with me?" I ask, and there my eyeballs go, getting wet all over again. "Did she tell you that? Oh, thank god! She hasn't replied to me in days. I didn't know what to think."

Aaron rubs his forehead. "What if I said yes?"

"Then I would call her and ask her why she's avoiding our chat."

"What if I said no?" he asks, tipping his head.

"Why would you ask that?" I force myself to choke out. "Did she say she *didn't* want to be with me?"

"I don't think she's aware there's currently even a question to answer, Morgan."

"There's always a question. Of course there's a question! That's the point of it being a break. It's a time-out! Anyone can end it if they want."

"A time-out from what?"

"From being together, from the *responsibility* of being together!"

"I'm sorry, I'm with Ruby, then. What's the difference between a breakup and a break?" he asks, apparently not realizing he's ignoring his rule about not giving anything away. "Other than the fact that you don't let each other move on?"

"Does she want to move on?" My voice sounds screechy in my ears. "Is it that guy from her class? It is, isn't it? Is this because Mac—"

"Are you talking about Shiloh? No, she's not moving on with him. Dude's like her brother."

"Then who?" I ask, anger and jealousy stoking the fire behind my rib cage.

Tell me, Aaron. Please, god, tell me.

"Nobody! I'm just pointing out how messy this is," he says, sounding frustrated. "But before you find out from her and get mad, I told her it was okay if she didn't want to respond to you for a little while."

"Why would you do that?!"

"Because somebody had to. I'm telling you the same thing.

It's like you both need permission to stop texting each other all the time."

"I don't want to stop texting her all the time!"

"Then why break up at all?" he asks. "That's my whole point!"

"Obviously, because we can't be together right now, but I don't want to lose her." I dig the heels of my hands into my eyes, because if the tears won't dry up on their own, then I'll shove them back in myself. "Does she really want to lose me? Did she say that?"

He sighs that awful sigh again. "If you two are hell-bent on not being together, then you seriously need to give each other space to figure out what that looks like. How are you going to do that if you're texting each other constantly and pining away?"

"I'm going to be pining away whether I text her or not," I say. "I'm supposed to just sit here and keep it to myself?"

"Yeah." Aaron frowns. "Yeah, that's kind of the deal, unfortunately."

"What about being friends, though? Lots of people break up and stay friends. That's all I was trying to do."

"People who are still horribly in love with each other can't usually jump right to being friends—not that I've seen, anyway."

I sigh. "I feel like you think we shouldn't have taken a break."

"I don't think you've taken one yet!" he practically shouts. "Maybe Ruby has if she's not responding anymore, but you haven't. I don't think you really want to either."

"We decided what to do together. Ruby even told you it was mutual too. I'm not going to burst back into her life and ask her to change her plans to accommodate me," I say. "I fully get that we're in a 'right person, wrong time' situation here. We're both just trying to survive it."

Aaron scrunches up his nose. "I always thought that was just something people said."

"Turns out it's not." I sigh. "So if you're sitting on any more sage advice, hand it over."

"I wish I was, honestly. For your sake and hers." He shrugs. "It just sucks, all around. It's not fair after everything you two went through just to be together . . ."

"I know," I say, wiping at my eyes. "We can't go on like we were. I get that! It just really freaking hurts!"

"Damn, I wish I could give you a hug."

"Me too, but I really can't have this conversation anymore," I say, grabbing a tissue. "I have another meet tomorrow, and . . ." I shake my head. "I'm fine. *I'm fine.* I have to be. Right? If we're taking a break, I need to give her a break. You're right."

"Morgan—"

"No, I can't keep staring at my phone, waiting for her to write back, knowing she doesn't want to. I need to give her space. I need to give myself space. I need to figure out what this all looks like without her. We owe ourselves that."

"Whatever happens, you don't have to go through it alone. You can talk to me whenever you need."

"Thank you," I say. "It really means a lot. I think right now I just need to be busy, though. Do you think we could ask

Danny to hop back on the call if he's still free?" I ask, taking a deep breath. "Or is that weird? I just need . . . I need to do something good to counteract how horrible this all feels."

"Okay," Aaron says, giving me a soft look. "Let me just text him and see."

I nod, taking a second to pull myself together, wishing Aaron really could give me that hug too.

Danny's face appears on my screen a minute or so later. He looks at me nervously and then pulls out his agenda.

"Where were we?" he asks.

"I was about to tell you two the numbers," Aaron says. "It looks like the drop-shipping cost would be around . . ."

Aaron fills us in on the projected expense, and I do my best to listen, lost in my thoughts no matter how much I fight it.

Ruby and I decided we need a break. *Together.* It's time I start respecting that. It's time I keep my word.

The next morning, for the first time since we got together, I don't text her good morning.

21

RUBY

Morgan didn't text today.

I knew it would happen eventually, but I didn't expect it to hurt this bad. I guess that's on me. Maybe I should have. What did I think would happen when I stopped replying, that she would go on forever? That I suddenly wouldn't care when she came to the same conclusion?

She gave up faster than I thought.

No, that's not fair; I know it's not. I'm the one who stopped replying first, and I'm the one who drove hours knowing it was likely things would end. I can't help but think I should have thought this through more before I left. I wish I could take it all back sometimes.

I fight the urge to send her a text asking where the hell my morning text is, even though I spent an hour talking to Aaron the other day about how talking to her so much was killing me. *Just another constant reminder of what I don't have anymore.*

My phone is a veritable land mine at this point, between my mother and Morgan.

Or, well, I guess not Morgan. Not anymore.

I pull the blanket over my head and roll over. Maybe I can just go back to sleep. Maybe I can stay unconscious until I hear back from Ben about the show—even though he said it would probably be a few weeks. He was over the moon when I went to talk to him about my chances of actually making it on the show. He implied I was almost definitely going to get it. *Almost.*

Wouldn't it be some kind of cosmic joke if Morgan and I broke up and I didn't even get on the show?

I groan and pull a pillow over my head.

No more thinking. Back to sleep.

Maybe tomorrow will be better.

It's about a week later that she posts it.

And by *she,* I mean Morgan, and by *it,* I mean a picture on her private Instagram. She has one she shares with Aaron and Danny about their fundraising and charity work, and a public one about her track career . . . but the private one is for friends and family only. The stuff she posts there is real—it matters—and it's strictly inner circle.

Morgan doesn't even have her own photo as the profile picture. Just a photo of her old dog, which could literally be any ancient golden retriever ever. Her username is even some fake name her brother used to order food from snack bars when they were little: Morgan Butole.

She died laughing when she explained that once, when Dylan was fourteen and they were on vacation at the beach, he gave that to a snack bar employee as the name for his order. He hoped and prayed that the people behind the counter would yell out *Mr. Butthole*, but they did not. Apparently, he's done it dozens of times since then, to no avail.

I called her Ms. Butthole for a solid week after she told me that story.

I've been forcing myself not to check Insta for days . . . but I guess that doesn't matter anymore. Not now that I'm staring at her post—a group photo of her and a bunch of other kids from her school.

I didn't even register the name on the post at first; I was just scrolling. I was scanning the pic, instinctively looking for my friends, figuring it belonged to someone safe like Everly or Aaron. But there she was instead, in the middle of the group, arms around the people on either side of her.

The little dots beneath the photo tell me there's more waiting for me. I swipe through a few more group shots and then see a selfie she took with a girl I don't know. I tap it hard, but there's no tag.

I flick my eyes down to the caption for a hint and am met with only a sneaker emoji. The relief that courses through me, realizing this is probably just her track team and not, like, a group date or something, is almost embarrassing.

Not that I think Morgan is going to stay single forever, but I don't know. We talked about it a tiny bit when we agreed to the break—she said she wasn't going to see anyone else, but does it still stand? Is it even still a break? Do we announce officially when it becomes a little more permanent, or will we just sort of fade from each other's lives like I originally thought?

Is that what I'm doing right now? Fading out of her life?

I click off the app, trying not to let it sting too bad that Morgan is out there with the track team making memories—or, no, I want her out there making memories. It's just that she's not going to tell me about it tonight when we FaceTime . . . because we're *not going to FaceTime.* We stopped doing that even before we stopped texting.

I miss it so damn much.

A sharp pang of regret shoots through me at the idea of never seeing her in that ridiculous scrunchie again, but I shake it off and get back to work, regretting picking up my phone on my lunch break at all.

I need to stick to what I know: grease and tools and the way cars fit together like glorified puzzle pieces. Sometimes I wish that my veins were full of fuel instead of blood, that I had strong metal instead of flesh for a heart.

After all, a broken-down car is an easy fix. A broken heart? Well . . .

Another week passes.

And we still don't talk.

I guess not talking is what we do now.

That's fine. I haven't been stalking her Instagram or anything. Or, I have, but only sometimes. I can't help microdosing my ex—and she really feels like an ex now, with nearly a month of not talking. But I'm doing . . . decent otherwise.

It's my birthday today. It's my birthday, and Billy bought a cake, and Shiloh is here with Stella Jane, who is basically the shop mascot now. Billy lets her come every single day so Shiloh doesn't have to pay for a babysitter or leave her someplace sketch. The toddler's growing on me, kind of. As much as a sticky little thing that always seems to have a cold can grow on you.

Before I catch myself, I start listing off in my head all the new pageant courses that she'll be eligible for once she turns three. My stomach flips at the thought of her up on the stage, even if she is the cutest kid I've ever met. I wouldn't do that to her. I wouldn't do that to anyone.

She'd win, though, I think, looking down at her sweet, crumb-filled face. Billy snuck her a cookie that Shiloh is definitely going to freak out about when he comes out of the bathroom—especially since we're having cake soon. Yeah, Billy is loving this new fun-grandpa role. He's kind of nailing it, honestly.

I asked him during our last family night, which Shiloh and Stella Jane have weaseled their way into now, why he didn't have any kids of his own, since he was definitely made for it.

He scrunched up his eyebrows, like I had just said the most ridiculous thing he ever heard, and said, "I did. *You.*"

I think he wanted to go in for a hug right then, but I think he also recognized that if he did that, I would fully fall apart.

And Stella Jane was on the couch watching *Bluey* with Shiloh while Billy and I were sorting takeout. So, no.

I still had to excuse myself to the bathroom to pull it together—not because I didn't believe him or had to convince myself, but because I knew he believed that, and I wasn't going to let myself question it ever again.

I realized that I wasn't about to fall apart because I'm an emotionally constipated mess . . . but because I'm not anymore. Because I can let him love me *and I can trust it.* I can reciprocate it, even.

I can't take all the credit.

Billy sort of insisted that I talk to somebody when I refused to get out of bed after Morgan and I broke up. We've only had a few weekly sessions, but it's . . . nice . . . to not have to figure it all out myself.

It definitely cut my bathroom breakdown in half that night.

I drop onto the living room couch next to Shiloh, who's looking like maybe he's having his own mini breakdown. Stella Jane has run off into the kitchen with Billy, which is probably for the best. I know Shiloh got in a fight with his ex's mom this afternoon, because he doesn't think her house is safe for visitation and she threatened to take him to court—which I didn't know was even a thing. And I know he needs to talk about it, but won't, not in front of Stella Jane.

Being a young parent seems *really* hard.

Shiloh watches Billy helping Stella Jane blow her nose in the other room. He smiles—Billy must have gotten all the crumbs off her face already.

“You’re lucky you have that guy,” he says, in the same wistful way I use to talk about Everly’s parents.

I guess Shiloh is as slow to figure things out as I was, when it comes to the grumpy mechanic in the other room.

“You have Billy now too,” I say. He looks at me, and I can tell he doesn’t believe me.

“Nah, this kinda stuff never lasts for people like me,” he says.

“I *also* used to think that.”

“That’s different.”

I’m about to point out that it’s really not, and/or stuff my therapist’s number into his hand, when Billy and Stella Jane start singing “Happy Birthday” in the other room. I didn’t know there were candles, but there are. Billy carries out a perfect little round birthday cake with a whole pile of candles on top making it glow. Stella Jane trots beside him, her little hand up in the air like she’s carrying it too, despite the fact that she’s about two feet too short.

Shiloh joins in the singing, dramatically belting out the words like some kind of opera singer, and I can’t help but laugh. Because yeah, they’re weird, and none of them are technically related to me, but I don’t have a single doubt anymore—I’m home.

This is my *family*.

Later, at exactly 11:59 p.m., just as my eyes start to drift closed, Morgan texts me: **Happy Birthday.** I wonder if she struggled with it all day. If she wishes we could FaceTime too—but I only let those thoughts play through my head for a second, one little microdose of longing, before I move on.

I type out **Thank you!** and add a smiley-face emoji before hitting send.

I never use emojis and rush to unsend . . . but it switches to read before I can.

Oh well.

I hope she likes it.

My mother texts me the next day. A simple **HBD**. She doesn't even bother to add *belated* or spell out the words.

I'm working side by side in the shop with Billy, and of course he notices the change in my demeanor. I look at him and shake my head, but he's still keeping an eye on me, even as I get back to work.

"Mom texted," I say before he can ask.

He waits for me to say more. He knows I've been tackling that in therapy. The other day, I spilled my guts to him when my therapist suggested writing my mom a letter. He sat by me at the kitchen table, not even trying to read it, just being there in case I needed him.

So yeah, he knows about how I miss her and hate her, about the Morgan stuff, and how secretly I'm worried that I used her to hide or as an escape from my life—the way Mom uses guys. He doesn't think that's true, but I pointed out that I've done more healing in the last month than I probably did in the last year.

Billy said the last year set the stage for all that healing I'm doing now, not that I was hiding from it. That I needed a little stability, a little love, before I could tackle all the hard shit. Maybe he's right—it was too fresh before. Too painful to unpack my mother when I didn't know where I stood—when I was sleeping in Billy's back room on a mattress Morgan's parents had donated. It's easier now that it feels like *my* room and *my* mattress and more importantly *my home*.

"I might go see her," I say, realizing only as I say it that it's true.

I know there's no real rush, but I don't know. I don't want it hanging over me. I'm not holding my breath that anything gets resolved, and I'm *definitely* not looking to move back in with her or anything . . . but maybe I could get some closure. Who knows, maybe we could work out some kind of fragile truce. A superficial kind of thing where I can call her and make sure she has gas money and not feel like shit when she texts me three letters a full day late.

"I could go with you, if you want," Billy offers.

"No, it's kinda something I want to do on my own, but thank you," I say as my phone buzzes again.

I expect the text to be from my mom, but it's not. It's Ben. *Oh shit.* In class today, he said he'd be reaching out with the show's decision.

"This is Ben. It's gotta be about the show," I say, and Billy smiles confidently, like he's sure I got it.

I read quickly, almost dropping my phone at the sight of his congratulations and his questions about when the scout can come to see if Billy's shop is suitable or if we need to film at the school.

Billy whoops and cheers as he reads over my shoulder, and we both jump up and down and make asses of ourselves in front of Shiloh, who catches on quick to what's going on and joins in the fun.

Later, after the scout logistics are all worked out and Billy has taken me and Shiloh and Stella Jane out to Mike's Hot Dogs for a celebratory dinner with Shelby, who's working till nine, I think about texting Morgan and letting her know.

I even open up my phone before I change my mind.

There's something I gotta do first. Someone I need to talk to.

Me:
Hey, Mom. I'd like to talk, if you're okay with me stopping by.

Mom:
...

22

MORGAN

Track meets are long.

The track at this school is nice. Nicer than the one at mine, it's a red velvety, rubbery material that's just springy enough, and banks just enough, to ensure that everyone running on it gets a PR. It's a pleasure to run on. Truly.

The problem is that I only get to run on it for about two minutes. Yep, literally—and it's a three- or sometimes four-hour event.

If I'm on the track for more than 2:05 or so, then things have *really* gone off the rails.

When it's not our turn to run, we all sit on the sidelines, scoping out our competition, chatting with our fellow teammates in the bleachers—something that's *way* more fun now that I've been hanging out with everybody more—plus stretching and then stretching some more, or doing quick little jogs around the building to stay at least somewhat warmed up. Some of us (okay, me) also spend a lot of time daydreaming about making one of the relay teams.

We distance runners have relays for a bunch of stuff: 1500, 800, and then hodgepodge ones that I swear somebody just randomly made up, like the distance medley relay, or DMR as we call it, where every person runs a different length. I was kind of hoping that I would make the 4x8, which is what everybody calls the four-person relay, where each person runs eight hundred meters . . . but I'm stubbornly still one second behind the junior in the last spot.

That's unfortunately a lot.

It's rare for a freshman to get on it anyway, *but still, a girl can dream.*

Currently, our 4x8 is composed of two seniors and two juniors, including our captain, Mika, who has been keeping an extra-close eye on me the last few weeks. I felt a little smothered at first, but I can't really blame her.

After Ruby left, I spent the next couple weeks trying to act like everything was fine. But that all fell apart after my call with Aaron. Ruby's lack of texting me back was bad enough, but once I stopped even trying to text her too? I . . . kind of started losing it a little, once even in the middle of practice.

We were on a long, cold run outside. One of my teammates had innocently asked me how Ruby was doing, and if she was going to come to our next meet, *this very meet,* actually. I instantly burst into tears. It was mortifying, truly.

I don't blame Mika for swooping in and watching me like a

hawk ever since. Her little freshie, supposed future face of the team, melting down in the middle of a jog across campus was bound to raise eyebrows.

I don't know who looked more weirded out when we got back, Mika or Coach. She excused me immediately and "voluntold" Mika to take me back to my dorm and make sure I got settled in—which I'm pretty sure was code for *find out what's wrong and fix it.*

It was awkward to tell her everything, but it felt good too, to finally open up to someone *here,* someone who only knew *me* and wasn't trying to take both sides. Mika is a good listener and didn't even act annoyed. She's probably the best captain I could wish for.

Which is why I'm not surprised at all when she catches me staring at the empty seat next to my brother—the one Ruby would be in if things were different—and immediately jogs over and invites me to run around the block with her. I check my watch; it's about time to start warming up before my race anyway.

"Lead the way," I say as I finish tying my sneakers. I wave at my brother, trying to play it off like I'm not missing Ruby right now, but I'm probably not fooling anybody.

The arena is pretty packed, so we take advantage of the athlete entrance—a long tunnel on the other side of the track that only students can use. It's the fastest way to leave, and it's currently filled with runners coming to and from the sidewalk outside at a decent clip. We pick up the pace to match the flow of runners, and I say a little thank-you to the universe for inventing automatic doors and inspiring whoever made this building to install them. There is nothing more awkward than having to jog in place while holding a door open for someone.

It's freezing cold outside, but nothing I'm not used to, since Coach decided to "toughen us up" with outdoor runs now that the temp is warm enough that she legally can. (Although how anyone decided it was safe for us to run outside as long as it's over twenty degrees is beyond me.)

The slushy remnants of last night's snowstorm make my shoes almost instantly damp, but it doesn't matter. I'll change into my track spikes when we get back inside. This time of year, I never travel with fewer than three pairs of shoes—outside sneakers, track spikes, plus comfy shoes for wandering around the arena before and after racing. There's really no other way to do it around here.

Mika makes it barely half a block before her heavy sigh sends a plume of fog shooting out into the air around us. I glance at her quickly, and then fix my eyes on the horizon, mentally preparing for her to give me some pep talk about how I'm thriving these days and shouldn't keep staring at the empty seat.

She's not totally wrong. It's funny how much better life gets when you *actually get out of bed.*

"I might need you in the four by eight," she says instead, and I nearly trip over my feet in surprise.

"Really?" I ask, and it's impossible to hide the excitement in my voice.

"Really," Mika says, looking slightly more stoic than I would prefer. "Karly's bad ankle is acting up. You think you can handle it? We *need* the points in this one. I'd rather run the whole thing myself than let the Moose win."

The Fighting Moose. Our biggest rivals. We've taken turns winning meets all semester, and typically it comes down to the last few races to declare a winner. Our 4x8 usually beats them easily, which is important, because our DMR team never, ever does.

"I can handle it," I say. "I'm just over one second behind Claribel. On this track, I can definitely make that up."

"Yeah, but so will everybody else. Besides, Claribel is four seconds behind Karly and maxed out on her speed. She trained all last year to shave that second off to make the relay team over you after Coach told us you committed. You're the variable. We need you to be Karly today, not Clari. Think you can kick it up another gear?"

"Five seconds?" I gulp. "You want me to shave five seconds off my eight hundred *today*?"

Five seconds is a lot. Like, *a lot* a lot, and we both know it.

"I want you to try," Mika says. "You have the solo eight hundred coming up. See what you can do without fully blowing out. If your time is way off, we praise god for pain meds and tape Karly all to hell."

"I'm definitely faster than an injured Karly," I scoff.

"That's what we're hoping," Mika says, abruptly turning around to jog back the way we came.

This is good.

This gives me something else to worry about, instead of the fact that—despite knowing better—I still held out a tiny bit of hope that Ruby might show anyway, the way she did last year at states. Seeing Dylan sitting alone earlier was like a gut punch, but now, knowing I have a shot at a huge race—the *only* freshman in the race, even—I'm glowing.

This is important. This is the kind of thing you can build a great day around.

I smile all the way back to the sidelines, where I trade my wet sneakers for dry spikes. I'm going to be lining up for my heat soon; Mika couldn't have timed it better if she tried. *Wait,* I think, realizing that she probably did.

I wouldn't put it past her to wait to tell me about Karly's ankle for maximum benefit—like right before an important race, to get me out of my head. A goal with no strings. I can control my time; I can push the pace or not. Unlike the internship application, where I'm at the mercy of many people, here on this track, it's between me, and my mind, and my feet.

I take a swig of water, grinning as my teammates surround me. They clamp their hands on my shoulders and shake, a good-luck tradition that we all take part in. The little shakes are a metaphorical baton, sending goodwill, luck, and speed each other's way.

I take my spot in the lineup. They've assigned me an outside lane, steep on the bank and pushed forward—not my favorite, by a long shot. I calm my nerves by running through the race in my head—when I'll cut in, what my strategy will be. I'm confident I can take down some of the people seeded in front of me easily, as long as they keep their elbows tucked.

I remind myself that everything is faster this year—my cross-country time, my 1500—so why shouldn't this be? I glance at Dylan while the officials are still busy lining everybody else up. He flashes me a smile and a thumbs-up, and I can't help but smile back. I'm going to do it. I'm going to PR so big, they won't even think of putting Karly on the track today.

I love you, Clari, but I'm coming for your spot.

The gun goes off, and it feels like I'm flying. Each step comes as naturally as breathing; each step takes me closer to when I can cut into the inside lane and join the fray.

A few heartbeats later and I cut left hard, passing a few runners, and find my spot among the jostling bodies that lead the pack. It's not long before the girl next to me throws her elbow into my ribs—it's subtle enough the officials won't notice, but hard enough to hurt. I'm not about to let a little pain stop me, though, not now with my dream on the line.

The fact that I'm so far ahead of the pacer lights running along the track tells me it's going to be a PR, *but will it be enough?*

I keep my eyes focused on the runner in first, Ashlynn. She's several lengths in front of all of us—famous on the college scene as much as a track star can be. I don't have a prayer of winning against her, but that's not my goal; my goal is to maintain the same distance behind her. If I can stay slotted right here, in second or third place depending on how good of a kick the runner on my butt has, I can get us the points and kill my old PR.

It will be harder in the 4x8, when theoretically we'll have enough of a lead that I won't have anyone to pace me . . . but right now I'm running behind a future Olympian, and that's motivation enough.

I blink and we're on the second lap. I stay steady, and when Ashlynn kicks, so do I. It's earlier than I normally would, but it feels right.

Seconds later, I'm crossing the finish line, stealing third right out from the school behind me before stumbling off the track and lying down the second I'm out of the staging area. The concrete floor is probably pretty nasty—but it's cold and solid and everything I need right now.

"We're still waiting for the official results, but how does a four-second PR sound to you?" Mika grins, leaning over me.

"Not like five," I say, pushing up to my elbows.

Does this mean Karly will still take the spot after all?

"Yeah, but once you factor in that elbow you took on the third turn and your shitty lane positioning, I think it will be. Pacing yourself off Ashlynn was brilliant. Risky, but brilliant. Coach almost shit herself when you picked up the speed so early, but I was all in on you. I knew you'd pull it off."

"Thanks, Mika," I say as she pulls me up to standing.

"You won't have that in the next race. It'll just be us and them after the first turn. Hopefully by the time you run, we'll have enough of a lead over whatever Moose they throw on your leg that it's just you."

"*I* won't have it, like specifically *me*? I'm definitely in?"

"You're definitely in," she says, laughing as I launch a sweaty hug on her.

"Oh my god, thank you!" I say, basically squealing the words.

Dylan walks up then, slurping a giant soda. "Amazing race,

Morgie," he says, ruffling my hair. I don't even care about his annoying-brother antics right now. Not when I'm finally getting a crack at the race I've been dreaming of since I committed. It was half the reason I *did* commit.

Their 4x8 is legendary, and sorry, Clari, but I'm hoping to stay. I'll slot into the injury spot while Karly recovers, but once she's back, I don't plan to go anywhere.

"I'm doing the four by eight!" I shriek.

"Like . . . the lumber?" he asks. I smack his arm, and he breaks into laughter. He knows these races as well as I do by now, and we both know it. "All right, all right, congrats. I thought you said freshmen never get to do it!"

"Never have," Mika says, "until now. Morgan, go fuel up. You've got about two hours before we need to warm you up again."

I nod, knowing there's an acai bowl somewhere calling my name.

We win the 4x8.

We win the 4x8, and I shave not just five seconds off but five *and a half*. Even Coach calls me her "little overachiever" the rest of the night. We wait nervously for the DMR, where our school finishes a half second behind our rivals.

Coach thinks we have it, but Mika begs her not to jinx it.

We all stare at the leaderboard, biting the skin around our nails, as we wait for them to finish calculating the points. I know Coach thinks she has it all worked out on her clipboard already—but it's not official until it's officially official.

Then the board updates, and we let out a collective cheer—we win the overall meet by two points.

We won! We really did it!

We all start jumping up and down, cheering and hugging, and then run to our people in the stands to do it all over again. It's amazing, it's brilliant, and it isn't until we're on the bus home that I realize something . . .

It's quiet as we drive through the cold night back to campus. Most of my teammates are dozing off; a few are tackling their homework or watching movies on their iPads. It hits me as I reach for my phone to reply to all the congratulations from my friends who streamed my race or Googled the results.

For the first time since Ruby and I broke up, I'm *really, really* happy. I'm happy and whole and, even better, *it doesn't feel like anything's missing.* It doesn't feel off.

I have the urge to text her; of course I do, it's Ruby. I'll love her till the day I die. Except the urge is different now. I want to text her because I want her to know that I did the thing I've been trying so hard for—not out of any sense of desperation or clinginess. I want to know if she's done good things too. I bet she has.

I'm not trying to hold on to something old out of habit. I want to know what's new.

I want to tell her something happy, and hopefully hear good news from her too.

Except I won't text her, though. I'll respect her radio silence and her boundaries. I lean back in my seat with a smile, content that my own happiness is enough, because it is.

Still, it's really nice to think of her without pain slicing through me. It's nice to feel proud of myself and want to share it with her, rather than feeling like it doesn't count because she wasn't here.

It feels healthy. It feels like progress.

It feels like hope.

23

RUBY

I take about a week to work up the courage to actually go over to my mom's.

I don't know why I decide to go today, when the producers are scheduled to visit Billy's shop later. The scout loved it, but the director and producers want to do a final check before deciding for real.

And here I am, deciding it's the perfect day to confront my mommy issues.

Maybe because if I wait any longer, it's already going to be time to film the show.

My mom has been texting nonstop since I agreed to come. I uncharitably wonder if she's only doing it because she's desperate to play doting mom for some new boyfriend. I always loved the first few weeks she was dating someone and on her best behavior.

As much as I'd like to believe that my mom had a change of heart and that she misses me the way I miss her, I'm going into this cautiously. I'm honestly not sure she's even capable of that—not after everything that happened last year.

Still, it's my mom.

My mom.

The person who sacrificed everything for me, and yes, I know that doesn't mean I owe her anything, and yes, I know that in a normal healthy relationship my mom would be the one who owed me—I didn't ask to be here. I didn't ask to be born.

But still, *it's my mom.*

And there were times that weren't awful. Especially before Billy left—and even then, we didn't fully hit rock bottom until Chuck started living with us. There were always the pageants, sure, but there were always going to be, I think. Even if she and Billy had made it work, or some other great guy. She wanted a do-over of the life she felt like she'd missed by having me so young. And since she didn't have a time machine, that meant living vicariously through me—whether I wanted to or not.

I miss our old life sometimes anyway. I'd be lying if I said I didn't. I loved making pancakes with her all the time or getting to push the buttons on the rice cooker and the microwave. It didn't matter that we couldn't afford anything else. I miss being little and thinking she was the whole world, and I miss her letting me.

I miss so many things from so long ago that sometimes I can't help but wonder if I'm even remembering the truth anymore, or just wishing for that sugarcoated version—one where my mom wasn't angry and hurtful and didn't slap me whenever she felt like it.

I don't know—a little of both, maybe.

I've lain awake more than my share of nights thinking about what a childhood like mine can do to somebody. How it could have made me mean and bitter too, and how it sorta did for a while, until I stopped letting it.

Billy had a lot to do with that, which I probably should tell him sometime. I'm sure he knows, though. And I know he's proud of me. I think he's going to be that person for Shiloh and Stella Jane too, or at least try to be for as long as they let him.

It's weird how this tiny town can forge such vastly different people. How Billy's life was a different kind of hard than my mom's, but still difficult. I'm glad he didn't give in to the bitterness either.

I still can't stop mulling over that incessant fear that I am more like my mom than I realize. That I loved Morgan because it was something to focus on. A salvation, a distraction, different from Tyler, but not all the way. Everly says I'm wrong; so do Billy and Shiloh, for whatever it's worth. They all think the fact that I'm even wondering about it is proof enough that I'm not.

My therapist doesn't know me enough to say either way yet, but her opinion is that if I'm thinking it through, it doesn't matter what I was . . . because I'll approach my next relationship aware of it and in a healthier way.

I don't think I'll be convinced by any of them until I see my mom. Until we talk things through. I doubt she'll have the answers, but maybe it'll help me find my own.

I pull onto the road that I used to live on, thinking about all of this, and realize that maybe I'm not here *despite* the producers coming today, but because of it. Because on some level I can't let myself step into the future—whether it's with Morgan or on TV or graduating college, or five thousand other things that could happen—until I know if she'll be there. Until I look at my mom and see if it's my own reflection staring back at me.

My car purrs to a stop right in my old spot at the front of the trailer. The grass has grown back into the ruts my tires left, but the blades are a sad winter brown now—the snow from the last storm melted away, but the sun's not hot enough yet to wake anything up. The sight pinches at my heart in a way I wasn't expecting—the space my life used to take up here all filled in with shitty weeds and dead grass.

Fitting.

I'm barely out of my car when Mom wrenches the door open—a grin on her face that sends guilt spiraling down from the tips of my ears to my soul, because it's her. *My mom.*

Behind her, I hear the dogs yapping. The sound that used to drive me nuts now instead feels familiar and nostalgic in a way that makes my stomach clench.

This used to be home.

. . .

Mom made coffee.

I stare at the dingy, stained carafe that she's set on the corner of the counter, not caring that it's adding to the scorch marks on the peeling Formica—the perfect match for the cracked linoleum under my feet. She leans against the counter awkwardly as I greet each dog. There are six now—or maybe still; I kind of blocked them out.

And now that I'm sitting down at our table, she's offering me coffee like I'm a stranger stopping by.

I guess maybe I am.

I resist the urge to rush down to my bedroom, to see if she's kept it the same, but just barely. I focus instead on figuring out the right answer to the coffee dilemma. If I say yes, then I bet she'll feel like I owe her something—there's always been strings attached to anything she offers. But if I say no, she'll probably take it as a rejection and get mad. Neither seems very appealing, but the longer I let the silence stretch out, the worse and weirder this all feels.

I settle on "I'm good, thanks," because that's the truth, and I'm done worrying about what will make her happiest at my own expense.

Mom scowls, but to her credit she doesn't flip out. Instead, she pulls a chipped mug out of the cabinet and pours her own cup.

I recognize the mug right away. It's from the holiday shop they held at school every year when I was little. She never had enough money to send me with any, but the parent volunteers always made sure I could buy something, "have the same experience," they said. I don't know if my mom ever knew—she was so against handouts—but she must have.

It's got a little snowman in a Santa hat printed on it. Probably not even worth the dollar I paid for it in third grade, seeing as it was already chipped even back then—everything in the holiday shop was donated castoffs from people in town; we just all pretended they weren't.

I was so proud after they helped me wrap it. I couldn't wait to run home and put it in front of the little dollar store tabletop plastic tree we had.

My mom laughed when she opened it. Laughed.

At the time, I thought it was a good thing. But with the benefit of hindsight, I wonder about it. I wonder if she cared or if she thought my sentimentality was ridiculous. I wonder if she was drunk and that's why she laughed. I'll never know how she really felt that day, but maybe I can figure out why she's using it now.

Is it to hurt me or has she been using it since I left? Is this a habit or a stab?

I hate that I have to second-guess everything, that I have to play defense with my mother instead of her being my safe space.

Mom finishes fixing her coffee—I see she's using sugar again—and takes the seat across from me. She seems to be waiting for me to say something. Maybe I should. Maybe I owe her an explanation for staying away so long.

I'm sure she thinks I do.

"How are you?" I ask, squirming a little in my seat. I'm desperate to end this silent standoff.

Mom smiles like a platoon leader who just realized victory is within her grasp. "Worrying about me now, are ya?" she says. "I didn't realize you still cared."

And there it is, the guilt trip I knew was coming.

"I never stopped caring about you, Mom. I just needed space after everything that happened. It was a lot, you know."

"It was a lot for me too," she says. "Not that it matters to you. You move in with the man who ruined my life and think that doesn't kill me? You let a girl turn you gay and pick a loser of an old man over your own mama? After everything I did for you?"

I squeeze my eyes shut, willing myself not to react. I know it's what she wants. When I open them, I see the cruel satisfaction in her face from knowing that her words hurt.

"Don't talk about Morgan and Billy that way," I say, the words coming out sharp.

"Why? You girls getting married or some shit? I know she didn't knock you up. Don't know why she'd want to be strapped to you otherwise, though," my mom says. "Her or Bill." My face must give something away because then my mom cackles. "Oh my god, she left you. You tore up your whole life and that girl still left you. Oh, honey." She slaps the table. "That's how it always goes for people like us, don't you get that yet? You can hide at Bill's, and you can screw anybody you want, but at the end of the day you're a Thompson girl like me. We don't get pulled up; we just drag everyone down with us."

And there it is. The fear underneath all the other fears. The feeling that there's something inherently wrong with me. Something bad in my DNA.

"That's not true," I say, weak and quiet.

"What do you think happened with Billy? Chuck? Hell, Donovan left last night."

New boyfriend? Must be. She's never meaner than right after a breakup.

This probably explains the coffee too. It wasn't for me; it was for her. She's probably been drinking since last night and trying to cover it up.

"I don't know about this Donovan guy," I say. "But Chuck was an asshole, and Billy had to get out before you—"

"Before I what? Got my filth all over his perfect morals?" She snorts.

"No," I say, not even sure what I'm saying no to anymore.

"Good, because he was already trash when I met him. He acts like his hands are clean, but you should ask him about all the girls he hooked up with while we were still—"

"Mom, can you just stop!"

She does, shockingly.

"Why did you come here?" she grits out.

"Because you kept texting me and asking me to."

"That's not it," she says. "I know why I'm texting you. I'm asking you why you finally answered me."

"I wanted to see you. I wanted to know . . . I mean . . . You're still my mom."

"Am I?" she asks, lighting a cigarette even though all the windows are closed. "Do you know how embarrassing it was to have people in town asking me questions about what my daughter was up to with that *girl*? I kept saying, 'She's experimenting. It's a phase.' You know how many people offered to pray for you? Any of them prayers work yet, Ruby? You done for good, or do you still need saving?"

And I know what she's asking. She's asking if I'm still bi. If I'm done *experimenting*.

Any hope I had that she had learned a lesson while I was gone—that she was going to accept me—dies in my chest. Its corpse flutters down behind my rib cage to be filed away with all the other disappointments and heartbreak I've experienced in my life.

"I don't need saving, Mom. I already saved myself." My voice is soft, but my words are hard.

My mom scoffs.

"I appreciate all the sacrifices you made when I was growing up," I say, continuing even as she grumbles something about me having a horrible way of showing it. "I will always love you as my mom. Always. But if you can't accept who I am, then I can't have you in my life.

"I'm good over at Billy's. And I can see you are over here too. You've got a fridge full of food, and a bunch of dogs, and you used to tell me that's all you really needed, right?

"But if you ever loved me, ever, then you have to stop texting me. You have to stop messing with me. I can't keep doing this with you. I'm not experimenting; it's not a phase.

I'm bi, and if you can't love all of me, including that, you don't deserve any of me."

A cacophony of barking dogs sets off behind me as I head for the door. I hear her laugh as I shut it behind me. At least I don't have to wonder anymore.

Because I know I'm nothing like my mother. *Nothing.*

24

MORGAN

The subject line says "Round one application decision," and I hold my breath as I click the email open. I squeal when the first sentence announces that I have officially moved on to the second round—which consists of one more essay and a Zoom interview with the hiring board.

"Oh my god, oh my god, oh my god," I say, force of habit causing me to reach for my phone to call Ruby. This still happens a lot, but usually I catch myself before I actually follow through. This time, I don't remember until it's already ringing against my ear.

I'm just about to hang up when she answers.

"Morgan?" Ruby says, sounding worried, because of course she would. We haven't spoken in forever, not even texted, and now I'm calling her out of the blue.

"Hey, hi," I say, my voice sounding strained. "Sorry, I didn't mean to call. Well, I did, but I shouldn't have."

"What's up?" she asks, her voice still sounding cautious.

"I'm sorry. I think it's just so ingrained in me to call you when I have news. Muscle memory or whatever. It's nice of you to pick up, but I really am trying to respect your boundaries. I honestly didn't register what I was doing until it started ringing this time. Usually I can catch myself. Sorry to bother you."

"It's all right," she says. The background noise quiets down around her. I can't help but picture her walking into Billy's office, maybe even kicking him out, so that she can have privacy and hear me better. That shouldn't send a little thrill coursing through me, but it does.

"It is?" I ask. "Are you sure? I'm not trying to run you over or whatever. I know you need space. Aaron told me, and, well, you had already stopped texting me back by then. I wasn't ready to get the hint, I guess, until he spelled it out."

"Yeah, sorry," Ruby says. "I should have had the guts to tell you that myself."

"Probably," I say, wishing that I wasn't sitting at the café on campus. I feel so exposed here in this crowd.

"For what it's worth, I've almost called you a hundred times too. And I'm really sorry I ghosted you instead of letting you know I couldn't handle all the texting, sincerely," she says. "I wasn't handling the breakup well at first, and I just—"

"It's okay," I say, letting her voice wrap around me and sinking into it.

God, I've missed her so much—more than I even

realized now that I have her voice back in my ear. I wonder if this accidental dialing could be the start of something new. Or a restart.

Yes, I know she just called it a "breakup" and not a "break," but she also said she's wanted to call me too . . . What if it's fate that I called her today, what if— But before I can even catch up to my thoughts, let alone restrain them, a whimpering cry rings out from Ruby's end of the phone.

"Oh shit," Ruby says. "Hang on."

She must set the phone down, because there's a little shuffling sound, and when her voice rings out, a high-pitched "Is that my Stella-Wella Bear I hear? What a big nap for my little lazybones!" Ruby sounds far away.

What is she doing?

Realization washes over me as I listen to Ruby continue to coo in my ear. Shiloh's baby. She said Billy let him bring her around the shop sometimes. *I guess that means Ruby helps babysit too. How . . . nice.*

Jealousy climbs up my throat, choking me out even though I try to ignore it. I feel dizzy and a little nauseous as I picture them playing happy family together already. God, the corpse of our relationship is barely cold, and she's— Are she and Shiloh . . . ? I should hang up. Probably. This isn't any of my business. *She did just say "breakup."*

Dammit.

"Hey, I'm back, sorry," Ruby says.

I don't answer her. I can't. I'm scared that I'll—I don't know—throw up or cry if I do. I was feeling so good about things before we talked. I know now that I don't need her in order to be happy, and I know I'm building a solid life without her at school . . . but I think Ruby will just always be a wound that doesn't heal for me. Maybe there's not a world where I don't ache when I hear her voice.

"Morgan?" she asks. "Did I lose you?"

Yes, I think. *Probably. And it's killing me, but I know I'll live.*

"Morgan?" she says again.

"Still here," I say cheerfully. Ruby isn't the only one who can paste on a pageant smile. I learned from the best.

I should probably let her go, but I'm not quite ready to yet.

"What was your good news?" she asks as the rustling picks up again. I imagine her fishing out snacks for the little babbling thing on her lap, acting like a mom.

"It's not important," I say. "It sounds like you're busy."

"Oh no, I'm not busy at all now," Ruby says, clearly not picking up on the fact that I desperately want to go. "Your timing couldn't be better. I just finished up some work. Now I'm stuck on babysitting duty until Shi finishes up. I was hoping she'd stay asleep, but Stella Jane has her own agenda. Don't you?" she asks the baby, her voice kicking back up into that higher pitch like she's talking to a puppy. "Yes, you do!"

There are some kissy sounds, followed by a little giggling. It makes me melt *and* want to throw my phone all at once.

"Wow, things must be pretty serious if he's trusting you with his kid."

"Yeah, you could say that. I'm glad Billy lets him bring her here. It helps him out so much. It really makes me appreciate—"

"I have to go," I say, ending the call before she can say anything else.

Because, oh. Oh, that hurts. Is she trying to rub it in my face that she's moved on?

The phone buzzes in my hand, Ruby calling back. I hit decline, sending her to voicemail. Then it buzzes again . . . and a third time. Now I'm not sad; I'm *mad.*

"Look, I called you by accident, okay," I snap when I pick up my phone. People are staring at me in the café now, but I don't even care. "I'm not ready to hear about you and your boy—"

"I'm an idiot," Ruby says, cutting me off. "I'm sorry. I didn't realize how that must have sounded until you hung up. Jesus Christ, thank you for answering. *I* probably wouldn't have if the roles were reversed! It's not— I need you to know that it's not."

"It's not *what*?" I ask. "You're not making any sense."

"Shi and I aren't like . . . That's not what I was talking about when I agreed it was serious. He's like a brother to me, and Billy and I have kind of taken them in. I meant like *the situation* was serious, babysitting a kid with no sense of self-preservation. Not that there's anyone I'm serious *with.* I'm not. I can't—well, I don't want to. I wouldn't anyway, not without letting you know—shutting the door on us or whatever. Didn't we have to do that first? You said that."

I gasp into the phone, my chest feeling tight, tight, tight, as I try to figure out what she's saying, and she's still going in my ear, frantic, something about missing me and—

"Hold on," I say, and everything goes silent, minus the kid, who's still squealing and babbling on in the background, but that's to be expected. "Okay, could you start over, please, a little slower." I wince when my voice comes out like a whine. "I just don't want to miss anything you have to say."

"Thank god," Ruby says, exhaling hard. "I thought you were going to hang up again."

"I'm sorry. I didn't mean to hang up. I panicked. I would have called back eventually, I think."

"You're better than me, because if you implied you had gotten serious with someone without talking to me, I think I would be done forever." Ruby goes silent for a second, and my eyebrows crinkle until she adds, "You're not, are you? Serious with someone?"

"God, no," I say.

"Okay, good. Well, not *good*. I don't know. Good for me, I guess. Good to know?"

She's rambling now, and it's freaking adorable.

"It's good to know that you aren't either." I smile. "You know, strictly for recordkeeping purposes."

"Yeah. Yeah, of course, recordkeeping." She laughs. "I'll, uh, I'll update your file accordingly. Still single, check."

"Oh god." I shake my head. "Are you feeling as awkward as I am right now?"

"Yeah . . . I'm trying not to put my foot in my mouth, and it's not really working. I'm just happy to hear from you and trying not to screw it up too bad."

"Likewise. Hey, fill me in, if you want. I'd love to hear more about this kid, Aunt Ruby."

"You're still such a dork," she says, and I can hear her

smile. "She just calls me Ru. Or actually, she doesn't pronounce things well yet, so it's more like Wu."

"Stop, that's so cute."

"I know," Ruby coos. "I've only known her a little while, but I swear I love this freaking kid. She's our little mascot now. And Shi is kind of family now too, in a way. He doesn't trust it yet, but neither did I for a long time.

"I think Billy's obsessed with this new grandpa role. Shiloh's like me; his parents aren't around to help him. When you asked if it was serious, I was thinking, like, his aunt and uncle that they live with are trying to force him to move out, so things are a little dire right now for him. I wasn't thinking about anything else."

"Yeah, that makes sense," I say. "I'm sorry he's having trouble."

"Me too. I wish Billy had more bedrooms. Worst case, Billy or I would sleep on the couch and give them the room until they can get a place, but yeah. Sucks," she says. "You'd love Shiloh, by the way. He came to the center with me last weekend, and we stuffed more backpacks for that program you set up last year. He was cracking Izzy up the whole time. She's going to try to get him into some affordable housing. She had him fill out a bunch of applications and stuff. I guess he might qualify for daycare help or something too."

"Oh, he's queer?"

"Yep, bi like me." I can hear the smile in her voice, and it's contagious. It wasn't *that* long ago that she wouldn't even say the word out loud.

“That’s really cool,” I say.

“That is not the word I would use.” Ruby laughs. “Like, you will die if we all ever go out anywhere together. He has the worst taste in people; like, seriously, shitty dudes are like catnip to him. It’s embarrassing to watch, but . . . sorry. I’m rambling. I don’t know what I’m even saying right now. I’m just so relieved you picked up.”

“Me too,” I say, fully meaning it. “I’m sorry for hanging up. It was immature. Even if you *were* seeing someone, it’s your right. Conversation or no.”

“I don’t want to,” she says.

“I don’t either, but . . .”

“But what?”

“I’m still over here and . . .”

“I’m still all the way over here. I know,” she says. “I got the show, by the way. So, that’s happening.”

“Oh my god! Congrats! I’m so happy for you!”

“Thanks. They loved Billy’s shop so much we’re gonna film here too. They already recorded some preinterviews with us all the other day—even Billy. He was so nervous, it was sweet. Oh, um, wait, what was your news? Now that we aren’t freaking out on each other.”

Right, my news. The whole reason I called.

“I made it to the next round of the internship application. It’s down to me and two other people now.”

“Yay! I didn’t doubt it for a second,” Ruby says.

Stella Jane must still be on her lap, because I hear a little voice repeat “Yay” over and over while clapping.

"Thanks. Thank your little cheerleader there too, but I definitely did doubt it. I'm nervous about how this round will go."

"That's because you don't always believe in yourself enough."

"Pot, meet kettle," I say, and she huffs.

"Yeah, fair, but I'm getting a lot better at that. Girls like us are tougher than we think. We gotta start giving ourselves more credit."

"I like that," I say. "We *are* pretty great."

Ruby laughs. "Yeah, we are, aren't we?"

"Oh crap," I say when an alarm goes off on my phone. "That's my *I have to get to practice* alarm."

"The life of a student athlete," she teases, and then we both go quiet.

I wonder if she wants to stay on the phone as much as I do.

Luckily, my question is answered almost immediately.

"Do you think . . ." Ruby trails off, sighing. "Do you think maybe we could do this again? Talk on the phone, I mean. No pressure if—"

"Yes!" I say, a little too eagerly. "Preferably without any jump scares in the middle."

"Yeah, no," she says. "Let's skip you hanging up and me panic dialing you over and over again next time too."

"Deal," I say.

"Good."

I can tell there's something else on the tip of her tongue. There is on mine too—specifically that *I don't want us to be done.*

The soul-searching I've done this last month and a half changed me, and it sounds like our time apart changed her too.

Instead of pushing things and risking ruining it, we both say our quick goodbyes. But I can call her again sometime. Text her too. I don't know if that will lead us back together or if we'll form a friendship out of the rubble of our relationship, but today, not knowing where we're going—but knowing we're going somewhere—is enough.

It's enough.

25

RUBY

We're filming tomorrow, and I'm freaking the fuck out.

Not in a cute nervous-jitters way, in a, like, *I'm going to throw up and then pass out and then maybe die* way. I continue my torment by staring at my ceiling for a while and then by staring at my phone.

I'm still happy about my call with Morgan the other night, especially since she agreed when I said, a little too desperately, that I hoped we would talk again. It's possible that she was just being polite . . . but then again, she did hang up on me earlier in that same convo, so politeness didn't seem to be a priority right then.

I roll over and hug my pillow, shoving my phone away. I'm too nervous to commit to calling. What if she doesn't pick up?

What if she doesn't still have the warm fuzzies from talking to me, the way I do with her?

I shut my eyes, letting myself drift a little, and try to remember last year, when I had performance anxiety before a big group project. It seems so silly and small now comparatively—this show I'm filming isn't going to be in a class of people I already know; it's going to be on TV. I'm going to be working in front of my favorite celebrity mechanic and trying to stay cool. Not to mention Ben, and Billy, and Shiloh, and the production crew, and most of my class. And then the show will end up in reruns and on streaming for all eternity. What if I say something stupid and it ends up going viral? What if I'm forever the dumb kid making women mechanics look bad everywhere? What if I make a face and they turn me into a GIF?

Shit. I'm spiraling, bad. I need to pull it together.

I nuzzle into the pillow more, taking a deep breath, and yeah, maybe I'm pretending this is one of the ten thousand times I nuzzled into Morgan, letting her heartbeat lull me into a sense of safety and calm, but who could blame me?

I think back to that big presentation last year. The way the warmth from her hand rushed through my body, cementing itself in my brain as I fumbled with the notecards. I was embarrassed by my scratchy handwriting, so I had tried to write the words loopy and pretty, like it even mattered. I was trying to be a good student, trying to prove to her that I could pull my weight.

Those notecards tried to kill me, but we didn't let them.

Morgan's confidence that day was like a balm to my frayed nerves. After years of being judged by all the kids at school, standing in front of them to help give our report was terrifying. It's no wonder that I dropped the cards nearly the second we got to the front of the classroom. Our classmates laughed when I accidentally scattered the notecards even more as I frantically tried to pick them up—another typical Ruby fuckup for them to make fun of me for. Morgan just crouched down beside me and helped. She hooked her pinkie in mine, reassuring me, and that blink-and-you'll-miss-it moment rewired my entire brain.

We pulled off the presentation. We got an A, even. I'm sure some people thought I let Morgan do all the work, but I didn't, and *she* knew I didn't, and that was all that mattered. That was the first time I had really, truly tried at something at school. When Morgan told me I was amazing after, for the first time in my life, I kind of believed she meant it.

And then of course I went and screwed it all up at the lacrosse party, but that's beside the point. As my therapist made me write on a sticky note, progress doesn't have to be linear.

I guess the show is kind of similar to that project, now that I think of it—as weird as that sounds. It's something I wanted. I went after it myself, got it myself, handled it myself.

Except now that I'm only kind of spiraling about the show, instead of full-on spiraling, I realize that I've opened a Pandora's box of memories by thinking about Morgan. Specifically, about how warm her hands were every time that her skin met mine. Whether it was the innocent nights we spent curled up on her couch watching *ShopTalk* for the five hundredth time or the less innocent nights where we roamed each other's bodies like cartographers, hell-bent on studying every curve, every dip, every gasp and sigh.

I groan and throw myself onto my back. Now is *not* the time to bring my libido into this.

My mind trips over the past again, dragging me back to the lacrosse party and how I had let myself feel my feelings about Morgan a little, just until I got scared and drunk and went running back to my former form of stress relief, hooking up with Tyler. (Well, tried to, anyway. He was a decent enough guy to realize that I'd had too much to drink and put me safely to bed instead.)

But I'm a changed woman now, aren't I?

Shit. Aren't I?

I sit up fast, my pillow falling to the floor as I fling it off me.

Am I repeating old patterns by not calling Morgan right now, or breaking a cycle? Am I being needy and scared, or do I just miss her and know that talking to her makes my day better? Am I so worried about using her as a distraction that I'm willing to walk away from something good just to prove I'm not?

These thoughts slide quickly into bigger ones, like: *Is there a universe where we could figure out how to make this work despite our busy lives? Would Morgan even want to?*

I know the purpose of this break was to figure shit out, but I guess now that I'm starting to understand myself more, this all feels like something we should figure out together, not apart. Like, are we both being stoic while secretly dying inside? Or just me?

There's only one way to find out.

I scoop up my phone, hesitating when I see the time: It's nearly midnight. She always was a night owl, though. *I hope that she still is.* I click onto Morgan's contact information, crossing my fingers. She picks up on the first ring.

"Hey," she says, "I'm glad you called. I was nervous to be the one to do it again."

I'm glad you called. She says it just straight up like that, setting me instantly at ease. We never talked about when I was filming, so I know she's not picking up out of obligation or concern. She means it; she's actually glad I called.

"Ruby?" she says, and whoops, because now her voice *does* have a hint of concern.

"Hi," I say, relief that I haven't completely forgotten how to talk spilling out of me. "Sorry, that was just really nice to hear."

Morgan laughs. "What was?"

"When you said you were glad I called. Well, that you answered at all feels like a win."

"Well, I *am* glad you called, and you don't have to worry about me not picking up, because I'll always answer when it's you. You're my favorite thing that's ever happened to me."

"Shut up," I snort.

"Okay, fine, winning the four by eight a couple weeks ago was pretty good too, but I think you still might have the edge."

"You made the four by eight team?" I practically shout. "Holy shit! Congrats. That's big, first freshman to do it!"

"I did," she says. "I am. I was subbed in last second because one of the other runners had an injury. My times were good enough that I got to keep my spot even once she was back. It caused a little tension between me and the junior I replaced, Claribel, but we worked it out. She's still first alternate by a landslide, and the way Karly's ankle keeps giving out, I'm sure Clari will be running it almost as often as I do, anyway, so. Yeah. It's pretty cool. I can't believe you remembered that I was the first freshman to make it. That's pretty deep track team lore."

"I remember everything," I blurt out. "I wish I could have been there."

"Dylan was there," she says. "It was . . . fine."

"Was it fine?" I ask. I shouldn't be picking at this thread—I know I shouldn't be—but I can't help it. For the first time, I consider that maybe it won't be *fine* when I film tomorrow. Morgan doesn't need to fill a hole in my life—I'm doing that myself—but she does such a damn good job adding to it even more. She pushes me to be the best version of myself, and I try to push her the same way. I bet she wanted me at that race. I bet I'll want her on set tomorrow too.

"It was the way it worked out," she says. "It wasn't *not* fine. I'm doing good. You don't have to worry about me."

"I know. It's not that." I sigh. "Are you in DC?"

Morgan doesn't answer for a long time, so long that I'm checking my phone to make sure we didn't get disconnected.

"No," she says eventually.

"Why not?"

She blows out a long breath and doesn't answer.

"Sorry, it's none of my business. If you don't want to talk about it, we don't need to. Are you at school still?"

"Yeah," she says, like she's admitting something she shouldn't.

I don't know what to do with this information. I don't know what to say or how to react. The whole reason I was going to give up filming was so she could have this DC experience that she didn't want to reschedule. *Now she's not even going? I'm sitting here alone, and she's not even . . .*

"I didn't want to go without you," Morgan says, cutting off my spiral just as it's picking up momentum. "I don't want to make you feel like it's your fault or anything. I still could've gone easily. My mom even offered to go with me. I just . . . didn't want to do it without you, at least not now. Do you ever feel like that? Never mind, you don't have to answer. I'm overstepping. Again. I—"

"Constantly," I cut her off. "It's why I'm calling, actually. I'm filming tomorrow and wish you could be here."

"Ahhh," she squeals. "That's so exciting! I can't believe I'm going to see you on TV someday. You're amazing, Ruby. You are so freaking amazing!"

Amazing. There's that word again.

This time, instead of doing the usual denying or downplaying or any of the stuff I usually do, I just . . . accept it. Because maybe I am amazing, and maybe she is too, and maybe we both make each other more amazing. Maybe we don't hold each other back at all but instead propel each other forward.

Maybe this break *was* the glitch in the system, not the way it was supposed to work out.

"I miss you," I say. "And not in a needy, user, codependent way. In an *I want to be there for your good things* way and an

I want you to be there for mine way, whatever that looks like."

"What are you saying?"

"I'm saying that I think we need to talk about this. I can't stop thinking about the way you looped your pinkie around mine when we were picking up the notecards last year, you know? I'm not sure we made the right call, at least not long-term."

"You kind of lost me," she says, and her voice sounds a little shaky, a little watery, just like mine does.

Morgan sniffles, and my heart cracks a little more and then reseals—a thousand memories flit in and out of my head, of all the times we made each other stronger and encouraged each other over the last year. When I was a constant cheerleader as she built up the Rainbow Athlete Coalition idea. When she sat beside me to register for my classes when I was scared because I didn't want to fail and I didn't trust that I wouldn't . . . and a thousand million other things big and small.

"What if we were wrong?" I ask. "What if we don't hold each other back? What if we make each other stronger? There have been so many things I've wanted to call and tell you about, like when I nailed my steering systems test or got a new client at Billy's or, shit, even the first time I made dinner for family night and didn't burn it.

"I want to tell you my good things. I want to hear yours. I want to be there, and not because I need you or can't handle things without you, but because I *want* you to be there. I don't know what that looks like to you, or if it even looks like *anything*. I know we're still hours apart and there are going be internships and jobs and other stuff getting in our way. But if you can see a path for us—if we keep supporting each other and go back into it knowing that the next four years are going to be hard but hard is worth it, then—"

"I don't want to be on a break anymore," Morgan says, beating me to the punch. "I thought it would be better for us, and in some ways, it was—I settled in here more and got closer to my teammates—but I hate that I can't tell you all about it at the end of the day. I still feel in this with you; I never didn't."

"You do?" I ask, grinning.

"Yes! God, yes!" she says, and I can practically picture her right now, throwing her hands in the air in exasperation like she always does. And suddenly, imagining it isn't enough.

I hit the FaceTime button, and she accepts. Seconds later, I'm staring at her smiling face for the first time in weeks.

"Hi," she says, holding her pinkie up to the camera like she wishes she could reach through the glass.

Yeah, I think as I hold mine up. *Yeah. Me too.*

26

MORGAN

We talked for two hours last night.

I think we would have talked till the sun came up if she wasn't filming today. Neither of us wanted to go, so like every cheesy college girlfriend, I asked her if she wanted to fall asleep on FaceTime, and she did. It was perfect.

We still have *a lot* to talk about before we officially "end the break," or however you want to put it. We both want to put safeguards in place. We're going to set some boundaries and expectations to make sure that we do things the healthy way. We both realize now that the mistake wasn't choosing to stay together when we left for college; it was the fact that we weren't letting each other, or our relationship, change. Just because we got used to being together every second we could in high school didn't mean the relationship had to end when we didn't necessarily want to keep that dynamic going.

It feels horrible to know that Ruby felt like she couldn't come to me about the show, but it feels even worse that my first solution for saving our relationship pre-break was us both giving up our dreams. *What was I thinking?!*

The next few years of college will be hard; we're both being realistic about that. The thing that we forgot was that it's temporary. Four years is a drop in the bucket when it comes to forever.

Who knows what will happen. A year from now, we might have a different opinion and break up for real, or Ruby might be done with her associate's and move here temporarily while I finish up. She might also decide she never wants to leave Billy's shop, and I may want to focus on work-from-home jobs and building up the coalition . . . but none of that is the point. The point is that we don't let ourselves or each other stay stagnant.

If I got a wish right now, of course it would be that everything is nice and easy and works out just the way we want so we can live happily ever after. Since I'm unfortunately bound by the laws of the physical world and not a magical one, the best I can do is promise myself that I really mean all of this—that I'm willing to take it as it comes with me and Ruby, even when it's tricky. If it gets too hard someday, we'll have a conversation, and if it doesn't, well, maybe we really will get that happily ever after—or as close as you can get in the real world.

Ruby left a while ago. She wanted to go to the shop and, as she put it, remind herself that she knows what she's doing in there before the bright lights make her forget. I fling open my laptop and check my email, hoping for a reply from Professor Dunner. I emailed her late last night and asked if I could have a meeting with her to discuss something important. I know it's a long shot, but she lives locally, and she's mentioned before that she spends a lot of Saturday mornings on campus because one of the soccer students here gives private lessons to her kid.

Probably not during spring break, but you know, wishful thinking and all that...

Most people are going home today, despite our dorms staying open all next week anyway, and I'm sure a lot of professors are also off on vacation or living their best not-stuck-on-campus lives. Worst case, I'll talk to her next Monday. In the meantime, I'll just prep for my interview and try not to obsess over the fact that I'm not there with Ruby today.

I quickly scan my screen and realize that my professor replied only ten minutes ago, saying that while technically school is closed, she'll be in her office for the next ninety minutes while Zoe is training, and I'm welcome to swing by if it's quick. Otherwise, she can put me in for her next office hours.

Hmm.

A part of me thinks I should just take the formal office hours slot, but... she did say I could swing by, and god knows I'm going to be obsessing over this all week if I wait.

I throw my clothes on to get ready, rushing over to the building her office is in. She's got the door cracked open, a bright light streaming out. I knock and open it with a smile, finding Professor Dunner perched on the edge of her giant chair. Her glasses are pushed down to the tip of her nose as she stares at her computer screen, typing away. She does a double take when she sees me, and it's clear that she didn't think I would actually show up this morning.

"Morgan," she says, leaning back in her chair. "I wasn't sure if you'd see my email in time. What time do you leave for DC today?"

"That fell through," I hedge. It's not technically a lie, is it? It *did* fall through.

It doesn't really matter that I'm the one who made it fall through, right?

"I see," she says. "Too bad; some of those meetings you lined up sounded interesting. Did you come to talk about your project proposal? Give me a second to pull it up here, but I believe it met all of the requirements and was already approved." She clicks around her computer to our class's shared drive.

"That's not why I'm here," I say. "You did approve it already, by the way."

"Then what can I do for you? If it's about our subject matter, my advice is to give your brain a break this week. I plan to do that as soon as Zoe's done kicking her ball around." She laughs.

"No, I'd actually like to discuss the internship opportunity with you a bit more. I have some questions. One question, really. It shouldn't take long, I promise. I'm sorry to bother you on break."

"I offered, didn't I? Don't be so nervous." She grins and gestures for me to sit down. I do as I'm told, taking the comfortable chair across from her. Professor Dunner sets her pen down, leaning back in her seat like she's sizing me up. I realize almost too late that she actually *is*, and sit up straighter.

Professor Dunner clasps her hands together. "You're wondering if I recommended you, I presume."

"No," I say. "Well, yes. I wasn't sure if that went into play this round or last. But that's not the real reason I came. Mostly I was wondering . . ." I trail off. A part of me can't believe I'm actually going to ask this, but a much bigger part of me is glad that I am.

"Go on," my professor encourages, tilting her head in concern. "Whatever it is, there's no need to be shy about it. Heaven knows you're not shy in class."

I swallow hard. *She's got me there.*

"I was wondering if you knew—which you might not, and that's fine—if the internship opportunity might be able to be partially done as a work-from-home position?" I wince. I would probably even cower before her if I thought it would help get me the outcome I wanted.

"Don't ask like *that*," she says, and I startle, bolting my eyes to her.

"Sorry," I say.

She looks disappointed, but before I can think about that too much, she snaps her fingers. "Don't apologize either. If you ask for something like you don't think you're supposed to get it, you *never* will. When you're asking to be accommodated or because you want something extra, then you *must* be confident. You *must* be sure of yourself. You are selling not only your skills, but this change, as best for the business. You want your potential employers to feel that you are not just the best person for the job, but the *only* person for the job."

She's not wrong, but that's *so* hard. I open my mouth to say as much, but she shushes me and gestures toward the door.

"You want me to leave?" I ask, shocked.

"I want you to start over from the top." She smiles.

I sit there confused and then realize that means she *literally wants me to leave and come back in.* At least I think she does? It feels like there is a nonzero chance that she might secretly plan to lock the door behind me as soon as I'm out—but that's something I'm going to have to find out the hard way, I guess.

I stand up and walk out, waiting in the hallway for a minute or two. I hear Professor Dunner go back to typing on her keyboard, and I can't tell if she's really selling this do-over or just completely unbothered by the idea that I might have decided not to come back in at all.

I am coming back in, though. I can do this. I've got this. I am *the best person for the job. The* only *person for the job.*

If I'm really going to make a difference someday, then I need to believe in myself—need to trust myself—in a way that I think I've lost sight of lately. *I "must," as Dunner said.*

I knock on the door frame and step inside with a bright smile. "Good morning, Professor Dunner," I say. "Do you have a moment to discuss the internship with me?"

She looks at me with narrowed eyes. *Have I already failed again? Am I supposed to* demand *she talk to me instead of asking? That seems obnoxious.*

Dunner keeps me in suspense for a few more seconds and then gestures for me to take a seat. "Are you here to find out if I sent in a recommendation for you?" she asks.

Okay, we really are going all the way back to the beginning, aren't we?

"No, actually," I say, planting my feet and leaning forward just slightly. "I'm positive that you already did."

That, at least, earns me a smile. "Are you? My classes tend to fill with the brightest and hungriest students this school has to offer. It's very competitive."

"I'm aware, but I'm also aware that I'm the best of the bunch. I'm the one you call on when no one else has the answer, even when my hand isn't raised. You would be doing this internship a disservice by not recommending me."

"A little too arrogant," she stage-whispers.

"Confident," I correct. "I have the highest GPA in the class. I've already founded my own nonprofit, like the ones that this organization works with. I understand both sides of the equation—I've embraced the boots-on-the-ground aspects, the struggles of running a nonprofit, especially the importance of getting the funding necessary to stay in the black. However, through my own organization, I've also taken meetings with politicians to urge them to codify what I feel should be inalienable rights for queer students—so I understand that side too. I've also filed a lawsuit against a former school that was infringing on said rights, which proves I'm willing to put my money where my mouth is when push comes to shove, and that I'm familiar with using the legal system to block or attempt to block unfair legislation. My GPA, my . . . *confidence,* my experience, and my tenacity all mean that I'd be an invaluable intern to any team in this field. Do you disagree with my assessment, Professor Dunner?"

"Not at all," she says, leaning back in her chair. "If you're so confident in having my recommendation, then what are you interrupting my spring break for this morning?"

"I understand that the corporation I'm applying to is composed of your former students, and that you were instrumental in helping them get things running several years ago. I also know that you have placed many interns with them over the years. As such, it stands to reason that you have an intimate knowledge of how things run over there. I was hoping you would be able to tell me whether or not they would be amenable to me conducting part of the internship virtually. I reviewed the job description, and it seems like once the legislative session ends in June, there is nothing they would require of me that couldn't be done off-site."

"Why do you need to be off-site?"

"None of . . . your business?" I try.

She shakes her head and mouths, *Too far.*

"Personal reasons?"

This time she tilts one of her hands back and forth, the universal sign for *so-so. At least I'm getting warmer.*

I think for a beat, grateful she didn't make me leave and start over again. Suddenly, the answer comes to me.

"Enabling me to work virtually would give me the chance to be more hands-on with my own organization during my off-hours. My internship would be the priority, of course, but seeing as it's only a twenty-hour-a-week position, I'll have ample free time to work on other ventures. This would also ensure that I am continuously aware of the needs of small nonprofits, because I *am* one. I would be better able to offer solutions and advice from the perspective of both a constituent *and* a coworker. I believe that will lead us to even more unique and out-of-the-box ideas than we have now."

"Bravo!" Professor Dunner says, clapping her hands. "That's exactly how you need to approach them during your interview. Showing them how this virtual accommodation is also in their best interest was a wonderful touch. You continue to impress me, Morgan."

I beam at her. "Does that mean I really did get your recommendation, then?"

"Of course you did. You said it yourself: I would be doing them a disservice had I not. It's out of my hands now—I want to make sure you understand that. I don't have any say in who they choose. You have to nail the interview and your request for virtual accommodation on your own. It does sound reasonable to me."

"Okay, as long as you think it's a reasonable ask."

Professor Dunner shifts in her seat. "I'm debating sharing this with you, Morgan, but in the interest of full disclosure, you should know that you are *not* the only student I recommended for the opportunity. Please be aware that despite your best argument, they may want someone in the office for the entire duration, not just the first several weeks. You *are* making yourself a less competitive candidate, even though your justifications are sound."

"Then I'll just have to be that much better than whoever else you recommended."

"Very well," she says with a smile. "If there's nothing else, I'd like to get back to my break, and I suggest you do the same."

"Have a great week off, Professor Dunner." I grin.

I jog back to my room, throwing some things in a duffel bag as quickly as I can. I know Mika was planning to leave this morning. If she hasn't left yet, there's a chance that if I give her gas money, I might be able to catch a ride. She drives right past my exit on the highway on the way to her parents' house. With a little luck, she'll be willing to drive an extra ten minutes out of her way to take me home or, if not, drop me at the McDonald's by the off-ramp so Dylan or an Uber can pick me up.

I wish she would answer my text!

If not, it looks like I'm heading to the bus station and crossing my fingers I can get home in time to catch Ruby's filming.

God, I want to be there so bad.

I zip up my bag, probably forgetting half of what I need, and rush out my door. When I'm just over halfway to Mika's on-campus apartment—it's technically on the way to the bus stop anyway; might as well check for myself—I see Mac walking toward me. I look away, hoping maybe she won't notice me, but of course she does.

Why does the universe love messing with me so much?

We've done a good job of completely avoiding each other after what happened in the library. We haven't talked once since and definitely haven't been remotely in each other's orbit. I've been avoiding her favorite study spots and the parties at that frat house her roommates like to visit. She moved her seat to the other side of the room the very next class and stopped popping up everywhere I was all the time. Here, now, is the first time we've been face-to-face alone since that fateful day.

I half expect Mac to scowl or take the opportunity to yell or at least get a dig in as she walks by, to blame me for what went down, but instead she just looks . . . uncomfortable.

Mac stops walking a little ahead of me, apparently letting me decide if I want to keep going or not. I appreciate that. I don't bother going too far around her—I'm not scared of her or anything—but I definitely pick up my pace a little, feeling complicated things about what happened between us.

"I owe you an apology," Mac calls before I get too far away. "I should have never tried to kiss you, especially not twice. You were being clear that night, but I thought you were being coy or whatever. I've done a shit ton of reflection on that. I don't want to ever put someone in the position I put you in again. For what it's worth, I'm sorry, Morgan."

I hesitate, and then come to a stop, finally turning back to face her.

"I genuinely mean that," she says, her face telegraphing her honesty. "I was out of line and then embarrassed, and I behaved very badly. I thought you were laughing at me when I realized you had a girlfriend, or that you were leading me on or something. Once I cooled down, I realized that *that* actually didn't matter. Even if you did do those things, you told me to stop after the first kiss, and I didn't. I should have listened immediately. I had no right to try again."

"Thank you for that," I say. "I know I could have handled things better too, before we even got to that day."

"Anyway," Mac says. "That's all I wanted to say. I'm not going to pretend we can ever be friends after this, but we'll probably have more classes together since the major is so small. If there's any chance we can be civil to each other, I would like that. But I don't want you to feel pressured in any way. I won't try to sit next to you or make conversation or whatever. I honestly just wanted to apologize and clear the air as best as I could."

"We can be civil," I say, giving her a somewhat friendly smile. "It doesn't have to be this big, awful thing that makes us both feel horrible forever. I did have a little crush on you at one time, I think. Or I knew you liked me, and I liked *that*. I should have squashed the flirting. I'm not saying what happened at the library was my fault, but I could have—"

"No, neither am I," she rushes to say. "I'm not excusing what I did. I don't want to be the person who hurts other people, and I believe that I did hurt you. I want to own it and say sorry. That's not who I want to be."

"Thanks, and I'm sorry for not paying enough attention to realize that your feelings weren't just playful banter anymore."

"You don't owe me an apology for that. I'm responsible for my behavior."

"True, but . . ."

"Let's just leave it at 'true.'" She hitches her backpack higher on her shoulder. "I have to go catch a ride. You have a good break, okay?"

"You too," I say, meaning it.

Mac gives me a nod and then turns back down the path to wherever she's headed. I jog the final bit to Mika's apartment, feeling lighter than I expected to.

I knock on the door, relieved when she opens it, her face scrunched up in confusion.

"How do you feel about taking a twenty-minute detour for a good cause?" I ask, flashing her my most charming smile. "I've got gas money!"

Mika rolls her eyes. "Get in here, freshie. Help me pack up some more snacks, then, so I don't have to listen to you whine. We leave in ten."

"Mind if I make a quick call first?"

"Not at all, as long as you call mine too. I can't find that stupid phone anywhere."

I grin and step inside. "Will do."

27

RUBY

"All right, Ruby, I think we have what we need from you as far as testimonials go. We'll do a reaction one either way at the end, once the winner is declared. That will probably take place in another week or two, since you're the first one we're recording. I'm going to take a small team to capture the last testimonials we need from Billy and Shiloh while you and Matty are filming," Andi tells me.

Andi's the director and producer of the show—a gorgeous and always sharply dressed Black woman, with natural hair and perfectly glossed lips. I watch her walk away, marveling over the way she's pulling off heels higher than even I ever could, and she's doing it while traipsing around a garage with a gravel driveway.

Her outfit stands in stark contrast to Matty's '90s grunge

style—it's clear this woman takes both her looks and her job very seriously, just like it's clear that I have a teeny-tiny crush on her, despite the fact that she's probably in her midthirties.

Andi reminds me of Morgan, in a weird way. Maybe it's the competence?

Oh shit, do I have a thing for competence? Is a competence kink even a thing? If it is, do I— *Okay, I need to focus right now, and not on that.*

Luckily, that's when Matty comes over and stands beside me with a friendly "Hey, Ruby" and a smile. He's talked to Billy more than he's talked to me so far, but I think that's a good thing. One, being in front of my TV hero just makes me extra nervous, and two, Billy liking him, even off camera, says a lot. It says I'm probably in good hands right now, even if my anxiety is still telling me I'm going to screw everything up.

"Looks like we're ready," Andi calls to us. "Matty, do you want to film the intro now or jump right into the segment? We're using the same setup for both."

He glances at me and then thankfully says, "Later," meaning we can get right into my part. I hope he can't tell how freaked out I am. The makeup department did a good job making me look less tired after my all-night convo with Morgan, but I still feel like it's obvious. Yeah, we did fall asleep FaceTiming together last night, but one of us (me) might have been pretending for part (almost all) of the time.

I was nervous, all right? And I liked being able to look at her whenever I wanted.

Billy's shop is lit up like the sun as I follow Matty into the bay where the 1972 Chevy Camaro is sitting covered in rust.

During my testimonials, I got to talk all about how I found this car in a junkyard about six months ago and have been slowly rebuilding it ever since.

Today, I need to fix some carburetor issues and get her purring again. I've already got all of the electrical and exhaust work done and rebuilt huge chunks of the engine. This carburetor is the last thing I need to do before I can finally start working on the flashy stuff—like the paint job and seat upholstery.

I assumed that aesthetic stuff was what they would want to film, since it has the most satisfying before and after in terms of visuals. But when Matty found out about the carburetor issue, he shocked me by excitedly asking if they could film me doing that instead.

Apparently, he thought his viewers would get a lot from me talking them through it. "It's more likely that they'll need to work on a carburetor than completely paint a classic car," he said. Plus, they're used to seeing him visit mechanics that specialize in car exteriors, and he's already filmed a couple for next season.

"Don't be nervous," he says, knocking my shoulder as I stare down at the still-closed hood of my car.

Well, I guess it is obvious, then.

"Easier said than done," I answer.

"You do this every day. It's just another repair job," Matty reminds me. "Ben says that you're one of the most brilliant students he's ever had come through his classes. This carburetor won't know what hit it."

"He really said that?"

"Really, really," he says, crossing his heart.

The gesture makes me laugh, breaking some of the tension. I flick my eyes over to my station, where a starter sits half-built. I'm fixing it for a single mom that Billy is giving a steep discount to, and I remind myself that yes, I do know how to do these things. I had planned to finish it after we film, like it was some kind of normal work schedule . . . but I know already that all I'll want after this is to crawl under my covers and hide until the wrap party that Shelby set up for everyone tonight.

No, scratch that, I'm going to call Morgan again and then *hide, preferably still on FaceTime. Unless she's busy . . .*

Whatever. The point is, I'm going straight to my bed and staying there, either way.

I take a deep breath and look back down at the car. As nice as it is to think about sleep and Morgan and even being called "brilliant," I need to clear my head and get to work. I need to perform—and not in a forced-by-my-mom kind of way. In my own way, by my own standards, doing something I love.

I'm going to be as amazing as Morgan always says I am. As brilliant as Ben thinks I am. I know I can be, because this car—this shop—is my element.

"I can do this," I say quietly.

"You sure can," Matty says. "Pretend the camera isn't here. Pretend I'm Shiloh, if it helps you remember to walk us through each step out loud. Whatever works for you works for me."

"Shiloh?"

"Yeah, they didn't tell you about the testimonial he's

recording today? When they were spitballing ideas, he told Andi he would like to talk about how you took him under your wing. He said he wouldn't be passing the class without you explaining each thing over and over until it sticks—that's what our viewers need too."

"Shiloh said that?"

Matty nods. "He *also* told Andi he wouldn't have ever gotten his shit together without you and Billy. Between us, though, Ben's shared some stories with me this semester that make me think your work there *isn't* done. Did you know he took his entire bike apart and left it all lying in pieces in a parking lot a couple months back? Ben had to move chunks of it to leave. He even texted me a picture." Matty laughs, and so do I.

"Yeah, I think I know something about that," I say, shaking my head. "I'm the one who had to put it all back together for him so he could ride home."

"Damn, that should have been an automatic A. I don't think Ben knows that part," he says, bumping fists with me like we're old friends.

It knocks even more of the anxiety loose from my skin.

"Ready to do this?" he asks.

"Ready." I smile, realizing that he waited for me to find my comfort zone—helped me get there, even—before kicking this whole circus off. He flashes Andi a thumbs-up.

"Quiet on the set," she yells, followed by "Rolling," and then we're off.

I talk Matty through what I've already fixed on the car, what I plan to do in the future, and what issue we're working on today. Matty has me hop in the car so he can record the sound of the engine turning over but failing to start. I go over my diagnosis of the issue next, acting like I just figured it all out so my reactions seem "real" for the show—or as real as they can be with someone yelling "Cut" every time I mumble, or the light looks funny, or one of Billy's real customers roars up on their too-loud motorcycle and then decides to stay and watch.

Once we're through all that, I pop the hood. I reach in, take the air filter off, and talk him through unbolting the carburetor from the intake manifold. We carry it over to Billy's workbench, which is much cleaner than mine, and get to work checking it out.

I hit my stride then. Once there's a part in my hands, and they don't look so clean anymore, I'm solid. I eagerly tell him about the pieces that still work, and how I was able to scavenge most of the parts I needed from junkyards all over the state.

I tell him how my goal is to restore cars like this full-time one day, but that right now it's a side business of our shop. Oil changes and replacing alternators and other boring day-to-day stuff, like brakes, are the bread and butter of any kind of car repair business.

Matty sprinkles in questions about how I got into fixing cars as we spend the next few hours working together. I know a lot of it will be cut down to segment length, but I appreciate that he sounds interested anyway. He seems to love hearing about the pageants and my relationship with Billy—especially how Billy helped me see a way out, and how I used my pageant winnings to pay for the program at my school. I also take the time to plug Billy's shop as being the one place in town that won't rip you off . . . I *really* hope that part doesn't get cut.

Eventually, I put everything back into place in the car. Before I know it, I'm inside it, turning the key. Matty lets out a little whoop when it purrs to life on the first try.

"A beauty queen mechanic, who woulda thought?" Matty says, looking at the camera. Breaking the fourth wall is kind of his thing, and he's taken a couple chances to do it while we filmed today.

I come up beside him and slam down the hood with a bang. He high-fives me, and then it's my turn to talk to the camera.

"*Retired* beauty queen *turned* mechanic," I correct, shrugging with a smile. "What can I say? Women contain multitudes."

"Couldn't have said it better myself," Matty says with a grin.

"Cut!" the director calls out.

The second they stop filming, Matty ditches his TV voice. "You're a natural," he says, looking at Andi, who has come to join us.

"She is," Andi agrees. "You two work great together. I loved the back-and-forth you had going during the repair. Congrats, Ruby, that was an exceptional segment you just filmed."

"Thank you," I say, trying not to blush.

Ben comes up next, hitting Matty in the shoulder and then yanking him into a manly hug full of backslaps with a "Hey, man, good to see you." Even though Matty is staying with him for the weekend, this is the first time they've seen each other today. Matty drove in from his own shop headquarters only about an hour before we needed to film.

There's a little crowd gathered outside of the garage, some lookie-loos from town and some of Billy's garage friends too. News spreads like wildfire in a town this small. Plus, Billy's already got Matty to agree to autograph like half the shop and stuff for his friends too, so it's safe to say the secret's out.

I head outside, scanning the crowd for Billy and Shiloh. They have to be done filming with their mini crew by now. My jaw drops when my gaze settles on Everly standing in the crowd instead, and I almost completely fall over when I realize who she's standing next to.

"Morgan?!" I shout, running over to her.

I wrap her in a hug, lifting her up to spin us around. She laughs in my arms, hugging me back just as hard. It feels so fucking good to hug her I'm not sure I'm ever letting her toes hit the ground again.

Morgan, unfortunately, has other plans. "Hi," she says, wiggling down but not letting go of me all the way.

"I see how it is, no hug for your best friend," Everly teases.

"Sorry, oh my god. I can't believe you're both here," I say, pulling Everly into her own tight hug.

"I was kidding," she says, shoving me off. "Go make out with your girlfriend. I can wait five minutes."

"She's not my girl . . ." I trail off, looking at Morgan—she looks just as unsure as I do.

"Uh-oh, you guys positive about that?" Everly smirks.

"Not at all," I admit.

"Me neither," Morgan adds.

"From here, I'd say you two look five seconds away from fu—"

"Okay, thank you, Everly," Morgan says, blushing furiously.

I wrap my arms back around her with a laugh. "What are you doing here? I thought you were on campus?"

"I was. I got Mika to drop me off on her way home for break. I can't take credit for Everly, though; she was already halfway home when I called to see if she could come too."

"You were?" I ask, looking over Morgan's shoulder at my best friend.

"Obviously," she says, waving me off. "I was supposed to be the big surprise until this one stole my thunder."

"I can't believe you're really here," I say, leaning back to look at Morgan.

"I'm so proud of you for doing this, Ruby. How could I not be? Plus, after our talk last night, I thought . . . I thought you might want me here too?"

"I always want you." I grin, but before I can get any sappier, or maybe even decide to kiss her, Shiloh's dragging me into a hug.

"You did it! AHHHHH!" he yells. I shake my head when he finally seems to realize that there's someone else with their arm around me too. Shiloh jumps back and gives me a wild look. "Is that . . . *her*?" he whispers, tipping his head toward Morgan.

"Shiloh," I say, "I'd like you to meet Morgan, finally, and also my best friend, Everly."

"Holy hell, Rubes," he says, his eyes darting between both of them. "You didn't tell me all your college friends were hot."

"Jesus, Shi." I groan.

"You didn't?!" Everly says, sounding offended. Thankfully

Morgan just lets out a surprised giggle at the whole thing.

"He's lying! I showed him both of your Instagrams. Plus, he's been in the garage when we've FaceTimed, Everly! Shiloh, what are you talking about?! You have seen her before."

"The digital world does *not* do you justice, my lady." He takes Everly's hand and bows down to kiss it. She gives me a *what the hell is up with this kid* type of look, but I notice she doesn't pull her hand away. In fact, she offers him the other one.

"Before we take this any further," he says, standing straight to give Everly a serious look, "are you taken and/or a lesbian?"

"Shi!" I yell.

"What! I'm just trying to figure out if I have a shot here or not!"

"You *don't* have a shot," I snap. "Everly, tell him he does not have a shot."

Everly pretends to think about it before she tucks her hands into her pockets with a little shrug. "I am very single and, sadly, very straight, or else I already would have married one or both of them." She grins, nodding toward me and Morgan. "So . . ."

Is she flirting with Shiloh?? Why is she flirting with Shiloh? Gross!

"So you're saying there's a chance," he says, stepping a little closer to her.

Morgan slides a finger into my belt loop, holding me tight. I put my arm back around her, enjoying the way she melts into my side.

As disturbing as it is, if Everly and Shiloh entertain each other, I'll have a little more time with Morgan, I realize as Morgan and I watch Shiloh pick a dandelion and present it to my best friend . . . It's not that far off from the way his daughter handed me one the other day when I was babysitting. *My dude has clearly got to stop asking Stella Jane for relationship advice.*

Okay, enough of this.

"They still have to film some intros and outros with Matty, but I'm done until the wrap party tonight. Do you want to go talk?" I suggest. "If not, can we at least leave before Shi and Everly make me lose my lunch?"

"Hey," Shiloh calls out. "I heard that."

"Did you actually eat lunch today?" Morgan asks. She knows me too well; I can never eat before I have to perform. I get too nervous.

I shake my head.

"What about breakfast?"

I shake my head again.

"Sounds like we're talking at the diner, then."

"Hey, Ev," I say, "is it okay if you meet us at the diner in a little bit? Morgan and I need to talk, but then I'd love to hang."

"Whatever," Everly says kind of dreamily. I notice her eyes never leave Shiloh's face.

"You sure?" I ask.

"Yeah, yeah, later." She smiles. "Shiloh and I have our own talking to do right now."

"You heard the woman," he says, a shit-eating grin plastered on his face as he waves us away. "Begone."

"Yeah," Morgan says, giving me a soft smile. "Let's begone. Together."

28

MORGAN

Walking into the diner feels strange.

I didn't expect that, since it hasn't been all *that* long since I was home for winter break. I guess it's more proof that things are changing.

Maybe this is growing up, or at least the start of it. It feels like I learned more about myself in the last month and a half than I did in the entirety of the last year. That's saying something, because last year was . . . a lot.

Not in a bad way. Well, not in an *all* bad way.

Growth is painful sometimes, no matter what you do.

I slide into the booth, half expecting Aaron to pop up any second with a pile of appetizers or something.

Ruby sits across from me, and I finally let myself really soak in the sight of her. My eyes trail over her face, snagging on her pouty lips, which are stained a distractingly perfect shade of light pink today. There's a smudge of grease on her cheek, and I consider telling her but then decide not to. It's so perfectly her. Tough and beautiful, strong and soft.

Her throat bobs as she swallows hard, and I reach my hand out, hooking our pinkies together. Her nails are short and well manicured, the soft purple gloss marred by a few scuffs and smudges from working on the car today.

I asked her once why she didn't wear gloves since quitting the pageants if she was still getting her nails done. She said because it felt like freedom after years of her mother forcing them on her. The manicures are a way to embrace beauty on her own terms, she told me, and the scuffs and scrapes on her hands are signs of a battle fought and won.

I knew she wasn't just talking about stubborn car parts either.

I look at her hands now, and I'm just so freaking proud—so happy for her that it's almost overwhelming. She did the big thing, the scary thing, the thing that could open the door to so much more for her in the years to come.

I can't believe I almost wasn't here to see it because of my own fear, my own selfishness.

I don't realize I'm tearing up until Ruby tugs my hand, pulling me closer so she can wipe them away.

"Are you crying because you're sad or happy?" she asks.

"Both. I think it's time we let go of high school," I say. It makes perfect sense in my head, but her smile falls and I worry she's misunderstood. "In a good way," I rush to clarify.

Her brows pinch together, and I want to kiss away that tiny divot as soon as it forms. The table between us suddenly feels like too much space. She's too far.

"C'mere," I say, sliding deeper into my side of the booth. "Will you sit next to me?"

Ruby gives me a strange look but slides out of her bench and into mine anyway.

It feels private sitting next to her like this, intimate. The hard wooden backs of the booths extend too high to see over. It feels like we're in a little cocoon now, and it's perfect.

I don't know how I ever thought we could give this up. I hope she's thinking the same thing.

I lean into her shoulder, and it smells like gasoline and steel and lavender and spice. The notes of her favorite perfume always did mix so well with the scent of Billy's garage. It's something so uniquely Ruby, and I hope she knows how much I've missed it. *I hope she knows what it does to me.*

Ruby presses her leg against mine, the heat of her thigh drifting down into my skin. I press back, a steady pressure, a shoring up that I hope we can apply to every aspect of our relationship. Ruby puts her arm back around me, and I snuggle in even closer.

"Different can be good," I say. "I realize that now. Things changing or being more complicated doesn't mean they're not worth it." I turn my head to look at her. "You're worth all of it, Ruby."

She smiles at me so fondly, so gently, it soothes every piece of me that I had to tape back together after she left.

"I missed you so much," Ruby says, a little bit breathless. "I didn't even get out of bed that first day you didn't send my good-morning text."

"I hated not sending it."

"Are you sure about this, though? Us? I am, but if you have any doubts . . ."

"I'm sure," I say, resting back on her shoulder. "It's going to be different from how it was in high school, but what isn't? We're not little kids anymore. We've changed so much this year already, let alone all the ones to come, and that's great. That's how it should be. My mom says that your college years are kind of like being a toddler all over again."

"As someone who babysits a toddler regularly, I can conclusively say she's wrong," Ruby snorts. "For instance, I have no intention of trying to stick my spitty fingers in a socket or wearing diapers."

I laugh. "I'm pretty sure Mom just meant that it's another period of rapid growth and maturing . . . although still with lots of ways to accidentally kill ourselves, if we're being honest."

"That's macabre," Ruby says with a little huff. Her breath fans out across my hair, and I swear to god, I will never take these small moments for granted ever again.

When I tell Ruby that, she pokes me in the side, right where I'm most ticklish.

"You will, though," she says.

"I absolutely won't."

"You will, and I will, and not only that, but we'll argue more and screw up and be inconsiderate and rude and probably let each other down dozens of times."

"All right, buzzkill," I say, a thread of worry slithering through my brain.

Is this all she thinks of us?

"We'll also fall more in love, and laugh a lot," she adds. "And grow more and change more and . . . we *need* to give each other space to do that. I want us to be able to jump at new opportunities and explore new things."

"I want that too, preferably within the parameters of our relationship."

Ruby leans forward, craning her neck so she can look at me as best she can without me giving up my spot on her shoulder. "Okay, nerd," she says. "I'm sure we can do that 'within the parameters of our relationship.' I don't want to keep breaking up either. It doesn't have to be either/or; we can do it together."

"Good," I say, "but stop pretending you're not as big of a nerd as me; it just comes out in different ways."

"Better, more useful ways," she teases, earning herself a side-eye.

"Different and *also* useful ways," I joke back.

"Okay, well, let's see if your poli-sci classes or my automotive ones come in more handy the next time your brother's car breaks down. Maybe you can recite some *Democracy in America* at him. Maybe his alternator will replace itself out of sheer boredom."

I laugh, but then pout. Ruby pulls me even tighter to her and squeezes my arm. "You know I'm kidding, right?" she asks. "Your work is incredible, and very important. I didn't mean to shit all over it with that joke . . . I mostly wanted to show off that I Googled some of the things you mentioned you were working on, just in case."

God, I love her.

"I know, and you're amazing, and your work is intimidatingly awesome. You filmed a show today. A show!"

"Intimidatingly awesome, huh?" She grins into my hair. "I can work with that."

"Good, because I mean it," I say. "Before we get to all the good stuff, though . . ."

"C'mon," Ruby whines, sliding the tips of her fingers underneath the bottom of my shirt. "Haven't we earned the good stuff yet?"

I blush. In any other situation, I would be kissing her right now, because yes, we have, and yes, I want that, and yes, I am as impatient as she seems to be . . . Except I know we need to talk more, and I know she knows it too by the way she keeps her hand from wandering any farther, seemingly content to trace the little bit of skin she can already reach.

"I can't wait to get back to the good stuff," I admit.

"I know, I know. I already hear the 'but' and can guess what you're going to say. We need to talk about what giving each other space to grow will look like." She pulls her arm back, inching away so there's a bit of space between us.

I frown at the expanse of air where her body used to be.

Ruby tips my head up to meet hers, looking somewhat sheepish. "Sorry, I want to be able to pay full attention, and if I'm touching you, I'm not going to be thinking of anything but how bad I want to keep doing that."

I melt a little and have to sit on my own hands to resist

pulling us back together. We need to take this seriously if we want it to work.

"That's a good idea," I reluctantly admit.

"I think, for me, I need to remember and believe that my career and dreams are just as important as yours and not let myself feel guilty about that."

"Good!" I say. "Yes, exactly, I feel the same. I was beating myself up so much over whether taking the internship was me putting myself first, but—"

"But that's not a bad thing!" she says. "We have to do that. We have to chase our goals and support each other for doing that. We have to accept that there's going to be sacrifices sometimes and that might mean going longer without seeing each other or not being able to talk all the time."

"It might also mean thinking outside the box about the opportunities we do pursue," I say. "Like this internship. I'm going to try to do some of it virtually if I get it. I made a whole case for it with my professor. It would mean we wouldn't have to be apart the entire time."

"But if you can't, that's okay too. Maybe I can ask Billy if I can work a little later during the week in the summer so I can have Fridays off without losing hours. Then I'd always have a three-day weekend to go visit you. I'm sure he would do it—especially if Shiloh keeps helping out."

"It's going to be complicated," I say. "But I'm in. It's worth it to me. Are *you* positive that this is what you want? I'd rather not get back together at all than go through losing you again over the exact same thing."

"Same," Ruby says. "And we have to commit to talking to

each other instead of letting things fester—even if it's hard things like jealousy or mini crushes or jobs we want that the other one might not think are ideal."

"Exactly. We have to love each other more than we hate all the complications, I guess," I say, my heart in my throat. "Do you think we can?"

"You've always been my favorite complication, Morgan," she says, leaning closer as her eyes flick to my mouth. "From day one."

God, I've missed her.

"You're mine too," I answer, swallowing hard. "Always will be."

My eyes slip shut as I close the distance between us. Ruby's lips are warm and soft, her tongue insistent. I let her in, sliding my hand up into her hair as she presses herself even closer.

"I love you," she whispers, our kiss turning frantic as we pour our love into each other.

I almost don't notice the clapping and whistling behind us, lost as I am in her scent and her skin and her hair and her, her, *her*.

Almost.

I giggle and Ruby pulls back, sliding her tongue along her bottom lip where I nipped it in my excitement. The clapping keeps up, and Ruby grumbles before leaning out of the booth, no doubt ready to yell at whatever pervert is watching us. Then she relaxes, motioning to someone as she scoots back against the bench.

Everly and Shiloh slide into the other side of our booth.

Shiloh throws in one last wolf whistle, and I hang my head in embarrassment.

"It took you long enough to get to the whole making-up-and-out part," Shiloh says, looking at his wrist, where he definitely does *not* have a watch. "I only have my sitter for another forty-five minutes, and I'm starved."

Ruby rolls her eyes. "You were sitting at the counter! You could have ordered."

"We couldn't risk it. We were too busy playing interference." Everly smirks. "Had to keep our heads in the game."

"Interference?" I ask.

"Did you two seriously not notice how no waiters bothered you this whole time?"

"Not really," Ruby admits.

"We were a little preoccupied," I add.

"We noticed," Shiloh says, waggling his eyebrows.

A fresh wave of mortification slices through my body, but I let it go when Ruby settles her arm back around me.

"Sorry, we just had a lot of catching up to do."

"Is that what the kids are calling it these days? *Catching up?*" Shiloh laughs.

A waitress glances over at us, and Shiloh flashes a big smile and a nod, presumably to let her know it's safe to come by. *Oh god, I'm going to need to leave her the biggest tip of my life after this.*

But then Ruby looks at me, *really looks at me,* and I look at her, *really look at her,* and I can tell—I'm positive—that this is just as worth it to her as it is to me. That she means every word she's said about letting each other grow without *letting each other go.*

Girls like us can go the distance, if we really want to . . . and yeah, *we want to.*

"I love you, Ruby Gold," I say, when I finally find my voice.

"I know," she says, a playful smirk taking over her face, but then she adds, "I love you too."

Epilogue

RUBY

"Check with Andi and see if we're set to film your exhaust repair tomorrow. Uh, could you also pop off an email to make sure we've got the releases signed by the students at Shepard High? I'd like to film their auto club between the other segments tomorrow if we can. After that, you're free to head out."

"Yep," I say.

"Oh, wait, if Roscoe gets up when you go to use the computer, could you please toss him in his pen on your way out? He's been passed out in my office for a while. He needs to go out. The old dog can use some sunshine, you know."

"Yeah, no problem," I say, marking everything down on the notes app in my phone so I don't forget. "Anything else?"

"Nah," Matty says, shoving his body back under the car he's working on.

"I've got two hours left on my shift, if you need—"

"Ruby," he says, poking his arm out from under the car and pointing his wrench at me. "Morgan is coming this weekend. I'm trying to get you out of here early. Take the hint. Don't make me chase you out with power tools."

"Okay, okay." I laugh, heading toward the office, where I know I'll find Andi.

Matty is the best boss I ever had—which Billy can never find out. He thinks *he* is. Like, Billy is definitely the best *dad,* but he always forgets to order parts or double-books us.

Or he did, anyway, until Shiloh took that stuff over about a month and a half ago. It turns out that what he's lacking in automotive expertise, Shiloh more than makes up for with his customer service and inventory skills—he's already doubled what we make selling off spare parts on eBay alone.

It still gets a little dicey sometimes, especially when he's sleep-deprived thanks to Stella Jane, but nothing like it was. In fact, Shiloh even switched his major to automotive management for next semester—since the courses he's already taken can count for either one. Billy says he has a shop manager position with Shiloh's name on it once he graduates.

This garage, however, is a well-oiled machine top to bottom, at all times. Home base for Matty's shows *and* his own projects. Everything is clean, beautiful, and state of the art.

I honestly didn't know what to expect when Andi approached me at the wrap party to say that I was "exactly what the shows were missing" and then ask if I would be interested in working for them and occasionally being filmed.

I looked at Morgan. We were fresh off our diner talk about not holding each other back, but I didn't think we would have to put it into practice so soon. She grinned and nodded at me, looking as excited as I felt. *Okay, then,* I thought. *We're really doing this.*

I got an email about a week later with details: a paid internship during the summer months, with on-screen cameos. If both parties wanted to make it a little more permanent after that, they'd work around my school schedule in the fall.

It requires a lot of travel to different states during filming, since we hop from shop to shop frequently bringing on guest stars, but their home base is actually not that far—pretty much smack in between my house and Morgan's school.

If things go well, it could turn into an actual job at his shop and *maybe* more than just cameos on the show. To start, I'm basically Matty's assistant, though.

So far, that's just meant getting to fix cars all day with my idol and sending any emails he doesn't want to shove off on Andi but also doesn't want to write himself.

I'm not going to lie, I was worried about leaving Billy's shop. Billy, on the other hand, said I was being ridiculous, and he would fire me if I tried to stay. Between Shiloh increasing the online profits and the way business has really picked up since the show aired, he could more than afford to replace me if he really needed to.

Weirdly, or maybe not weirdly since they're the same age and into the same things—not to mention the fact that both of them still go by their childhood nicknames—Billy and Matty have struck up a solid friendship. Sometimes I feel like they talk even more than Billy and I do, which is wild because I literally talk to Billy almost every single day.

They've even recently discussed that Billy might have a place at Matty's shop too, which, believe it or not, is a fully operational garage fixing cars for the general public whenever we're not filming. *That would be awesome.*

If Matty thinks I have a lot of knowledge and experience, he should see Billy under the hood. Actually, he probably knows. Billy corrected him on a couple things last time he came to visit.

Billy says he'll never fully close up his little shop in town—too many locals depend on him—but that he could see a future where he brings on a couple trustworthy mechanics so he can come here . . . especially if Shiloh really does take over as shop manager someday.

I'm cautiously optimistic about all of this.

Who knows where the future will lead any of us, but taking risks and swinging big is the key to opening doors. I learned that the hard way. I won't get anywhere by always doing what other people want or expect or by limiting myself when things get hard or intimidating.

If I hadn't forced myself out of my comfort zone, I would never have found the love I have with Morgan or embraced who I really am. And I *definitely* wouldn't be standing here in front of Andi asking scheduling questions as a real member of the *Mastermind Mechanics* team. Sometimes I still feel like this is all a dream.

"If we can be at the school at ten a.m. tomorrow, that

would be ideal," Andi says, reading my notes over my shoulder before I even get a chance to open my mouth.

Yeah, her efficiency is still hot.

"Okay, so we could film that *and* the other stuff he already has on the schedule?"

"Yes, if the students come in at eleven ready to film. I need about an hour to set up and test the angles, plus another fifteen to mic them up and let them get their jitters out. We have to be done filming by one to also do the exhaust repair, but that should be plenty of time."

"Sounds good," I say. "I'll plan to be there at ten, and I'll make sure Matty knows to be on set by eleven fifteen at the latest."

"Perfect," Andi says. "Are you heading out?"

"I have to email the school to confirm the releases are all signed, and then, yeah, I just have to put Roscoe in the run and I'm off."

"I'll send the email. Take Roscoe out and keep walking," Andi says with a wink before turning back to her desk. "Don't forget to tell Morgan I said hi."

Maybe I should be embarrassed that everyone at work knows how gone I am for my girlfriend, but I'm not.

How am I supposed to contain my excitement over the fact that she's able to do the rest of her internship virtually, just like she asked—meaning she's moving here with me for the rest of the summer? Like, I can't. No one could. Morgan gets to save the world while sitting next to me, in the finished basement apartment that one of the camera guys rented out to me for dirt cheap. It's a lucky thing too. Nobody was going to rent to a nineteen-year-old with no credit history beyond the fraud committed under her Social Security number by her now-estranged mother.

The cameraman, Dave, and his wife, Jenna, insisted I stay, even knowing Morgan was going to be staying with me for most of the rest of the summer. They said they didn't care—as long as we respect quiet time from ten p.m. on, which won't be a problem, given how I generally have to be at the shop by six a.m. on filming days.

Dave and Jenna are great, high school sweethearts who've been together twenty-plus years with twin toddlers that I love to babysit. They joke I'm never allowed to move out, and honestly, other than the fact that they keep fighting me on my actually paying rent and insisting that babysitting for them is enough, I'd probably be happy staying forever.

They're already giving me a deal on my room, so living in their basement for free—babysitting or not—feels like taking advantage. Especially since Shiloh and Stella Jane come to visit so much now that she's besties with their twins. It's pretty cute seeing them all run around the yard together.

I can't wait for Morgan to be here too.

I walk into the back room, where Roscoe is passed out on the couch. He's a thirteen-year-old boxer dog that's gone mostly gray. He's partially deaf and snores like the devil but is also the sweetest boy alive. I think he's given me back my love of dogs, something I thought was permanently ruined after living with that pack of feral Jack Russell terriers at my mom's for so long.

Roscoe groans and slides off the couch, demanding pets before agreeing to follow me out to the massive dog run that Matty has set up for him in back of the production offices. It's less of a run, really, and more of a full-sized fenced-in dog park. Every employee is welcome to bring their dogs to work and use it, as long as their pets are well behaved with the staff and gentle with Roscoe.

Today, there's a little Boston terrier named Stevie ping-ponging around inside, which really gets Roscoe's little nub of a tail wagging. She's one of his favorite dog friends.

I let Roscoe through the gate and watch him zoom around the yard faster than any old dog should be able to. The Boston's mom, Nora, is one of the show's location scouts. She looks up from the shady bench in the corner of the pen where she's working on her laptop and gives me a wave, and then reaches into her bag to pull out the treats. Roscoe and Stevie come barreling over the second they hear the bag crinkle. It's possible that Roscoe's love for Stevie might be slightly food motivated, but if everyone's happy, who cares?

I'm just turning to leave as a car pulls up with a glowing Uber sign in the front window. Morgan steps out, grinning. I rush over, completely shocked, and can't help kissing her while the driver pulls her bag out of the trunk beside us.

"What are you doing here?! I thought I was getting you at the bus station in a couple hours?"

"I took an earlier one. I couldn't wait anymore," she says, still smiling.

The Uber driver gives us a nod before driving off, and then

it's just me and Morgan, alone behind the garage. *I couldn't be happier.*

I'm tempted to bring her inside and show her around. This is the first time she's been able to come and see this place . . . except I'm not quite ready to share her yet. Instead, I grab her luggage, and I lead her over to where I'm parked. She probably thinks I'm opening the passenger door for her—chivalry and all—but instead I set her bag down and spin us around, caging her between my arms and walking her back against my car. I kiss her good and proper now that we don't have an audience.

"But your car," Morgan says when I move to her neck. She must be remembering that first day we met, when I almost murdered her for putting her hands on my baby.

"Forget the car," I murmur, going gentle in her arms.

She lets out a sigh as I trail kisses against her cheeks, her eyelids, her nose, that little spot at the edge of her jaw that makes her shiver.

Yeah, I love my car. And yeah, it's a symbol of how far I've come.

But I love Morgan even more, and we are too.

ACKNOWLEDGMENTS

Huge thanks to my agent, Sara Crowe, for her never-ending support, advice, and enthusiasm, and to my editor, Stephanie Pitts, who was immediately on board when I said I felt like there was more of Ruby and Morgan's story left to tell!

I'm also so grateful to have such a wonderful and talented team behind the scenes at Penguin helping to bring this book to life. My sincere gratitude to the wonderful Matt Phipps and the amazing Madeline Art, who both stepped up immensely to get this book across the finish line; to my publisher, Jen Klonsky, and my publicist, Lizzie Goodell, along with Felicity Vallence, Shannon Spann, Alex Garber, and everyone at Penguin Teen; and to my very patient copyeditors and proofreaders, Kat Keating, Janet Rosenberg, Cindy Howle, and Misha Kydd.

Also, my eternal gratitude goes to Jeff Östberg for bringing Morgan and Ruby to life in yet another gorgeous cover illustration, to Kelley Brady for creating such a stunning cover design, and to Suki Boynton for the interior design.

And last but never least, thank you to all the readers and book people who help to get my stories into the hands of the people who love them. You're the reason I get to do this. Thank you, thank you, thank you!

JENNIFER DUGAN is an awkward romantic who writes across many genres and categories. Her debut young adult novel, *Hot Dog Girl*, was called a "a great, fizzy rom-com" by *Entertainment Weekly* and "one of the best reads of the year, hands down" by *Paste* magazine, although she is best known for *Some Girls Do*, which took TikTok by storm. Her other novels include *Summer Girls*, *Playing for Keeps*, *The Last Girls Standing*, and *Melt With You*. Jennifer has also collaborated with artist Kit Seaton on the graphic novels *Full Shift*, *Bite Me*, and *Coven*, which was a GLAAD Outstanding Original Graphic Novel nominee. She lives in upstate New York.

JLDugan.com
@JL_Dugan

DON'T MISS THE BEGINNING OF MORGAN AND RUBY'S LOVE STORY

READ ON
FOR MORE FROM
JENNIFER DUGAN

CHAPTER 1

EVERYBODY SEEMS TO THINK THE SUMMER AFTER YOUR senior year is the stuff of legends. That it's two months of pure teenage bliss or something. It's almost as if there's this big conspiracy surrounding it, like, sure, kid, throw your cap in the air, cue up that hit pop song you will definitely hate by fall, and then you, too, will be guaranteed the most epic summer of your life. I mean, we all know that's not how it actually goes down, right?

Even though I won't kick off my own senior year for

another couple of months, I've already witnessed way more than my fair share of post-senior summers. It's a hazard of attending a tiny school—you can't really be picky about how old your friends are. But yeah, I think I can conclusively say that frantically searching Target for extra-long twin bedsheets while freaking out about what to major in does not an epic summer make.

So no, I don't buy into that whole post-senior-year magic thing. I think *pre*-senior year is where it's at, and for me, that starts right here in this tiny breakroom—with a stomach full of butterflies and a brain full of fireworks.

This is going to be my summer, no doubt about it.

I take a deep breath and slide my finger down the crisp page in front of me, searching for my name on the corkboard of destiny. Seriously. That's what we call stuff like this at Magic Castle Playland. It's not a bulletin board; it's a "corkboard of destiny." It's not a list of job assignments; it's a "character reveal chart." I swear to god everything here is about as whimsical as it is rusty.

I look lower, past the names of the ride operators and the food service people, over housekeeping and maintenance, until I get to the costume crew. I pause at the listing for princess. It's not my name. Okay, that's fine, disappointing but fine. I knew it was a long shot when I put in for it. My finger dips even lower, gliding past the prince, and the pirates, and all the furry park mascots, until it hits my name: Elouise May Parker. I drop my head against the board. No, no, no. Not again. I can't. This has to be a mistake.

My best friend, Seeley, nudges me out of the way. "What's it say?"

"I'm the hot dog."

Pity flashes in her hazel eyes. "It could be worse."

"Could it, See? Could it really?"

"Yeah! What if they put you in housekeeping and you were stuck in the bathroom by Swashbuckler Bay?" She shudders, cracking herself up.

"It's not funny." I pout, but technically, yes, that would be worse. I mean, the bathroom crew finishes every shift smelling like mildew and old diapers, so . . .

Seeley holds up her hands. "Hey, I'm just kidding, but it's going to be okay, Lou, promise."

She's right. I know she is. This is a minor speed bump. I mean, it's not like anybody died or there's a giant meteor about to strike Earth or anything. But still, there are so many things I have planned for these last few months before we're sucked up in the frenzy of senior year, and playing the hot dog isn't one of them.

I glance back at the list, letting out a little humph, and then look back at Seeley with an exaggerated frown. She bursts out laughing, shaking so hard her teal hair tips right into her sun-kissed face. Seeley's always got it a different color these days, almost like a mood ring. The happier she is, the brighter her hair gets.

Meanwhile I'm her slightly duller, significantly paler sidekick. My skin doesn't tan—it just burns—and my hair is this permanent mousy brown color because it doesn't hold dye. My dad calls it "caramel brown," which makes me think it's been way too long since he's actually seen any caramel.

Seeley grins and shoves her bangs out of her face as we start to walk toward the main stage for orientation. "Seriously, what are the odds that a vegetarian ends up in a hot dog suit two years in a row?"

"Shut up. What did you get?" I almost hope it's something awful like the Scrambler, where she's guaranteed to clean up tons of puke on the daily. It's only fair we both suffer.

"The carousel." She shrugs, her lips twisting into a smirk.

"I hate you."

"No you don't." She laughs. "Besides, would you honestly rather have Marcus or Brynn in charge of the carousel? They'd have Butters and Racer scratched all to hell from day one."

"I would kill them."

Seeley crosses her arms. "Exactly. So really, you should be thanking me for helping you avoid a lengthy prison sentence."

I snort, running my hand along the rock wall. This is the only time of year I even dare to touch it, the only time when it's still sort of semi-clean—well, as clean as the filthy old rock wall of a run-down amusement park can be, anyway. But tomorrow the gates will open, and everything will be sticky from the sweat and garbage of our less-than-stellar clientele.

I drop my hand, smiling at the familiar sight of co-workers finding seats and talking excitedly to everybody they haven't seen since the last time the cold broke in our unforgiving little mountain town. Most of them aren't townies like me; some of them live in neighboring areas, and some of them—the lifers, as I like to call them—follow the seasons. They spend their summers up here where it's a little bit cooler, and the winters down south where the weather is mild.

You don't realize how many people it takes to run an amusement park, even an old midsize one like ours, until you try to cram them all into the seats at Mr. Johnny's Magic Emporium. Even though our little rust bucket can't compete with the corporate giants, we have some cool stuff here—a couple roller coasters, some games, enough rides to pass an afternoon, and, of course, our namesake: a tiny pink castle smack-dab in the middle of the park—and it takes tons of people to keep it going each day.

Tons of people who are currently causing a human-shaped traffic jam right ahead of me. I take a sharp right and turn down the lower path to hit up the amphitheater's side entrance. Seeley follows close behind me, stepping hard on the back of my sneaker, so hard my heel pops out. I glare at her, grabbing onto her arm for support as I fix my shoe.

"Sorry." Her voice lilts up like this isn't an offense punishable by death.

"Hey, Seeley," a boy says, nodding at her as he walks by. It's Nick, because of course it would be Nick when I'm hunched over looking like I don't know how to operate a shoe. Seeley lifts her hand to wave and nearly sends me sprawling. Thanks for that, universe.

MORE BOOKS
BY JENNIFER DUGAN

WITH KIT SEATON